The
Red
Boots

Linda Kuhlmann

ISBN: 978-0-9858333-3-6

There's something in the core of me
That needs the West to set it free.

'Connemara'
by Oliver St. John Gogarty

CHAPTER ONE

Ireland

A tall figure dressed in black paused in the shadows as a Dublin Garda patrol car passed by. Illuminating his watch, the figure checked the time. Quickly, he darted across the street, being careful not to break the silence before dawn.

The Pearse Gallery was dark except for a spotlight on a statue near the window. The light illuminated a poster announcing the premier show for Shannon O'Toole's world art tour.

While walking to the back of the gallery, he removed a small computer with wire leads from a black canvas bag. He carefully connected the leads to the alarm keypad outside the door. After disabling the system, he used a three-inch blade to enter through the metal door.

In the faint light coming from the next room, he could see the bins of surplus art and statues. Walking around a large desk in the center of the room, he went through the doorway to the front of the building.

On a pedestal to his right stood the small bronze statue of a nude woman, gleaming under the single light overhead. The body was athletic and elegant. Her long hair flowed out around her, as if blown by an unheard wind. Her head was turned to look over her shoulder, where a few strands fell, covering her left breast.

He reached over and flipped off the light over the statue.

In the darkness, he picked up the statue and stood for a moment holding it gently in his hands as if it were a priceless gem, his breath the only sound.

He knelt down and set the statue on the floor. Taking a dark cloth from his bag, he wrapped it carefully and placed it into the bag. Again, he checked his watch before lifting the now heavy bag to his shoulder. He started to leave the room, but stopped.

Turning to look back at the empty pedestal, he reached over and turned the overhead light on, then left through the back of the gallery.

CHAPTER TWO

Shannon pressed the heels of her hands across the clay cheekbones on the jaw line of the man's bust, which was mounted on a slab of bog oak. She'd found the rare piece of wood, preserved in the Irish peat bogs, during a short visit to see her grandparents in Clifden, County Galway.

She sat back, looked at the bust, and frowned. After a moment, she picked up more clay from the small pile next to the statue and began to fill the cheeks back in.

"Damn!" Frustrated, she pushed a stray lock of auburn hair from her forehead with the back of her clay-covered hand. She'd been struggling with this particular statue for over a year.

Looking around her studio, Shannon sought inspiration in the myriad of shelves containing statues, some finished, others, still in progress. Her studio was the only place she felt free to be herself.

She saw a sculpture of a rearing Appaloosa she'd created from memory and sighed.

"I'll not finish you today," she said to the bust of her father, a lilt in her voice. "I'm not sure I'll ever finish you. It seems horses come easier to me than the image of your face."

Outside her window, she watched the water of the River Liffey slowly flow past her apartment in Temple Bar. The vibrant colors of the fall leaves reflected in the water. She'd lived in Dublin for years now, but it really wasn't her home – she didn't know where her home was.

Her eyes landed on an unframed black and white photo, one corner folded over. The three people smiling at her took her back to the year when she was eight – the day when her life had changed forever.

She'd gone riding with Jake, the boy in the photo. He was a

couple of years older than her and was her best friend then. They'd ridden to the pond on her ranch in Oregon, where she was born. Until that day, it had been her home.

"You ride like a girl," she remembered Jake had said as they dismounted.

"I AM a girl, you dork!" She'd laughed, ran to the dock that hung over the clear water, and plopped down, dangling her small red cowboy boots over the water's edge. Mount Hood was reflected near the other shoreline.

She watched as Jake skimmed flat rocks across the water's calm surface. They jumped and danced until the rocks plunged into the pond, creating continuous rings that grew around the point of entry. A cloud crossed over the sun as young Shannon's thoughts turned to her parents.

"I heard them arguing again last night," she said, looking up at the mountain.

"Everybody heard!"

"But, you live in the cottage away from the main house. How did you hear?"

"Kid, everyone can hear when they're going at it—" Jake stopped, then added, "I'm sorry."

"You'd better just mind your own business…and…and don't call me 'kid'." Shannon was jealous of the love that Jake and his parents had.

Just then, the cloud moved and the sun beat down, warm and bright. Shannon ran her fingers through her hair. "I hate the way my mother always keeps my hair cut short."

"Then, let it grow. That'd make her crazy."

"I would if I could." Shannon smiled, looking down at her boots. She jumped up and stood next to Jake.

"She already hates my boots, but I love them."

Shannon could feel Jake's dark eyes on her. She turned and saw the expression on his face, one she'd never seen before. His eyes stared into hers. Before she knew it, he pressed his lips softly to hers, then quickly pulled back.

"What was THAT for?" she exclaimed.

"I-I-I don't know…" Jake stammered, thrusting his hands deep into his pockets.

Before she could think, Shannon punched Jake in the stomach, then ran to her pony.

"Race you back!" she yelled as she jumped on Skye and tried to ride like the wind. She knew that her pony couldn't outrun Jake's tall gelding, but it was a game they'd played since her father gave her Skye. Jake always let her win. But, today was no game. She pressed her lips together, still feeling the tingle from his kiss.

As they neared the barn, they pulled their horses to a stop and watched as Shannon's father was putting luggage into the ranch's van. Shannon's stomach started to hurt as she recognized her own sapphire- blue bags.

The harsh ringing of her telephone startled Shannon from her memories. She wiped her hands on a towel and looked at her watch as she walked to answer it.

"Oh, my god," she exclaimed. "It can't be that late!"

She thought of her show tonight. Suddenly, she froze, remembering that she'd totally forgotten her appointment with her mother. With a shaking hand, she picked up the receiver.

"Shannon, here."

"The gallery was burglarized!" the voice on the other end said.

"Thomas?"

She was rarely glad to hear his voice, but was relieved it wasn't her mother. Thomas was the manager of her step-father's gallery. He was also her fiancé.

"Your nude was stolen," Thomas added.

"What? That's absurd. Who would want—"

"It doesn't matter - the important thing is the burglary. I can't tell yet if anything else is missing..."

Shannon thought of the statue. She hated that piece, but she'd had no choice. Thomas insisted she complete it for this upcoming tour. Now, more than ever, she dreaded seeing him tonight.

"Has anyone seen Nikki, yet?" Shannon asked.

"I have no use for Nikki Conroy any longer."

She heard her front door open and slam shut.

"Where are you?" she heard her mother call out in her shrill voice she used when she was upset.

Shannon realized she was holding her breath and sighed. "In

here," she yelled.

"I've got to go," Shannon said into the phone, then quickly hung up.

"I thought I told you to meet me..." Sarah Pearse began, entering the studio, an attractive woman in her mid-fifties, slender and elegantly dressed, with artfully-placed blonde streaks in her short auburn hair. She was also a woman who liked to get her way.

"I know, Mother. I'm sorry. I just got busy and...and forgot."

Shannon became frightened as she watched the anger rise in her mother's face on seeing the bust.

"What the bloody hell..." Sarah began, placing her hands on her hips.

"You can't come in here!" Shannon said, in a small attempt to protect her sanctuary, but was immediately sorry.

"Watch your tongue!" Sarah snapped, raising her hand.

Shannon cringed, but no strike came. She picked up a cover for the statue, then stopped, surprised that for the first time in her life, Shannon simply didn't seem to care what her mother thought.

Sarah nodded toward the bust. "I thought we were through with HIM!"

"Maybe you are, but I'm not." She dropped the cloth next to the base of the statue, then got up to wash her hands.

"D.J. Hamilton was a liar. He tricked me into marrying him, and you know how impossible he was to live with."

"No, I don't. I was only eight when we left, remember?" Shannon was surprised to see a rare hint of sadness in her mother's eyes. "Didn't you love my father – when you married him?" she asked.

"I was young..." Sarah began. "I doubt I really knew what love was then. He promised me the world. Instead, he ruined my life!"

As Sarah pulled off her gloves, Shannon looked at her mother's expensive clothes and large diamond ring. "It seems you've landed on your feet."

Shannon quickly walked past her mother and went to the kitchen, putting some distance between them. She rarely stood up to her mother and usually lost when she did. She filled a glass of water from the tap and slowly drank it down in an attempt to slow her beating heart. She cringed when she heard her mother's footsteps.

"William is the best thing that happened to me," Sarah said from across the counter.

"I don't trust him." Shannon looked past her mother into her living room.

"How can you say that after all he's done for you."

"For me? He bought that gallery for his own schemes. You just don't want to see it."

"He did it to give you a venue to sell your art."

"I hate being on display in that awful place. And, the thought of this tour makes me sick. Why don't you just take the pieces to Paris — you're better with those people than I am."

"But, the public wants to see you. William has gone to a lot of trouble to set this up. You'll do as you're told, young lady, and will show some gratitude."

Shannon was amazed at how her mother's words could make her revert back to feeling like she was ten again. *Will I never grow up?* she thought to herself.

"I'm sorry," Shannon finally said.

"That's more like it." Sarah put on her gloves. "Now, I want to talk to you about what you're going to wear tonight. I don't want you showing up in those damned boots you insist on wearing."

Shannon looked down at her red cowboy boots, one of the small gestures of independence she'd kept throughout her life. She and her mother had been circling back to these same crossroads for years.

"I'd prefer—" Sarah continued.

"I know what you want," Shannon interrupted, knowing it was futile to argue. She wondered if she should mention the theft and decided against it. Her mother probably already knew and was simply ignoring it.

"And, you're hair! Look how disheveled you look in that long mess."

"I like it this way." Shannon looked at her mother and added, "But, I'll put it up tonight – the way you like it."

"You were going to meet me at the bridal shop," Sarah said as she sat on the sofa. "How're we ever going to get you fitted for your wedding gown if you don't—"

"Mother, there isn't going to be any wedding—"

"Shannon, stop this instant. We've been over this a hundred

times. Thomas is—"

"Your choice, not mine!" Shannon said, then walked into her living room. "I'm never getting married – to Thomas or any man."

Sarah crossed her arms over her large breasts and waited.

Shannon sighed and added, "I don't want to end up like you and my father."

"But, you saw how miserable we were in Oregon on that filthy ranch of his."

Shannon thought back to the rolling green hills behind her father's house that led up to Mount Hood, then looked sadly at the large, white- capped mountain in the painting hanging over her mantel.

"You may have been unhappy…," Shannon said in a small voice, "but it was the best time of my life."

CHAPTER THREE

At dusk, Shannon walked past the newsstand in front of the Pearse Gallery, a green cape flowing around her long, sinewy legs that matched her eyes.

"Hi, Ronan," she said to the man who owned the stand.

"Shannon O'Toole," the man said in a broken brogue. She recognized the lilt in his voice, similar to the Gaelic spoken in the village of Clifden. "I hear you're gonna be famous tonight."

Before she could answer, an older man in a dark suit came up to the stand and bought a newspaper. She saw the headlines: DUBLIN'S SERIAL KILLER STILL AT LARGE.

Shannon shivered and pulled her cape close around her as she walked on. She thought of Nikki, a teacher she'd known at her art school, who worked evenings at the gallery. But, Nikki hadn't been to work for awhile.

As Shannon entered the back door of the gallery, she felt relieved to hear the large door shut behind her. The familiar room was cluttered with packing material, canvases and statues waiting for shipment. A desk stood in the center of the room, covered with paperwork, printed shipping labels, and a stack of mail.

Thomas Aherne, an unctuous man, looking confident in his tuxedo, frowned at Shannon as she entered. He ran one hand through his dark hair as he nodded in response to the rambling of an officer wearing a Garda uniform.

"I'm sure it was an expert who did this, Mr. Aherne," the short, stocky officer said, looking at a small tablet in his hands. "It may be the same culprit that broke in here before, but this new alarm system must've been disarmed very carefully, sometime in the early morning, so it could be reset after he left—"

"He?" Thomas interrupted loudly.

"We're assuming one man did this job - at this point. The lock was picked with utmost skill. He knew what he was doing, alright. But, you, being the director and all, probably already know this."

"Manager," Thomas corrected. "And, yes, I do." He sighed, looking at the officer's badge. "However, Officer Murphy, we have a show starting now. Can we pick this up again tomorrow?"

"Of course, Mr. Aherne." The officer tipped his hat to Shannon and smiled with a sheepish grin. "Good evening, Miss O'Toole. I hope we find your statue very soon."

"Thank you," Shannon said softly, a little embarrassed. She laid her purse on the desk, aware that Thomas was watching her. He seemed to be upset about something other than the burglary.

Thomas took Murphy by the arm and began leading him to the back door as the officer continued.

"Me Maggie's working for you now."

"Yes, she is," Thomas sighed.

"She's a good girl, she is. I'm sure she'll fit in here nicely. She has only one year left at her art school. Then, maybe she'll be as famous as yourself, Miss O'Toole…with a lot of hard work, that is."

Shannon nodded, then took off her cape and placed it next to her purse.

"Maggie's very satisfactory…for now," Thomas said, then once again turned the older man toward the door.

Just then, Shannon heard loud laughter coming from the large gallery and frowned. Sighing heavily, she walked to peek through the open doorway to the front of the gallery. Numerous people were already mulling around her art pieces, Champagne flutes in hand, filled to the brim with the golden liquid. Shannon looked back at Thomas and saw her opportunity. She slid out of the back room before he could yell at her for being late.

She walked to a counter at the back of the high-ceilinged room, where a tall redhead stood in a black dress that covered only the necessities over her voluptuous figure. Maggie Murphy was going to the art college that Shannon had attended, and was recently hired as a part-time receptionist at the gallery.

"Hi," Shannon said.

"Shannon!" Maggie's face lit with excitement. "You look fabulous in that melon-colored chiffon dress. I'm sure Thomas will be pleased…" Maggie's eyes fell to Shannon's feet and she stopped.

"Thank you," Shannon said, while Maggie stared at her. She hated the dress, since it'd been chosen for her, but she smiled down at her boots.

"What a devil you are," Maggie finally said. "Those boots go everywhere with you, don't they?"

"Pretty much." Shannon looked around the room, then turned to Maggie again.

"Any word from Nikki?"

Maggie's long hair fell over one shoulder as she struggled to open a Champagne bottle. "No. She hasn't been in class all this week. I called her apartment, but no answer. I think she ran away again, like she did when she went to Greece. But then, I wouldn't be here if she was doing her job."

A loud pop sounded as Maggie pulled the cork out of the bottle.

"Oh, I'm so nervous," Maggie continued as she wiped a small spill on the counter. "This is my first show since I started here. Look at them all." She waved her arms to encompass the filled room.

Shannon looked around, but didn't see any faces she knew.

"You won't have any pieces left for the Paris show!" Maggie said excitedly. "Oh, I wish I could go."

Shannon frowned. She hated the thought of her upcoming tour. But, then, she wasn't very happy with her life right now.

"Has Thomas said any more about your missing statue?" Maggie asked.

"No, not yet. He didn't have a chance. Your father is still back there asking a lot of questions and telling your secrets."

"Oh, my Da never lets up." Maggie rolled her eyes to the ceiling. "That's the way they are, aren't they?"

Shannon didn't answer. She didn't know how fathers really were. There was William, her step-father, but he wasn't exactly what she called 'father' material.

"I wonder, Shannon O'Toole," Maggie giggled, her hand on her hip. "Now, did you use a mirror or a photograph to make that likeness of yourself in the nude for that statue?"

This time, Shannon rolled her eyes. She was glad the statue was gone. "I'll never tell," she said, then walked away.

Just then, two people walked into the gallery, and Shannon was happy for the first time that evening.

Liam O'Toole was a husky man. His silver hair glistened in the overhead lights of the gallery. He was a proud man who lived where the sea and the rocks were a part of life. His wife, Moyna, stood next to him, a beautiful, small woman with sky-blue eyes and a warm smile that was given generously.

"Granma, Granda," Shannon exclaimed and ran into her grandmother's arms. "Oh, I've missed you." The familiar smell of lavender enveloped her.

These two people had been her anchor during a time of her life when she was uprooted and confused. For one precious year, she had lived with her grandparents in their small stone cottage in Clifden. They're gentle manner and soft-spoken Gaelic had given her a sense of belonging that she needed most after her mother had taken her away from her father.

"Now, Love," Moyna sighed, her eyes twinkling in her beautiful, tanned face, as if she knew a secret. "You didn't think we wouldn't be here, did you now?"

"Well, there's that old badger that used to come up to me cottage," Liam roared, pointing to a statue of an animal standing on its hind legs. His voice carried across the room, and Shannon noticed numerous people turning to look their way. "I remember how he'd run like the dickens across the clon when I'd come near 'im."

Shannon laughed. "You two hardly ever leave Clifden. Are you staying with Aunt Elva?"

"Yes," Moyna answered, raising her hand to the silver Celtic cross necklace that she always wore. "I haven't seen me sister in so long."

Shannon felt a twinge of guilt that she had been ignoring her aunt, but they never really got along. She was too much like Shannon's mother.

"Let me look at you," Moyna said, holding Shannon at arm's length. "You're much too thin—"

"We'll be heading back t' home in a couple of days," Liam interrupted, with a wink. "Must be back in time for the Connemara Pony Show. I've got me horse entered agin'… but then, you'll be leavin' on your grand tour, as well."

Shannon's grandfather was a leading member of the Connemara

Pony Society of Ireland. His horses were from the native Irish breed dating back to the fourth century, BC. Suddenly, she missed being near the horses and that part of her past.

As she looked at the expression on her grandmother's face, Shannon knew she must have seen the sadness in her eyes. She smiled now and nodded. "I'm sure he'll win again this year."

"We're so proud of you," Moyna said, softly laying her hand on Shannon's arm. "And, when you're through with your tour, maybe you can come stay with us for a bit. I'll put some meat back onto those bones."

Shannon's smile broadened at the thought of returning to Clifden. "I'd like that very much."

Just then, her smile faded as she saw Thomas walking toward her.

"Hello, Mr. and Mrs. O'Toole," Thomas said in a polite, businesslike tone. "I didn't know you were coming tonight."

"Didn't tell you we was," Liam said, stepping closer to his granddaughter.

Thomas took Shannon's hand and pulled her toward him, slipping his arm around her waist. "Shannon, you must visit with our other guests, too. I'm sure the O'Toole's will understand."

"Now hold on there," Liam said to Thomas, placing a protective hand on Shannon's arm.

"It's alright, Granda…Thomas is right. Help yourselves to some Champagne. I'll come find you as soon as I can."

"Don't you worry about us," Moyna said, patting Shannon's hand. "We'll have a look around ourselves."

When they were out of earshot, Shannon turned to Thomas as he pulled her away, her green eyes flashing with anger. "That was rude! You didn't have to—"

"All of these people are here to see you, sweetheart," Thomas cut in, an edge to his voice. "The least you can do is spend time with them, as well."

Fuming, she remained silent as Thomas led her away, wishing she could someday tell him what she really thought. But, she knew she wouldn't dare. She was too afraid of him.

"Why did you hang up on me today?" Thomas whispered to her. "You know I hate that."

"Mother came in. I...I had no choice."

She was glad when they were approached by a couple and tried to smile as she met the Devlins of Kilkenny. Then, she was introduced to the Bayles of Waterford, south of Dublin. After so many new faces, Shannon's head began to spin.

She noticed a strange man that stood out among the handsomely-dressed crowd. His tall, muscular body strained the seams of his tweed jacket; his wavy, dark hair was cut shorter than most men she knew. He was staring at her from the counter where Maggie stood. When he saw her looking at him, he turned, picked up a glass of Champagne, and disappeared into the crowd.

"Here we are," Thomas said, pulling Shannon's attention away from the man. They stopped before an older couple, who were obviously wealthy. The man wore an Armani suit, and the small, slender woman next to him was covered in jewels.

"John and Laura," Thomas said, "I'd like you to meet Shannon O'Toole. The Greenburgs are from America."

"Mr. and Mrs. Greenburg," Shannon said, shaking the man's wide hand. "William, my step-father, introduced us at a private reception held at my mother's house."

The man and William had conducted some business behind closed doors that night. Thomas had been there, as well. Shannon remembered there was something about John Greenburg she didn't trust.

"Oh, yes," Greenburg said, smiling at Thomas as if he knew something only he and Thomas shared. "I remember now."

"How long will you be staying in Ireland?" Shannon asked Mrs. Greenburg.

The petite woman shifted her sable stole up onto her shoulder, looking bored. "Too long, I'm afraid!"

"But, Laura," Thomas began, "I'd hoped to take you two on a tour of the city—"

"I'm not interested in seeing the city," Laura said, cutting Thomas off. "John, I need a refill."

"I'll do that for you," Thomas insisted, taking her glass. Then, he walked toward Maggie.

Shannon smiled at the Greenburgs. "If you will excuse me," she said, then slipped away from the unpleasant couple, smiling to herself as she heard the man grumbling behind her.

She looked for her grandparents and saw they were talking to a large woman with her hair piled high on her head, so she walked toward the back of the room.

"Would you mind if I ask you something, Miss O'Toole?" a deep voice said softly behind her, making her jump. She turned and saw the strange man now standing too close to her elbow. His eyes were darker than his hair.

"That all depends," she replied. Suddenly, she felt as if she should run away as fast as she could, but her feet wouldn't move.

"I'd like you to come with me."

"And, where would you be going?" she asked shortly, but she'd heard her voice quiver.

"I'll tell you when we're outside." The man grabbed her arm. "I want to ask you some questions about—"

"No, I don't think so," she said, pulling away from his grip. She quickly walked away from the man, hoping that her knees wouldn't buckle now.

In one corner, with a shaking hand, she tried to look busy as she turned a bronze statue of a cormorant, a bird that had reminded her of Thomas as she'd created it - greedy and voracious. The man she'd just met seemed worse. She took slow, even breaths to control her racing heart, then turned slightly and watched as the man walked to the other side of the room. He stood near the door with his arms crossed, staring at her. She looked down to avoid his eyes.

"Stop fidgeting with my display," Thomas said behind Shannon, making her jump. He placed his hands on her shoulders and turned her to him. "It was perfect the way it was." He reached down and reset the bronze to its original position.

Shannon didn't respond because her throat was too dry.

"Who was that man you were talking with?" Thomas looked at the stranger.

"I…I don't know. I thought you invited him."

"I'm sure I didn't. What did he want?" Thomas asked as he pushed a loose hair back behind her ear.

Shannon shivered at his touch. "I didn't wait to find out. He gives me the creeps."

She saw her grandparents waving at her from across the room

and tried to smile, wishing she could relax.

"What's up with you?"

"I'm just so nervous…" Shannon began. She glanced over Thomas' shoulder and said a silent prayer when she saw the strange man leave.

"You'd think this was my first show, like Maggie," she said, pulling the strand of hair back toward her face where she preferred it.

Thomas looked over at Maggie and winked. Shannon saw Maggie blush.

Slowly regaining her calm, Shannon looked around the gallery. She noticed an art student making notes on a pair of butter fairies she'd created last spring. She thought of the mythical characters of the Irish underground world she'd recently chosen for her work: the slippery leprechauns, the mischievous pookas, and the cluricauns, with their silver buckles. They'd reminded her of herself - a shadow of the person she really wanted to be.

"You will soon be world famous, darlin'," Thomas said, turning back to Shannon. "And, it's a great success, I might add."

"How do you know?" she asked. "We've just opened."

"I let a few of my best customers preview your work last evening and three pieces were taken. Today, two more have sold."

"You're forgetting that last night, something else was taken. It never made any sense to me why the thief only stole the one piece - the nude. You wanted it finished for this show."

Thomas looked around the room. "I know," he said after a moment.

"I don't understand how the alarm was disabled so easily. William just had that installed before the—"

"See her?" Thomas asked quickly, discreetly pointing to a very large woman in a gray dress, wearing a white seal coat. "She wants to commission you to do her bust."

Shannon frowned, then leaned into Thomas, so as not to be overheard.

"I'm not sure I have enough material!" she whispered.

Thomas threw back his head and laughed heartily. Then, he kissed Shannon deeply.

"I love you, Shannon O'Toole. Even more, now that you'll be a millionaire."

Shannon looked at Thomas in disbelief. "You know I don't do this for the money," she said, frowning.

"But, darlin', I DO! Tomorrow, when we're in Paris, let's finally get married."

Shannon looked toward the door and sighed deeply as she saw her mother walk in.

"You know why I'll never get married," Shannon said softly, looking back at her mother.

Shannon's mother, wearing a full-length mink coat, walked into the gallery on the arm of her second husband, William Pearse. Sarah led her younger husband over to where Shannon and Thomas were standing. Shannon knew her mother had seen her grandparents, but was ignoring them. They were always a reminder of where Sarah'd begun, and she hated the reminder.

Offering her cheek to Shannon for the obligatory public kiss, Sarah said loudly, "What an exciting night!"

Shannon reluctantly kissed her, then quickly pulled away.

"Shannon, dear, you look pale," Sarah said in her sing-song voice she used in high society.

"Thomas just gave me a shock and told me how much I'll be worth."

"Oh? And, how much would that be?" Sarah asked Thomas.

"After this tour, over a million!"

Sarah rubbed her heavily-jeweled hands together. "How wonderful! Isn't it, darling?" she said, looking at her husband.

"Yes, marvelous," William said to Sarah. He was a handsome, successful businessman, with an elegant flair about him in his perfectly; tailored tuxedo. But, Shannon knew more about him than most people.

"Hello, my dear," he smiled sweetly to Shannon, as he ran his hand down her arm.

Shannon stepped aside, out of William's reach.

Thomas walked away.

William looked around the room and smiled, nodding to some of the people. Then, he removed a gold case from his pocket, took out a cigarette, and lit it. Shannon saw a flash of light reflect off the ruby ring with the crest on his right hand. William leaned toward Shannon, his dark hair glistening in the overhead lights.

"You look stunning in that dress, my dear. And, from the look of things, you're a hit. Maybe I should keep you closer - to keep an eye on your future."

"I wish it were all over," Shannon said, feeling suddenly very tired. "I just want to go home."

Shannon saw her mother look down at her feet for the first time. She swallowed hard, knowing what was coming next.

"My God, Shannon Eileen, what do you mean by wearing those god-awful boots to this show! I've told you a million times to get rid of them."

"I always wear them," Shannon said, trying to sound convincing, but she knew it was useless. She'd just have to bear through her mother's disapproval again.

"Someday, I'm going to burn them."

"That'll never happen," Shannon said, then was sorry. The stern look on her mother's face made Shannon wince.

"We'll see about that."

Shannon saw William's face change as he looked across the room. She turned and noticed Thomas was leaning close to Maggie, whispering something in her ear.

"For now," Sarah continued, "the most important step in your career, young lady, is selling your work. If no one bought your art, what good is it?"

"It means more to me than the money," Shannon snapped back, tired of the same old argument. At least her mother had gotten off the subject of her boots.

William took Shannon's arm and said, "Come with me."

He steered her toward the backroom, and Shannon went along, as she always did. William pulled the thick drapes across the doorway between the gallery and the workroom.

"Now, Shannon," William said, his words echoing through the rafters of the high ceiling. "You need to understand the importance of this tour. We will be together every day...showing your work to the world."

"I don't want to go. I don't want your version of wealth."

"I made my wealth before I married your mother, remember?" William was twisting the crested ring on his finger.

"Yes, I know all about your wealth, more than you think. My

Granda knew you when you were a servant's son. You probably found some way to steal the old man's estate—"

William grabbed Shannon's wrist. "I have given you everything," he cut in. "The best schools, started your career. I even financed this gallery to give you a place to sell your precious art."

"Yes, I know all that," Shannon said, wriggling her hand free. "SHE never lets me forget it," Shannon yelled, hoping that her mother would hear. "Who is she trying to impress?"

"We merely want you to remember your place."

"My place," Shannon said. "That's all I ever hear. My place is in my studio, working. Not here, hawking my wares to the rich and famous of Ireland. That's Thomas' job."

William was about to speak, but Shannon cut him off. She had stayed silent too long.

"Why don't you go do something else, like play with one of your precious racehorses at The Curragh and leave me alone! You love those animals more than anything else in the world," she yelled as she began to walk away.

William grabbed her and pulled her to him. "You little—" He stopped, staring down at Shannon. "If only..." he said in a soft voice that Shannon had never heard before. Just then, Sarah walked in.

"What's going on here?" Sarah yelled.

"Mother, I..." Shannon began, pulling herself free from William's grasp.

"William," Sarah snapped. "John Greenburg is looking for you in the gallery."

William nodded and left the room.

"What were you doing in my husband's arms?" Sarah accused, her hands on her hips.

"What?!" Shannon put her hand to her head, replacing a strand of hair that had fallen out of a barrette. She'd seen her mother's jealous attitude with William and the gallery's receptionists, but never before had it been aimed her way.

"When I walked in here, you were throwing yourself at him!"

"You're crazy," Shannon replied.

Sarah slapped Shannon hard, then stopped. "Oh, Shannon...I..." Sarah walked away from Shannon and began pacing the room, her high heels clicking on the tiled floor.

Shannon rubbed her cheek. This wasn't the first time she'd felt her mother's hand. She knew that her mother wasn't worried that she'd hurt her, she was more afraid that her slap might have left a mark on her daughter's face and someone would notice.

Sarah straightened herself and stood by the desk.

"We're not happy with your attitude lately," Sarah said.

"Why am I not surprised. I'm never good enough for you," Shannon said finally.

"You're a wealthy, well-known sculptor in Ireland. After Paris, the WORLD will know you! Do you think you can act this way during your tour?"

Shannon remained silent, standing with her arms crossed, watching her mother. She had learned to ignore these lectures and was through letting her mother dominate her.

"Dear," Sarah continued, softening her voice, "I'm only taking your career into consideration—"

"That's all you've ever considered," Shannon yelled at her. "Never what I wanted."

"That's not true," Sarah said indignantly. She began to rifle through the papers on the desk, avoiding Shannon's eyes. "Why you haven't married Thomas yet is beyond me. He's perfect."

Shannon stared at her mother. Her ability to switch conversations so quickly still astonished her. "Maybe for you," she snapped.

"What's that supposed to mean?"

"You've been pushing me into marrying Thomas ever since William bought the gallery. I told you before, I'm never getting married. Look at what it did to you and my father."

"D.J. Hamilton didn't want anything to do with either of us. Remember?"

"That's what you've said all my life," Shannon retorted and turned away from her mother.

Sarah picked up a letter from the desk and stared at it.

"Besides," Shannon continued, "I don't love Thomas..." Shannon turned and saw her mother's pale face and the envelope in her hand.

"What is it?" Shannon asked, walking over to her.

Sarah tried to hide the envelope, but Shannon took it from her and looked at the address. It was from her father! She stared at her mother in disbelief.

"What can HE want now?" Sarah yelled into the room.

Shannon saw that the envelope had been opened. She quickly took out the letter and read out loud.

"'My dearest Shannon. Once again, I'm writing to you, asking that you return to our ranch - you belong here in Oregon.'"

She stopped and looked at her mother.

"What does he mean, 'once again?' I never got any letters from him."

"I have no idea," Sarah said. She reached for the letter, but Shannon pushed her hand away and continued to read.

"'The Diamond H hasn't been the same since you left. Please come back. It's vital that I see you now, I have something important to tell you.'"

Shannon paused and looked at her mother's flushed face. She finished reading the letter.

"'Come home, Shannon. I love you, Your Dad.'"

William walked into the back room with a disapproving look. "Shannon, you must come back. People are beginning to leave—" He stopped when he saw the letter in Shannon's hand.

"No," Shannon said.

"What do you mean 'no'?" William said fiercely. "You can't do this in the middle of a show. This will not be allowed in Paris."

Shannon looked at her mother, then at William. Just as Thomas walked into the room, she tried to stand a little taller and said, "I'm not going to Paris."

"What the devil—" Thomas began.

"Nonsense," William said. "You can't give up your career now and go running off to some horse ranch in Oregon."

Shannon looked at her mother, her eyes narrowed in anger. "Why did you open my letter?"

"I didn't—" Sarah began. "You haven't seen your father in over twenty years. Now, he expects you to just come running?" She paused, then added, "Go to Paris, Shannon, and forget about him."

"Not this time, Mother. I'm going home."

Shannon took her father's letter, grabbed her purse and cape, and ran out the back door.

CHAPTER FOUR

Bridget McDonaugh, a young woman with long strawberry-blonde hair, pulled back in a ponytail, stood before a window in her apartment. The streets below were crowded with people reveling in the night. She wished she could have gone to Shannon's show, but her father had needed her in his pub.

Shannon was the one who gave her the nickname "Brid." Brid thought of when she and Shannon first became friends at boarding school, when Brid was nine. Her aunt had decided that Brid was too wild and needed more discipline, so it was her aunt's money that had paid for the school. Being from a close family of six kids, Brid had hated the school, but Shannon was the only one who understood her homesickness.

Looking at her watch, Brid saw that it was late, but she knew Shan- non wouldn't mind if she stopped by. She grabbed a bottle of Champagne and walked out of her apartment.

In the hallway, she met Maggie Murphy, the young girl who lived in an apartment on the floor above.

"Hi," Brid said with a smile, but her smile faded when she saw the bruise under Maggie's left eye. "My Lord, girl, what happened to you?"

"Oh, I, huh, fell...outside of school. I'll be fine," Maggie stammered, then ran up the stairs.

Brid was beginning to worry about that girl, even though she'd only known her for a short time. She knew that Maggie was now working at Shannon's gallery, to earn money while she was going to art school. But, recently, there was something different about her. She'd been staying out late and was secretive about where she'd been. Brid had also noticed the sharp, expensive clothes Maggie was now wearing.

None of my business, Brid thought to herself. She turned and placed a key in the lock to Shannon's apartment, which was next to hers. They'd shared keys with each other when Shannon moved in.

Brid knew something was up when she saw all of the lights on in Shannon's apartment, illuminating the soft, cream walls of the high-ceilinged room. Shannon's usual habit was to turn off a light as she left a room 'to save energy' she would say.

"Shannon!" Brid called out. "Are you home?"

"In here," Shannon said from her bedroom.

Brid passed the table next to the red velvet couch, where a statue of an Appaloosa stood, a copy of an ancient Chinese spotted horse she'd seen Shannon create in one of their classes together. Brid knew about Shannon's father's horse ranch in the U.S. and had always secretly hoped that one day she'd get to see it.

She walked to the kitchen and grabbed two glasses, then went down the hallway. She stopped and peered into Shannon's studio. She smiled at the unfinished bust, then continued to Shannon's bedroom.

Brid stopped when she saw clothes strewn all over the room. An open suitcase lay on the bed. Another bag sat on the floor, containing sculpting tools and sketch pads.

Shannon stood in front of her closet in jeans and a red sweater. She had numerous dresses slung over one arm. A chiffon dress was crumpled on the floor of the closet.

Brid set the glasses on a desk and poured the bubbling liquid into each. Then, she took the glasses and sat on the bed, watching Shannon for a moment. Shannon folded the dresses and placed them into her suitcase. Brid handed Shannon a glass.

"Sláinte!" Brid said, smiling again over the rim of her glass. "To your success."

Shannon gulped down her Champagne.

"Going somewhere?" Brid asked casually, and refilled Shannon's glass. She saw the tension in her friend's face and knew it must have something to do with her mother.

"Yes." Shannon took a deep sip. "Oregon."

"You're kidding! Isn't that where your Da lives?"

Shannon bristled at the familiar name for her father, set her glass down, and walked toward the closet.

"Yes, but I doubt I'll ever call him 'Da.' He'll always be 'D.J.' to me. He hasn't done all that much for me all these years, remember? He never came after me…"

Brid watched Shannon with a puzzled look, then smiled as she saw Shannon shove a pair of expensive, red leather cowboy boots into her suitcase on top of the dresses.

"Okay," Brid said. "Let up. What's happened?"

Shannon pulled the letter out and handed it to Brid.

Brid looked at the envelope, then quickly read it. "This is the first letter you've ever received from him."

"I know."

"Why do you think he wants you to come now?"

"I don't know."

Brid looked again at the letter. "He says it's important."

"Yes…" Shannon sat down on the edge of the bed. "Oh, what am I doing?"

"You're frustrated, that's understandable. Look, your mother took you away when you were young, then shoved you around to boarding schools all your life. You've never felt at home here in Ireland."

"I know, but—"

"No 'buts' about it. I think you should go. It's what you really want, right?"

"Yes…, but what if—"

Brid held up her hand and stopped Shannon.

"No 'what ifs', either. It's time you stood your ground on this and go see your Da."

Shannon looked up at the large, metal sculpture of an old oak tree hung over the bed. Brid watched as tears welled in her friend's eyes, imagining the memories that flooded through her mind.

"I don't know what I'll say to him," Shannon finally said, wiping her face. "I've been so angry at him all these years."

Brid nodded, then saw a black and white photo lying on the bed and picked it up. Three people were standing outside a horse corral: Shannon, around age eight, a tall, slender man, and a boy, around the age of ten or eleven. A dark puppy with large paws sat next to Shannon in the photo.

"You were so cute. That's your Da in the middle, right?"

"Yes, that's D.J."

"Who's this guy?" Brid asked, pointing to the young boy.

"Jake McLeod."

Brid looked at the photo again and raised her eyebrows. "He's Irish?" she asked. "But, he doesn't look Irish."

"His mother was a Nez Percé Indian," Shannon explained. "His father manages D.J.'s ranch." She looked at the photo. "He was the first boy I ever kissed."

"What?! You never told me about him."

"I know…I'm sorry. It was just a silly kid-thing that happened a long time ago."

Brid watched her friend for a moment, then asked, "Do you still like him?"

Shannon shrugged, then took the photo from Brid, smoothing out the folded corner.

"He's cute, in a sort of rugged way," Brid said, looking over Shannon's shoulder. "I'd fall for him in a minute."

Shannon frowned at Brid. "You'd fall for Thomas, if he wasn't such a weasel," she said.

"No way!" Brid exclaimed, shuddering. "Thomas is more like a snake than a weasel. I've never liked him."

Shannon looked at her friend, then stood and turned toward her suitcase. "He can be an okay guy…sometimes," she said.

"He's too stuck on himself…and he likes to keep secrets."

Brid watched Shannon mindlessly rearranging her clothes. She looked at the photo again. "Will you see Jake when you go to Oregon?" Brid asked coyly.

"IF I go to Oregon!"

"Oh, I think you'll go."

Shannon smiled for the first time and picked up her glass, raising it in the air.

Brid raised her glass and clanked the rim against Shannon's. "To Oregon!" she toasted.

"Yes. To Oregon," Shannon sighed and then emptied her glass. She placed the photo into a side pocket of her smaller bag. "I thought you were working late at your Da's pub tonight?"

"I was, until my brother, Sean, returned from America early. He took over my shift. How did your show go?" Brid asked.

"There was some creep there that scared the bejesus out of me."
Shannon wrapped her arms around herself.

"What'd he want?"

"He said he wanted to talk to me, but that I had to leave with
him. I'd just seen the headlines about that killer still out there, you
know, and was freaked out."

"Yeah, I wish they'd catch the bugger. You don't think this
guy...?"

Shannon started pacing. "Probably not...he was just odd."

"Did Thomas know who he was?"

"No." Shannon frowned as she slumped onto the bed. "All he
could talk about was how I'll be a millionaire - after this tour."

"What?" Brid said in surprise.

"That's what he said...shortly before I announced I wasn't going
to Paris."

"You said that?"

"Maybe I shouldn't have. Mother and William were there."
Shannon shivered.

"Oh, my God," Brid said. "What did SHE have to say?"

"Mother flipped out, of course, forbidding me to go to Oregon.
William, huh..."

"What?"

"Oh, nothing."

"You know what your mother is like when she gets angry," Brid
said.

Shannon sighed heavily and they both looked out the window.
Brid saw the lights twinkling on the water from the Halfpenny
Bridge.

"Maybe I should just forget D.J.'s letter," Shannon said as she got
up and started to take the boots out of her luggage.

Brid reached over and stopped her.

"You just told me you were going to see your Da."

Shannon looked at Brid and frowned.

"It's about time you started doing what YOU want to do," Brid
continued, "not what that arsehole, Thomas, or anyone else tells you
to do."

Shannon's face began to relax a little, and Brid giggled.
"Especially, since you're going to be a millionaire!"

Shannon laughed.

"You're right."

"Good girl!" Brid said. "Oh, I ran into Maggie Murphy in the hallway just now. She looked beat up, but said she'd taken a fall by her school today."

Shannon stopped for a moment.

"That's not the first time I've seen her like that." Brid continued.

"Maggie was working at the gallery tonight," Shannon said. "She didn't have any marks on her then."

Brid jumped at the sound of a key in Shannon's front door. "You expecting someone?" she asked softly.

The door opened and slammed shut with a loud bang.

"Shannon!" Thomas yelled.

Brid jumped off the bed. "I'd better go."

"Shannon O'Toole, where the hell are you?" Thomas yelled louder.

Brid hugged her friend, then said softly, "Don't forget what I said. Call me if you need me!"

"I'll be okay," Shannon said, hugging Brid back. "Thanks."

Brid kissed Shannon's cheek. "Luck!" she said as she walked out of the bedroom, passing Thomas in the hallway.

"What're you doing here, Bridget?" Thomas asked angrily.

"Just leaving," Brid replied, without stopping.

In her bedroom, Shannon's smile disappeared as Thomas entered. He was still wearing his tux from the show, but his tie was undone and his shirt looked crumpled.

"What's gotten into you?" Thomas yelled.

Shannon continued packing. "I'm going to Oregon."

"The hell you are," Thomas said as he took the boots from Shannon's suitcase and furiously threw them toward the closet.

Shannon stood looking at Thomas, shaken by his anger.

Thomas sighed and smiled. She watched as he tried to collect himself. It was like seeing a chameleon change colors. He walked to her and rubbed his hands up and down her arms.

"What's gotten into you lately?" he asked. "One minute we're get- ting married—"

"That's what you want to believe."

"What's that supposed to mean?" Thomas demanded.

"You know…"

Thomas grabbed Shannon again. "I don't like your attitude. That will all change…after we're married—"

"There you go again."

Thomas stood silent for a moment, staring down at her. She tried to pull away, but he held on tighter. "You're hurting me, Thomas."

"Why won't you listen to reason?" he asked, softening his grip. "You're throwing away a great opportunity. Paris will be so good for you - for us."

Shannon looked away from Thomas. She was so tired of always letting others control her life. She finally pulled away from him and walked to her closet.

"I don't care about Paris."

Thomas went to her and turned her back to him. "But, you said you hated your father."

"I know…I've decided…it's time I confront him."

"Why now?"

Thomas waited, but Shannon was silent.

"Why not wait until after Paris - after we're married?" he asked.

Shannon saw her father's letter on the bed. She took a deep breath and looked at Thomas, determined. "Paris will be there when I get back. Besides, if you love me, like you say you do, you'll wait till I've finished this."

Thomas pulled her into his arms and kissed her cheek, her neck.

"Darlin', your future is what's most important," he said as he pulled her sweater down from one shoulder, trailing his lips where the fabric had been. "Your show in Paris will make you famous worldwide."

"Is that what you want?" Shannon asked, her arms hanging at her sides, her skin crawling.

"Yes, more than anything in the world." He saw the look in her eyes and added, "Except for you, of course."

Shannon looked around her room and saw the sculpture hanging over her bed. Then, she looked down at the boots lying on the floor and slowly smiled. A new feeling was rising in her — one of freedom, stemming from her new confidence, or maybe the Champagne. She knew what she needed to do.

"If that's what you think is best," she sighed.

"Brilliant. I knew you'd come to your senses."

Thomas continued caressing Shannon, as he slowly guided her toward the bed.

"No, Thomas," she said, pulling away from him and straightening her sweater. "You know that I want to wait until…after we're married. I was raised a good Catholic girl, remember?" The truth was she didn't love him. She'd only loved once in her life.

Thomas came to her again, but she went to her suitcase and began re-folding the clothes inside. "Besides," Shannon said, "I need to finish packing. We're leaving in the morning, right?"

"Yes, on the noon plane to Paris."

Shannon took Thomas by the arm and steered him out of her bedroom, down the hall, to her front door.

"Then, you must be leaving me, now," she said, opening the door.

"Make sure to pack your wedding dress," Thomas said, a wide grin on his face. "And, forget those damned boots."

"Goodbye, Thomas."

Thomas kissed Shannon fiercely, then left.

Shannon shut the door and leaned back against it, taking deep breaths. She looked around, seeing the world she'd created for herself. Then, she saw the large oil painting hanging above the fireplace and slowly began to relax.

She walked to her telephone. Her hands shook as she reached for the receiver, but she calmed herself and dialed.

"Metro," a woman's voice answered.

"I would like a taxi sent to Welling Apartments on Temple Bar."

"Absolutely. It will arrive in twenty minutes. What will your destination be?"

"Dublin Airport."

Shannon hung up and walked to her bedroom, smiling to herself. Slowly, she picked up the boots and placed them back into her suitcase.

***

Late at night, a black car drove under an archway of one of Dublin's parks.

The Red Boots

The car stopped near a large ravine. With the engine still running, the driver, dressed all in black, got out and opened the trunk. He looked around him, then removed a large, black bag from the car. The man carried the bag over one shoulder to the edge of the ravine, then dropped it to the ground and rolled it out of sight. He got back into the car and drove away.

In the dark, the bag tumbled down the hillside. The moon came out from behind a cloud just when the bag came to a stop. The top of the bag had opened, revealing a woman's long red curls circling her ashen face and lifeless, green eyes that stared into the night.

CHAPTER FIVE

Michael O'Sullivan walked into Garda Headquarters, went to the lift, and punched the button hard, angry that he'd been pulled off the murder team to work on some fraud investigation. He also hated having to return to the section he'd worked in when his father was killed.

When the doors opened, he cringed when he saw the two occupants in uniform.

"They found her body in North Park last night," Jeff Whelan said to his partner, ignoring Michael as he stepped onto the lift. "It's strange that all the victims are naked when we find them. It seems to be the killer's style."

"Makes it harder to identify them," Jeff's partner said.

"Another one?" Michael inquired.

The other officer nodded sadly. "Maybe. It's been four months since the last killing like this. That makes three this year, and we still don't have a lead on the six cold cases from the two years before. We're no closer to ending this than when we started."

"Michael," Whelan said, smiling too broadly. "Haven't seen you since-"

"You're right, Jeff," Michael said, cutting Whelan off. He looked at the other man and smiled, "Paddy, you're looking fit as a fiddle."

Paddy Graham smiled and looked down over his protruding stomach. Michael imagined the man was unable to see his own shoes. He hoped he'd never have to work with either of these two again. The drug case they'd been on together, before Michael moved to the Criminal Investigation Unit, had ended in a fatality.

Whelan and Graham were Michael's partners when he worked at the local Garda unit, but they'd complained he was too hard to work with. They said he didn't follow the book, too much of a rogue.

Michael agreed with them, but had argued that on some cases, you had to throw the book out and follow your own instincts.

He'd gotten used to the other men dancing around him, when his father was Chief Superintendent of the Dublin Metro Garda. He'd begun to follow in his father's footsteps, like he wanted. But later, Michael learned that he thrived on the adrenalin from working in the eye of a murder case, which made others nervous.

A 'ding' was heard, the lift stopped, and the doors opened. Michael nodded to the men and began to walk out. A tall man, dressed like someone in an American Western movie set, bumped into Michael.

"Sorry," the man said with a voice that surprised Michael. He'd expected a much different dialect than one he'd most likely hear on the streets of Dublin. The man tipped his white Stetson hat to Michael as the lift doors closed.

Michael shook his head. Cowboys, he thought to himself and turned into the large open room.

"Top-o-the mornin' to you, Deidre," Michael said to the woman at the front desk in a sing-song voice his mother had used when he was young.

"And, to you, Michael O'Sullivan." Deidre was the receptionist, an older woman with graying hair that only the tips revealed the red color of her youth. Michael respected Deidre because she seemed to know everyone and everything.

"You're looking beautiful as ever."

One of Diedre's eyebrows rose higher than the other. "Smooth talker. You'd better get your butt into Dugan's office. Ever since he arrived, he's been drummin' his fingers on his desk as if he were playin' a Bodhran."

"I'm on my way," Michael said with a smile. The last time he'd heard the native drum being played was in a pub down in Temple Bar.

As he walked through the maze of desks and cubicles, he thought of when he was a teenager and Innis Dugan was made his father's partner. Years later, after Michael graduated from Garda College, his father was shot and killed while walking up to their home. Michael was there that night. Shortly afterwards, Dugan had been given his father's position as Chief Superintendent. That was the moment

Michael decided he wanted to be a detective. His father's murder was another unsolved, cold case.

Michael hesitated at the familiar door, then knocked.

"Come in," Dugan said, then looked up as Michael walked in. "Oh, 'tis you, Michael. I'm glad to see you decided to finally come to see me."

Michael noticed that Dugan's hair was white now. Then, he saw Neville Murphy sitting in one corner of the office and smiled.

"Neville," Michael said, shaking his father's best friend's hand. "It's been too long since we've seen each other."

"I agree," Neville said, nervously settling back into his chair.

"Do you two mind?" Dugan said from behind the large desk.

Michael smiled at Dugan, then slid into a dark brown chair. He was hit by the memories that flooded his mind. He never got used to this having been his father's office once. "What's so important that you have to pull me back here, Dugan?"

Dugan slid a thick file across the desk. Michael picked it up and began thumbing through it, while the Chief continued. "I was just asked to cooperate with a Special Agent from the American Internal Revenue Service about a large money-laundering scheme they think is linked with a business here in Dublin. You just missed him."

Michael thought of the tall cowboy he'd bumped into at the lift. "I've never worked in money-laundering," he confided. "I only know that most of these cases are linked to some illegal action, like drug trafficking, and the money is then sent overseas to be made to appear as legitimate cash. With today's internet and wire transfers, it's increasingly difficult to trace."

"You've always been a quick study, son," Neville said.

Michael looked again at the file. He came to Neville's report on a gallery robbery and stopped at a photo of the stolen statue. He looked up at Dugan. "What's this?" he asked, turning the file so the two men could see the snapshot.

Dugan looked at Neville.

"There's been a theft at the Pearse Gallery," Neville said, avoiding Dugan's eyes. "I was the originating officer, but the Chief feels we need—"

"That gallery's been hit a few times recently," Dugan interrupted. "And...we think there may be someone inside...and this theft's possibly linked to the laundering scheme. I want you to head the investigation."

"But, I've been working on the serial killer cases," Michael said, still in denial and hoping to sidestep this new assignment. "And, I just heard there was a new victim—"

"Whelan and Graham are the new team. I need you on this."

Michael grimaced. "Why me?"

"I don't have enough time or men for this now," Dugan continued, raking his fingers through his hair. "You've got the art background. It's all in there," he said, nodding to the file. "The American will be contacting you."

Michael sat in silence. He'd grown up with an appreciation for the masters. His mother was an artist, and she'd taken him to the Dublin National Museum every Saturday when he was young. He watched Dugan's face, thinking to himself that the man was hiding something.

"Besides," Dugan continued, smiling, "your superior tells me you're the best we have in our Investigation Unit, even if no one else wants to work with you. Neville's agreed, though I'm not sure why. While you're working on this, you can share Neville's office here, so we can keep in touch."

Michael looked at Neville, then again at the file in his hands. It felt very heavy now. He could sense the frustration building inside of him, but he knew he had no choice.

"I'll see what I can do."

Michael and Neville walked out of Dugan's office together.

"I'm glad you're here, Michael," Neville said, as he led the way to the break room. He poured two cups of strong, black liquid, then went toward his own, small office. Michael followed, wincing at the taste of the familiar, thick sludge that must have been stewing all morning.

"You guys still haven't learned how to stop and make a fresh pot?"

"'Tis the only thing available up here when you're in a hurry and in need." Neville chuckled as he sat behind his desk. He looked at Michael. "How're ya feelin' about the new assignment?"

"I don't like it. I'm the only one who knows the most about these murders."

"Aye, but sometimes a change gives us a fresh look at things. Besides, you never know when you might accidentally stumble onto a new piece of information along the way. Just keep your eyes and ears open."

Michael nodded as he sat in the only other chair in the office. Those were his father's words.

"How's your mother?" Neville asked. "Is your aunt still living with her?"

"No, she got her own place, just a few months after..." He looked out the window behind the older man. "Ma likes her independence and won't leave her house, even though my sisters have asked her to move in with them."

Neville was quiet as Michael looked around the sparse room. He was astounded that after all the years that Neville had worked for the Garda, his only furniture was his desk and two chairs. A black and white photo of his wife, Joan, and daughter, Maggie, sat on the desk in front of him in a gold frame.

Michael turned toward the open door when another officer in the blue uniform passed by. "Tell me about this theft."

"I interviewed Thomas Aherne, the gallery manager." Neville said after a moment. "He didn't seem to care much about the entire thing, just wanted the investigation over with."

"What made you think so?"

"He was more interested in that artist, Shannon O'Toole - the one who the statue was made after."

Michael nodded. He'd seen the photo.

Neville continued. "This is the third time this year they've been bro- ken into. I noticed that the back door lock had been tampered with, but it seemed strange to me that the alarm system was disarmed so quickly. It was one of those new wireless access control systems that's controlled with a computer."

"Do they have a guard on duty after hours?"

"No. This is the strangest case I've seen at that gallery. In the others, a few select oil paintings were reported stolen. But, this one, the only thing taken was that statue."

Michael made a mental note and remained silent.

"Did you know me Maggie is working at the Pearse Gallery

now?" Neville touched the frame of the picture on his desk.

"No, I thought she was still in art school." Michael had grown up with Maggie. She was like a little sister to him, even though he knew Neville had secret hopes that Michael would think of her in a different way.

"She's just about finished. Took this job to advance her career, she said."

"How long has she been working there?" Michael asked.

"A couple of weeks. She's even got herself a flat in some fancy apartments on Temple Bar. All grown up, she is now."

Michael could hear the sadness in Neville's voice. After his wife's death, Neville had seemed to put more of his attention on his daughter, much to Maggie's dismay.

"I'm sure she'll be just fine," Michael said. "Da always said it was hard to let go, when I wanted my independence. Look how I've turned out."

"I've known you since you were in nappies. There's only one piece of advice I'd be given ya."

Michael held his breath.

"Don't be so hard on your partners. They may save your life, someday."

Michael sighed and smiled.

Just then, the same officer in uniform called to Neville from outside the door, "Come on, you old coot, lunch is awaiting us."

Neville stood up and turned to Michael. "Well, I must be going. Would you like to join us?"

"No, you go ahead. Mind if I use your desk for a few minutes?"

"Not at all, make yourself 'ta home." Just before leaving, Neville said, "Dugan wants the file left here."

Michael nodded, then watched as Neville and the other officer walked out together. Then, he closed the door. Shrugging out of his jacket, he hung it on the back of Neville's chair and wondered to himself how Neville could work in such a neat environment. His own desk was always littered with paperwork, and he'd have to push everything out of the way to make room for a new file.

He pulled out his Nokia mobile handset and turned it on. He loved gadgets, and he was delighted that a new TV-to-mobile program allowed him to keep up on the latest news. A reporter droned on about the stock markets.

Slowly, after taking a long sip of the already cooling liquid, Michael went through every page, categorizing and storing the information away in his mind. He'd been blessed with a photographic memory, which annoyed the other staff in his office. He was able to recall the names and descriptions of every culprit he'd investigated.

Michael stopped scanning the papers and looked at his Nokia when the announcer said, *"A woman's body was found this morning in the North Park by a jogger...,"* while a composite of a woman's face was flashed onto the small screen.

Just then, Michael's cell phone rang. He turned down the volume of his Nokia and answered, "Detective O'Sullivan."

"Detective, I was given your number to call." The man's voice on the other end trembled.

Michael waited.

"My wife and I saw the newscast." Silence filled the air. "We think the young woman found in the park last night was our daughter, Nikki."

"What is your name?" Michael asked, thankful that not everyone in the Garda knew that he'd been taken off the serial killer cases yet.

"James Conroy. I'm a groundskeeper at Kilkea Castle."

Michael thought for a moment. The castle was less than an hour from the city. "I understand. Where do you live, Mr. Conroy?"

"Castledermot, County Kildare. Nikki works in Dublin at the Pearse Gallery."

Michael wasn't surprised to hear the man speak of his daughter in the present tense, as if she might still be alive. He'd been in the same state of denial for a long time after his father's death.

"Why do you think this woman may be your daughter?"

"She was on vacation for awhile. Then, when she was supposed to return back to work, we learned they haven't heard from her in over a week now. It's not like her..."

Michael was silent for a moment, then asked, "Could you arrange to come into Dublin this afternoon?"

"Yes." Conroy hesitated. "My wife would like to come, too."

"No problem. Just give me a phone number where I can reach you in the next half hour after I've made arrangements on where to meet."

James Conroy gave Michael his number, then hung up.

Michael put his cup down on the desk with a thud as he remembered Neville's words about the fact that Maggie worked at the Pearse Gallery. He scribbled a quick note for Neville, grabbed his coat, and left Garda Headquarters.

***

Chicago

It was three in the morning when Shannon disembarked from the airplane at O'Hare with dark circles under her eyes. Dazed, she walked toward the gate of her connecting flight.

A petite, dark-haired woman in a tight-fitting uniform was helping the person in the queue in front of Shannon. She overheard the woman's nasal voice say that the next flight was delayed for three hours because of a storm. Shannon waited her turn, then walked up to the counter.

"I just heard that this flight has been delayed. Is there another flight I could take to Oregon from here?"

The woman typed on the keyboard in front of her, then shook her head.

"I'm sorry, but this is the only one for now. All the others are full. You'll just have to wait."

Shannon thanked the woman, then picked up her bag and walked away. She was relieved to see a small, busy bistro still open nearby. Looking around, she found a table with a single man typing on his laptop, an iPod plugged into his ears, and his black-rimmed glasses hovering on the tip of his nose.

"Excuse me," Shannon said to the man, gently touching his shoulder.

The man looked up and removed one earphone.

"Would you mind sharing your table?" Shannon asked.

He pushed his glasses up and smiled as he shook his head, then moved some papers to one side, put the earpiece back in, and continued typing. Shannon dropped her suitcase onto the floor next to her and sat down. When a waitress came over to the table, she ordered coffee and a sandwich.

Shannon looked around the room and noticed an attractive bartender and one blonde stewardess eyeing each other. The bartender had a rugged, tanned face, with a small moustache on his upper lip. Shannon noticed a short man with wavy black hair, wearing a blue dress shirt, walking up to the woman. He laid some money onto the bar and said, "My treat, Marsha." Shannon watched the bartender frown as he took the money and walked to the other end of the bar, keeping his eyes on the blonde.

Just then, the woman was joined by two pretty, brunette stewardesses and two men in pilot uniforms. They stored their small bags near the end of the bar. Loud laughter erupted from the party at something the blonde said. The man in the blue shirt put his hand on the blonde's shoulder as the bartender placed drinks on the bar. Shannon noticed something in the bartender's eyes. Was it concern? Fear? Or, could it be jealousy? It was like watching a live mini-drama on television.

Then, it struck her. This was exactly the attitude she'd seen in Thomas for the past few months. He watched her all the time, as if she was his possession. He'd begun to scare her, but she didn't know why. Now, she knew. He was insanely jealous and obsessed with her. God knows why her mother thought that he was perfect for her. Shannon had done everything to dissuade him, but she realized she had to break off the engagement before it was too late.

Pulling out her cell phone, Shannon turned it on. She was not surprised to see five calls were from Thomas, eight from her mother, and two from William. There was one from Brid. She deleted all the messages, except Brid's. After listening to it, she checked her watch and called her friend. Brid wouldn't mind her calling now, even though she'd probably been at the pub late the night before.

"Brid, it's Shannon. I'm in Chicago with a three-hour layover."

"Chicago?" Brid said, yawning. "So, you ARE going home."

Shannon was silent for a moment. *Home*, she thought. She didn't have any sense of where home really was for her now. "To Oregon," she said softly.

"I'm so glad you called. There's so much going on here - you won't believe it."

Shannon could hear the panic now in her friend's voice.

"What's up, Brid?"

"There was a newscast today…about another murder. The Garda found a body this morning. They haven't come out yet and said who it was, but when I saw that composite photo...I thought of Nikki...Nikki Conroy."

Shannon sat stunned in disbelief. There was activity all around her, but she only heard a roar, like waves crashing upon rocks.

Brid paused, then added, "Shannon, are you still there?"

"Yes. I'll call you when I get to Oregon."

Shannon quickly disconnected and sat staring through the crowd passing by. Across the aisle, she caught her own reflection in a pane of glass and thought for a moment that she saw Nikki's face.

CHAPTER SIX

Ireland

Thomas was framing a Matisse print in the back room of the gallery. A commercial played on the television sitting at the end of the long counter where Thomas worked. Something on the print caught his eye and he looked closer at the signature. Puzzled, he removed the print from the frame, turning it over in his hands. His experience in the art world had taught him a few things, but this was a new one.

He looked up as the door opened and Maggie walked in.

"Hello, Thomas," Maggie said with a slow smile. He watched as she turned her head slightly, causing her hair to fall over her left eye.

"Maggie, you're late again."

"I know, I just—"

An announcement came on the television.

"Reporting again on a woman's body that was found this morning in the North Park by a jogger," the male announcer said. "The woman was strangled and had been dead for many hours. This is the ninth murder that may be related to the serial killer, but the police are still unsure if they're all connected."

Thomas dropped the print onto the workbench and stared at the screen. While the announcer continued, photos of the crime scene appeared. Unconsciously, Thomas picked up a thick picture wire and began wrapping it slowly around his hands. Just as the back door opened again, this time with a loud bang, a composite of the victim's face appeared on the television screen.

Thomas dropped the wire.

"NO!" Maggie gasped.

"Thomas," Sarah yelled as she stormed into the room, followed by William. "Shannon's gone—" Sarah stopped and stared at the screen.

"No identification was found on the body," the announcer continued. "The Garda is appealing to anyone with information about this woman."

"Oh, my god," Sarah said. "That looks like Nikki!" She looked between Thomas and William, as if Maggie wasn't even in the room. William's eyes were glued to the screen.

"We haven't seen her for two weeks." Sarah looked at Thomas, then added, "Wasn't that about the time you and Shannon became engaged?"

Thomas simply shrugged, picked up the print, and said, "It's a crazy world out there, nowadays." He glanced at Maggie, then gave a side glance toward William.

When the newscast changed to the weather, Thomas turned off the television.

"Maggie, you'd better unlock the front door," William said. "I'm expecting someone early this morning."

"But, what if that's Nikki?" Maggie asked, pointing to the now-blank screen.

"I'll call the Garda later. Now, go."

Maggie shook her head in disbelief and left the room.

"What did you say about Shannon?" Thomas asked Sarah.

"I went to her apartment this morning to help her pack, but she was gone!" Sarah said in a shrill voice. "That snit, Brid, said she didn't know where Shannon is, but I know she was lying."

Thomas and William remained silent.

"What are we going to do, if that IS Nikki?" Sarah asked.

"We will do nothing," William interjected. "We don't want to get involved with this now."

"How could you just let her go like that?" Sarah said as she turned on Thomas.

Thomas stared at Sarah for a moment. Then, he swallowed and asked softly, "Who?"

"Shannon!"

"We've been through this before," Thomas said with a sigh. "I didn't let her go. Your brat tricked me into thinking she was going to

Paris with me."

"Have you called her?" William asked.

"Yes, numerous times. I only get her voice mail on her cell phone."

"Well, we all know where she's gone - to her father's ranch in Oregon. What're you going to do to get her back?" Sarah demanded with her hands on her hips.

Thomas smiled and tried to ignore Sarah's temper tantrum. Yet, he loved to see Sarah riled. Her Irish eyes, wild with fury, always excited him. He wished that once in awhile Shannon had her mother's passion and was less meek.

Sarah paced the room, rubbing her hands together. "Shannon needs to get to work if she's going to be ready for the show next month in Rome. We've already had to change our plans for the Paris event without her."

"I may know of a way to get Shannon back," William said. "It may take a few days to set up."

Sarah stopped pacing and looked at her husband.

"You know how she obeys anything you wish of her?" William asked Sarah.

"Yes," Sarah said, a smile beginning to cross her lips as she saw the look in her husband's eyes.

"We'll arrange a show, somewhere close to where she is. Then, you and Thomas will go to this ranch and take her away for the show."

"Once we have her..." Thomas said, then looked hopefully between Sarah and William. "Brilliant! I know a fellow in a San Francisco gallery. I could talk to him about—"

"San Francisco?" Sarah interrupted. "But, that's too far away. No, we need something closer to that awful place."

"I have a contact in Portland," William said. "John Greenburg."

"I thought Greenburg is from Seattle," Thomas said.

"He is, but he has connections all over the world."

"John and his wife were just here for Shannon's show," Sarah said, rubbing her hands together. "Are they still in Dublin?"

"Yes," William said. "He's leaving later this morning. So, get that Matisse framed and in the crate in the next room."

Thomas watched as Sarah walked to the large desk and began

opening the mail. He walked closer to William and said softly, "I'm concerned about this Matisse, there's something about it—"

"Just finish the job," William said curtly and turned away. "I'll ask John to make the Portland arrangements for us. Besides, Greenburg owes us."

***

Entering the Pearse Gallery, Michael saw the poster for Shannon O'Toole's tour. He noticed that the photo of the woman could have been a model for the nude statue that was stolen. He picked up a postcard, which was a smaller version of the poster.

As he walked around the different areas of the gallery, he was impressed with the collection of Irish painters' oils displayed on the walls, such as Barry and Grogan.

On one wall, a single large painting was hung. Michael saw the name of the gallery's owner, William Pearse, on a gold plaque at the base of the painting. He was standing with his right hand clasping his lapel and looked like a formidable man.

In one corner of the room, he noticed a large, open crate with a Seattle address on it. He quickly noted the name and address, thinking to himself about the paper trail if this was shipped by air freight. He began planning how he was going to get access to the gallery's financial records.

"Michael?" a small voice said from the back of the large room.

He turned and saw Maggie standing near a curtained doorway. She quickly walked behind a long counter.

"Hi, Maggie." Michael was surprised at how much she had changed since he'd last seen her. She was wearing a simple black dress, but her figure and long, red hair made it seem exotic.

"What're you doing here?" Maggie asked.

"I just talked to your father and heard you were working here…" Michael's voice faded away when he saw the dark bruise under her makeup. He reached up and gently touched her face. "That must hurt."

Maggie brushed his hand away and turned, knocking some papers off onto the floor. Both Maggie and Michael bent to pick them up.

"It's nothing," Maggie stammered. "I fell from my bike the other day." She grabbed the last paper and put the stack on the counter.

"I'm sorry," Michael said. He handed Maggie the papers he'd

46

retrieved, after noticing the letterhead from a Portland gallery on the top sheet. The name below the signature line was the same as the one he'd seen on the Seattle crate.

"It wasn't you who made me fall..." Maggie said, than she put the papers in a folder. "Thank you, Michael. Is there something I can do for you?"

Michael saw Neville's eyes in his daughter. "How long have you worked here, Maggie?"

"Just two weeks - right after Nikki Conroy..." Maggie looked out the window, her body trembling.

"Do you know Nikki?"

"We were...are...she works at my school...That's how I knew about this job."

"Do you know where Nikki is?"

Maggie looked at the counter and began to rearrange a statue of an owl with glittering, dark eyes. Michael saw that the placard under the owl read: "*From the Land Under the Wave*" and was reminded of a childhood legend of a countess who'd saved Ireland from the famine.

Just then, he heard voices coming from the room in the back of the gallery and noticed that Maggie's hands were now shaking. He decided to take a different tactic.

"I'm here to see Thomas Aherne...with some questions about the robbery. Is he here?"

"Yes," Maggie said, looking nervously behind her as the voices raised an octave. "But, he's busy right now."

"I picked this up about Shannon O'Toole's tour. Do you mind if I keep it?"

"No. They're for the public."

"Is she available? I need to talk to her, too." Michael put the postcard in his jacket pocket.

"No, I think she's gone to America to see her Da."

"Where in America?"

"Oregon."

Just then, a voice from the back was heard and Maggie caught herself. She straightened. "I think you should come back tomorrow, Michael. Now's not a good time."

"I think not," Michael said, then walked toward the back room. He paused just outside the doorway and watched the three people through an opening in the curtain.

He recognized William Pearse from the painting. *The woman must be his wife, Sarah*, Michael thought to himself. He was surprised to see that Pearse looked much younger than his wife.

The other man in the room was as tall as Pearse, with similar dark hair. But, his demeanor was guarded, his eyes shifting around the room as if his mind was elsewhere. Michael followed his eyes and saw the edge of a painting he recognized – a Monet, or at least a very good reproduction.

"When we're in Oregon, Thomas," Sarah said, smiling to the other man, "I could continue making the wedding arrangements for you and Shannon."

"I don't give a damn what you do," Thomas said flatly to Sarah. "I know what I'll do with her when I get my hands on her again."

"But…" Sarah began.

"You raised that conniving little bitch—"

Michael was startled when Thomas' voice was cut off as William thrust his large hand around his throat. Thomas' eyes widened and his mouth opened, but no sound came out.

"You will do as you're instructed!" William said in a low voice. "And, you'll remember to talk to my wife with respect."

Thomas nodded and was released. He rubbed his neck and stepped back out of William's reach, a dangerous look on his face.

Michael walked into the room.

"I'm sorry to disturb you, but I'm Detective O'Sullivan with the Garda." He smiled and flashed his badge to the three people in the room who looked at him in surprise.

"Are you here about the blasted theft?" Thomas said. "I've already told the last officer all I know about it. I don't have time-"

"I just have a couple of questions. You must be Thomas Aherne, the manager here."

"Yes," Thomas said arrogantly.

On a hunch, Michael played a card that Maggie had just dealt him. "I'd like to know more about Nikki Conroy, whom I believe was one of your recent employees."

Watching the glances around the room, Michael smiled. His hunch had been right. At the mention of Nikki's name, Sarah fidgeted with the skirt of her red dress, while William had difficulty lighting a cigarette. Thomas only stared at Michael with disinterest.

"Mr. and Mrs. Pearse," Michael said to the other two. "I'm delighted to make your acquaintance. I've heard so much about you." Just then, he heard the front door of the gallery open and close.

"Yes, well, we must be leaving. We're late for a charity event for the Garda, you see."

"Of course," Michael said, stepping aside for William and Sarah to pass. He'd been warned by Dugan about how much money the Pearse Gallery donates to his agency. When the curtain was pulled back, he saw a large man in a gray suit walking toward the counter.

Michael turned to Thomas, who was coolly going through the papers on the desk. He noticed that Thomas shoved some picture wire and tape into a drawer, then slammed the drawer shut.

"I don't know what you mean by coming in here and disrupting everything," Thomas yelled at Michael.

Michael felt his blood rush through his veins. He knew he was on to something, but he wasn't on the serial killer cases anymore. He tried to remember his assignment. "About the theft, I understand you had a new alarm system installed."

"Yes, Mr. Pearse had it installed just before this last break in."

"Would you please show it to me?"

Thomas walked to the back door and pointed to the box, then he went back to the desk.

"Who knew how to disarm it?" Michael asked after he'd inspected the wiring mechanism and opened the door. He also noted the condition of the lock on the outside.

"Mr. Pearse, myself, and Maggie."

"Not Miss O'Toole?"

"She wasn't here when it was installed." Thomas looked bored.

"Where is Miss O'Toole now?"

"Frankly, I don't know," Thomas replied.

"When was the last time you saw Nikki Conroy?" Michael asked quickly.

Thomas stared at him for a moment. "I haven't seen Nikki in…some time now." He shook his head. "I just saw the news today," he added. "What a waste."

"What do you mean?"

"She was the best I ever had."

"Best what?"

"Employee, of course. What did you think I meant?" Thomas stared at Michael, understanding crossing his face. "You don't bloody think I…"

"We don't know who the victim in the newscast is just yet. In a murder case, Mr. Aherne," Michael said smiling, "everyone is a suspect."

Michael began to walk out of the room, but stopped and turned.

"I'd advise you and Mr. and Mrs. Pearse to stay in the country."

"But, that's ridiculous," Thomas yelled. "Shannon's tour has just begun, and we're scheduled in Rome in two weeks."

"You'll need to cancel the tour," Michael said, then walked out of the gallery through the back door.

***

Reflected in a mirror was a single spotlight, illuminating Shannon's bronze statue, standing on a pedestal in a corner across the room.

From the doorway, a soft light beamed into the room as the man walked in wearing a dark suit, his face hidden in the shadows.

He took off his gloves and went to the statue, his back to the mirror behind him. His hand came up and softly caressed the statue's face and body, as if it were the woman standing in his bedroom.

He thought of her soft, warm skin that his fingers longed to touch. But when he remembered her words, his anger rose up.

"Shannon O'Toole," the man said harshly, "You will never say 'no' to me again!" And he threw the statue at the opposite wall.

In the mirror, a large hole could be seen in the plaster where the statue had hit. The bronze lay on the floor below it, unscathed.

CHAPTER SEVEN

Oregon

Raindrops streamed down the window when Shannon's plane landed at Portland International Airport. She disembarked and walked through the sea of strangers to the baggage claim area. Looking around her, she saw signs directing her to where the car rental agencies were located. There was a non-stop barrage of announcements over the intercom, which she could barely understand.

Shannon looked around, hoping to find something familiar, but she realized there was nothing here to remind her of the day her mother had taken her away, except her now faded memories.

Every day, in her grandparents' cottage in Clifden, she'd known in her heart her father would come for her. She'd sat in her room on a blanket chest that stood by her window, watching and waiting, her little legs curled under her until they fell asleep. Then, one day, after she was taken to her first boarding school, she'd stopped waiting.

Someone bumped into Shannon as she stood at the back of the crowd in the rental line. She looked at her watch and realized she'd been waiting for half an hour. The couple ahead of her were finally at the counter.

The clerk, a tall black man, dressed in a dark blue jacket and gray slacks, had a strained smile on his face.

"Now, I know my secretary at my dental practice ordered me a Cadillac," the large man in front of Shannon said in a heavy southern drawl.

"I'm sorry, Dr. Preston, but I don't find any note of the reservation here. Perhaps if you'd call your secretary back in

Texas..."

The heavy-set man reached over the counter and grabbed the clerk by the lapel.

"I want you to look again young man, or call your supervisor - now!"

The clerk removed the man's hand and took a step back. Straightening his jacket, he smiled slowly. "I AM the supervisor," he said lightly, then looked back at his computer screen.

"I'm afraid I only have a Ford Taurus available—"

"A Taurus?" the Texan yelled.

"It is my last vehicle..."

Shannon was about to turn away when she caught a slight wink from the clerk's left eye that was aimed at her.

"As you know, there's a dental convention in town," the clerk continued. "All of the rental agencies have been hit pretty hard. I'm sure you'll understand, being one of the attendees."

Finally, the Texan agreed, took the Taurus key, and the couple left. Shannon went up to the desk and noticed that the clerk looked very tired.

"How may I help you, Miss?"

"I would like to rent a car for two days," Shannon said.

"Do you have a reservation?"

"No."

"I'm sorry, but we only have one car left available. It's one of our premium vehicles - a Mercedes."

Shannon looked at the clerk in surprise. "But, I thought you told that man—"

"I'm afraid he has a record of returning his vehicles damaged. Besides," the clerk smiled slyly, "you're my last unreserved customer today."

"Are you sure you don't have anything less, huh, ostentatious?" Shannon asked nervously. She was afraid her father would think she was trying to impress him if she drove to his ranch in an expensive car.

"I'm afraid not, this really IS our last vehicle."

"I'll take it," she sighed, handing him her credit card. "Do you have directions to The Dalles."

The clerk took a map out of a stand on the counter and drew a long line with a yellow marker, then handed it to Shannon.

"Just follow this line and you'll have no trouble."

After Shannon signed the agreement, the clerk handed her a key.

"Walk through the double doors to your right," he said. "Your car is in slot twenty-three. Have a nice trip, Miss O'Toole."

"I appreciate all of your help."

As Shannon walked out of the terminal, she could smell rain in the air. In Ireland, it rained a lot, carrying the smell of peat. Here, there was an earthy, almost metallic smell. *Finally*, she thought, *something familiar.*

She watched as other passengers were being met at the arrival area and was glad no one was there to meet her. Her stomach was full of butterflies.

Shannon placed her luggage in the trunk of the silver car, then got in. The smell of new leather was strong and the seat felt cool at first. When she looked through her bag for her camera, the photo of herself, her father, and Jake fell from the pocket onto the seat next to her. After re-checking the map, she started the engine and pulled out of the parking garage, following the traffic away from the airport, the city.

Shortly after turning east onto Route 84, Shannon was glad to see the highway opening ahead, winding alongside the Columbia River. As the sun cut through the clouds behind her, she began to relax. She set the cruise control and turned on the radio. The announcer on the first station surprised her, the English dialect was unexpected. She turned to a station with music, a Country band that sounded similar to a group she'd seen perform in Brid's father's pub in Temple Bar. A woman's voice was singing something about getting wings to fly.

For the first time in years, Shannon felt truly free and alive. She slowed the car when a sign appeared for Multnomah Falls. Glancing quickly to her right, she could see the wide ribbon of water cascading down the mountainside. She sped up again.

After awhile, she passed a sign advertising The Bridge of the Gods and realized she was tired and hungry. She turned off the highway at the Cascade Locks exit sign. Slowing her car, she noticed the quietness around her. She lowered her window and smelled the fresh, pungent odor of evergreens.

Shannon stopped at a small roadside diner. As she stepped out of the car, she became aware of the rushing water below the span of the bridge that she could see in the distance. She stood for a moment, realizing her shoulders were tense and her fingers were stiff from driving. She wondered if her anxiety was more from the anticipation of seeing her father again - or the fear.

At the window of the diner, she ordered a hamburger and coffee to go. Looking around her, she really didn't see the buildings or the people. On the drive, she'd been rehearsing in her mind what she would say to her father when she saw him again. Her deeply hidden anger was beginning to surface, just as it had over the years whenever she'd allowed herself to think of him. But, this time, she didn't try to push it back into its hiding place. She wanted to wear it like an armor, to protect her heart.

"You're not from around here," the waitress said as she packaged Shannon's order.

"I used to be…" Shannon started, then looked over at the bridge. "What's the Bridge of the Gods?"

"It was a natural rock bridge, until it fell thousands of years ago. The Native Americans around here say it had something to do with a war between two mountains, Mount Hood and Mount St. Helens." The woman shook her head. "Now, there's talk of a new casino going in here. Some like the idea, some hate it. It'll change everything, but, life goes on!"

The woman handed Shannon a sack containing her food. "Enjoy."

"Thank you," Shannon replied, then walked to her car.

As she left Cascade Locks, Shannon frowned when she saw the remnants of a huge fire in the area. Tall, thick branches, black and naked, reached toward the sky, while the ground below was charred and covered with ash. When she saw a large bald eagle perched on a dead branch of a tree next to the river, she stopped the car, rolled down her window, and grabbed her camera. She smiled as she took the photo. To her, the eagle was an omen, a sign of new things to come.

She drove up the ramp to the highway again. While eating her burger with one hand, she neared Hood River, where two wind surfers were skimming over the dark water with their colorful sails shining in the setting sun.

Then, she saw large platforms standing suspended at the river's edge, and pictures in her mind of Native Americans fishing on those platforms panned before her like a reel in a movie.

As Shannon placed the empty sandwich wrapper into the sack, she glanced down at the photo lying on the seat next to her. Her mind wandered back to images of her childhood on the Diamond H Ranch:

- Shannon's father giving her her first pony at age five.
- Jake giving Shannon her first kiss near the pond on the ranch.
- Little Shannon standing in the hallway of the ranch house, listening to her parents argue in the den.

She remembered now the words she'd heard that night:

'You lied to me about your money,' her mother had said. 'All you care about is this god-damned ranch.'

'*That's not true…*' her father tried to explain.

Then, Shannon was again eight years old, looking out of the back window of the car leaving the ranch as her mother took her away, saying, "*D.J. sent us away. He doesn't want us here.*"

The sun began to set in her rear-view mirror as Shannon saw reflections on the river of the hills around her, soft colors, like a Monet painting. Noticing a thin ribbon, carved on the hillside to her right, she recalled an article in a magazine on the airplane about "The Oregon Trail." Crude roads had been cleared by the pioneers, carved by the large wheels of their wagon trains. She shivered to think of the hardships those people must have experienced in their search for a new home. She felt as if she was retracing their footsteps, maybe returning to a home she had once known.

Shannon left the highway and drove into The Dalles, a city built on a hillside, the Columbia River its front yard. She passed a large church with a tall steeple and wondered if that was the church she'd gone to as a child. She couldn't even remember any young friends from that time in her life, other than Jake. It was as if it all had been taken away from her.

She wondered what Jake was like now. Panic grabbed her when she thought that he might be married. She hadn't even considered that an option before she'd made her decision. Most of her life, she'd never learned to trust her instincts. She'd left that to others. Now, here she was…about to take a giant leap into a world she couldn't even remember, fearing what she might find.

Shannon parked the Mercedes in front of an old, red-brick hotel, located next to a restaurant called "David's." She got out, retrieved her bags, and walked into the lobby of the hotel, tired and jet-lagged.

A short, round woman with sparkling eyes and salt and pepper hair pulled back into a bun, stood behind the reception desk. Shannon noticed an older, silver-haired man, with red suspenders holding up his pants, sleeping in a chair in a corner by a large fireplace.

The woman smiled. "Hi, can I help you?"

"Yes, I'd like a room for two nights. I don't have a reservation."

The woman opened a large book bound in red leather. After awhile, she smiled at Shannon. "I have our finest room on the top floor still available."

"What, is there a convention here, too?"

"I beg your pardon?"

Shannon shook her head, immediately sorry for the sarcasm that must have been in her voice, but she was exhausted. "The room will be fine, Ma'am."

"Please, call me Janet. I always think of my mother when someone calls me that."

"Thank you, Janet." Shannon signed the large registration book. On the counter, she noticed a tourist brochure for Joseph, Oregon, picked it up, and placed it in her purse. Then, she looked around the lobby while Janet turned to get the room key.

The plaster walls were a soft cream, trimmed with dark mahogany wood. Gold wall sconces and a large chandelier in the center of the ceiling softly lit the room. Shannon could see that the fixtures were originally piped for gas, but had been converted to electric at some time. Heavy, dark olive drapes framed the enormously tall windows. Damask-covered furniture surrounded an old chessboard that sat on a Mission-style table in front of the fireplace.

"This is a lovely hotel," Shannon said.

"It's been in my family for three generations."

Shannon could hear the pride in Janet's voice and smiled.

"Room three-twenty,' Janet said as she handed Shannon a long, old-fashioned key, attached to a gold medallion bearing the room number. Janet nodded toward the older man sitting in the corner.

"My husband, will help you with your bags." She looked at the man in the corner and yelled, "Walter!"

Shannon jumped, then saw the old man awaken and start to push himself from the large chair.

"That won't be necessary," Shannon said, holding a hand up to stop the man. "I only have these two bags. I can manage them myself."

Walter sighed and happily relaxed back into the chair.

"Are you visiting relatives?" Janet asked.

"I guess you could say that. Do you know where the Diamond H Ranch is?"

A shadow fell over Janet's face. "It's outside of Dufur, just south of here. Does your relation live there?"

"D.J. Hamilton…he's my father."

Shannon saw Janet quickly glance at Walter, who was now fully awake.

Just then, the telephone rang. Janet quickly turned and answered it.

Shannon noticed Walter had picked up a newspaper and was now hidden behind it. She took her key, picked up her bags, and walked over to the old elevator, pressing the number three button. She watched Janet walk quickly over to Walter. Just before the elevator's door closed, the couple looked back in her direction.

The hallway was dark, except for one wall sconce. Shannon found her door, unlocked it, then fumbled in the dark for a light switch. She was surprised to feel that there were two buttons on a switch plate. She pushed a button and sighed with relief when an overhead light came on.

A deep red area rug covered the shining wood floors. The high bed had a canopy of Battenburg lace, and the welcoming, thick, feathered Duvet and pillows were of the same material.

Shannon placed her luggage on the stand provided, which was next to a washstand containing a flower-painted bowl and ewer. She walked into the adjoining bathroom and sighed when she saw a deep, claw-foot tub. She promised herself she would take a long, hot bath - after she finished one thing.

She went to the heavy, ebony phone. Reading the card next to the phone, she found what she needed to do to get an outside operator.

"What city and state, please?" a voice asked in the phone's receiver.

"Dufer, Oregon."

"What listing, please?"

"Daniel Hamilton," Shannon said, a little shyly.

She heard some clicks, then a ring. She held her breath for a moment. Then, a man's voice answered.

"Hello," he said.

Shannon's hand began to shake.

"Hello," the man said again.

Quickly, Shannon hung up.

***

Ireland

It was night when Maggie entered the elaborate hotel and rode alone up the elevator to the top floor. She wondered why he wanted to meet in Newbridge, so far from Dublin. But she didn't care, as long as she got what she wanted.

She was nervous as she stepped out of the elevator because of what she had to tell him. Maggie knocked on the penthouse door. After just a moment, the door opened and she walked inside.

"You're stunning." His voice behind her was unusually raspy. His breath came in gasps as he slowly removed the orange cashmere wrap from her shoulders.

"Thank you." Maggie said. The dress she wore did not work with her skin tone, but he'd sent it to her to wear this evening. After all, it was a Prada.

A flash went off, blinding her for a moment. She realized he had taken her photo. "What'd you do that for?" she asked coyly.

He did not answer as she slid her arms around his neck. He ran a finger slowly across the top of her white breasts and leaned down and kissed her shoulders.

"Remember what you promised," Maggie said, 'about my

career?"

He nodded, then said, "Say nothing to anyone."

"Of course."

Maggie shivered and took a deep breath, fighting down the jitters in her stomach. "You bruised my face last time. I had to make excuses about it."

She felt his hands tighten on her skin and she shuddered. "You know I like it when you resist," he whispered.

He picked her up and carried her to the dark bedroom. As she lay on the bed, she saw an object in one corner, illuminated by the light from the next room. As he undressed her, she could just make out the shape of the object. Her eyes widened with understanding.

Just then, he roughly grabbed her arms and held them over her head. She knew what was coming and closed her eyes to the pain. His hand covered her mouth to muffle her cries.

Much later, the door to the penthouse opened and Maggie walked out. She stepped into the empty elevator, wincing as she raised her arm to press the lobby button.

As the doors closed, she smiled.

"What would Da do if he knew what I'm planning?" she said out loud in the empty elevator. She had ambition. She wanted more from life than what her mother had. A Garda detective did not earn that much.

But for now, what she saw in that room was her little secret!

CHAPTER EIGHT

Ireland

Michael peered through one of the small glass panes on the thick doors and saw the enormous man he'd come to respect, leaning over a Gurney in the large, sterile room. Quietly, he opened the door and stepped in, slowly letting the door close behind him.

"The victim's face is congested," Glen Flannery's booming voice echoed against the gray walls as he made his visual examination of the body before him. Michael saw a wireless microphone strapped over one of Flannery's ears, then saw the light on a computer nearby blink as the man talked. "Her eyes have petechial hemorrhages, which indicates that death was due to asphyxia. Deep grooves in the neck tissue mean that the victim was strangled with some kind of ligature, a constricting band of approximately one-quarter inch in size."

Michael watched silently as Flannery's eyes gazed down the naked woman's body. His stomach roiled when the drape across the midriff was brushed aside, revealing the woman's bruised torso. He knew the medical examiner had seen hundreds, probably thousands of cases much worse than this, but Michael never got used to it himself. He admired people like Flannery for doing a job he'd never consider.

"Abrasions and contusions on her arms and body have a yellow tinge, indicating they are older wounds. Yet, there are some newer contusions on her face and hands, which show the victim had struggled against her attacker prior to asphyxiation."

Flannery picked up the woman's left hand. "Lividity of the muscles show that time of death must have been sometime before midnight..."

Michael's throat seized, and he could hardly breathe. When he tried to clear it, Flannery suddenly looked up, pausing the recorder.

"Michael, what the devil are you doing here? Whelan and Graham told me you were off the serial killer cases."

Michael looked around the room, expecting to see them lurking in a dark corner.

"Graham called before I began my examination." Flannery said. "They'll be here in half an hour."

"Well, technically, I'm not..." Michael began as he stepped closer to the Gurney, then stopped when his eyes fell on the fiery red hair that surrounded the woman's pale face.

Young, he thought to himself, *too young*. But then, to him, violent death at any age was a waste. He looked up and saw Flannery smiling at him.

"You guys wouldn't last five minutes in here, if you had to face something like this every day."

"That's why you're over there and I'm here, Flannery. How do you know this is one of the serial killer's victims?" Michael asked.

"I'm not sure, not until I'm able to complete my examination. So, if you don't mind." Flannery turned back to the body.

"What does 'petechial hemorrhages' mean?"

"See those red streaks in the whites of her eyes? It's the blood leaching from ruptured capillaries...caused by sudden pressure in the veins."

Flannery picked up a scalpel and was just about to make an incision when Michael cleared his throat again. "Uhm," he began, "can you wait on that for a few minutes? I brought some people I think you'll want to meet. They might be this young woman's parents." He took a few steps back when he saw the fire in Flannery's eyes.

"Jaysus, Mary, and Joseph, Michael! I can't have anyone viewing the body right now. I'm in the middle of my exam."

Michael looked at the woman, then back at Flannery. "Well, couldn't you just...throw the drape over her, leaving only her face visible? These people are looking for their missing daughter."

Flannery was silent for a moment, then he nodded.

Michael turned and left the room.

The waiting room was softly lit, which made Michael squint to see after the bright light of the exam room. He hated this part of his job. When Neville told him he'd found Nikki Conroy's name on the missing persons list, Michael had asked Neville to have her parents meet him here at the morgue.

"Oh, I hope they're wrong," Michael heard Mrs. Conroy sigh as she looked hopefully at her husband sitting next to her. She was a small woman with graying red hair.

James Conroy sat stiffly in his tweed suit, his hat in one hand.

"Maybe Nikki's just playing one of her tricks on us," Mrs. Conroy continued. "She's probably off somewhere with her new boyfriend, like she did when she went off to Greece on holiday."

Conroy remained silent. He slowly placed his arm around his wife and hugged her close, letting her tears fall onto his jacket. When he saw Michael, he stood up.

"You may go in now," Michael said softly.

Conroy helped his wife to her feet, and they followed Neville toward the examination room. Michael watched as their steps slowed the closer they approached the large, double doors. He couldn't imagine what it must be like to dread the possibility of having to identify a child in a morgue.

He caught a glimpse of Mrs. Conroy's face and knew that, even at that distance, she had recognized her daughter. They continued to walk closer in silence, each step taken carefully, as if the earth was as soft as a bog and would open up and swallow them at any moment.

"Mr. and Mrs. Conroy, this is Medical Examiner, Glen Flannery," Michael said in introduction.

Flannery nodded to the couple, but remained silent.

Michael watched as Conroy's wife suddenly crumbled against her husband. "NO!" she yelled, as if the exclamation alone would stop the awful reality she was now facing. Conroy held onto his wife, his eyes never leaving the body in front of him.

"How?" he asked Flannery.

"Strangulation."

Conroy and Michael's eyes locked. Then, Conroy nodded. "'Tis our Nikki," he said softly. Michael could see the hatred rising in the man. Then, Conroy's voice changed to a low, dangerous tone.

"Mr. O'Sullivan, promise me you'll find whoever did this to her. I want to look into the eyes of the man who murdered my little girl."

As Michael and Neville followed the grief-stricken parents toward the exit, Michael spoke to Neville in a hushed voice, so as not to be overheard.

"Please take Nikki's parents home. I'm going to stay here until Flannery is finished with his exam."

"Aye." Neville looked at the couple ahead of them. "We're going to hear about this from Dugan."

"I know. Will you be okay with that?"

"Aye," Neville said softly.

"When you find the right moment," Michael added, "question the Conroys about that new boyfriend of Nikki's."

"I'll do it." Neville followed the parents through the exit.

Back in the examining room, Michael watched patiently as Flannery moved the dead woman's hand closer to a light nearby.

"This is interesting." Flannery said as he leaned in to take a closer look. He turned and retrieved a pair of tweezers from a tray next to him and plucked something from underneath one long, red, manicured nail. "We've never had any DNA before—"

"DNA?!" Michael interrupted, stepping closer.

Flannery placed a small strand of dark hair on a tray, then examined it under a microscope.

"Damn!" the Examiner swore loudly.

"What?"

"This hair is broken - no follicle." Flannery looked up at Michael. "No follicle - no DNA. It's a dead end."

"No, it's not!" Michael exclaimed. "We now have the color of the murder's hair. It's the only identifying piece we have."

Michael was still excited as he watched Flannery continue his investigation, the Examiner's voice droning on in a monotone to the computer. Then, Flannery paused the recorder once again.

"What's up?" Michael whispered, even though there was no need.

"Take a look at this."

Michael reluctantly stepped closer to the body. He felt strange, now that he knew her identity.

"What do you make of this?" Flannery asked.

Michael looked at Nikki's throat, where the scalpel in Flannery's hand pointed. The furrow around her neck was an ugly, dark color.

"I don't see any…" Michael stopped. He leaned in closer to look through the large magnifying glass that hung suspended from the ceiling over the Gurney. Then, he saw it. A faint glint of light on something shiny. "What the…"

"I know. Surprised me, too."

Flannery pulled the glass closer to the body. Michael stepped back a little as the wound around Nikki's neck seemed to jump out of the lens.

"Some kind of metal filings are imbedded in her skin," Flannery said. "But, I don't remember any evidence like this from any of the other murders."

Just then, Michael's cell phone rang. He looked at the screen and cringed when he saw it was the number for his office.

"I've gotta go," he said, closing the phone without answering. "Let me know when you find out more about those filings," Michael said, then left.

Outside, just as Michael was turning the corner of the building, he saw Graham and Whelan drive up to the entrance.

CHAPTER NINE

Oregon

A white Cessna flew east up the Columbia Gorge, the rising sun shining on the plane's logo of a black diamond with a yellow H in the center. It cruised past Crown Point and the city of Hood River. At The Dalles, the plane banked south, then eventually flew over the small town of Dufur and the luscious valley at the foothills near Mount Hood.

Jake McLeod was now a dark-haired young man with a chiseled face - the mark of his half-Irish, half-Nez Percé Indian ancestry. His hair hung slightly over the collar of his Chambray work shirt.

He steered the plane low over a herd of Appaloosa horses in a large fenced meadow, scattering the herd with the noise of the plane's engine. He was proud of the stock he'd introduced to the Diamond H Ranch.

Beyond the meadow, he saw a lone horseman riding toward the Cascade Mountain range.

"Now, what's Larry doing?" Jake said to himself, shaking his head. He'd heard the rangers' reports of a cougar sighting in the area. "Charlie'd better have a good reason for sending that boy up there alone."

Jake smiled with pride when he saw the ranch's name atop the massive log gateway leading onto the property. The Diamond H was his home. Jake was born here, his parents had died here, and now he was the ranch manager.

He banked right toward a two-story ranch house that his father helped build. Flying low, Jake saw Daniel Hamilton, the owner of the Diamond H, walk out onto the wide porch that wrapped around the house. Most people called Dan "D.J.", but only those close to him were allowed to call him by his name. Jake saw Dan look up and shade his eyes with one hand.

Tipping a wing of the plane to his lifelong friend below, Jake flew to a grassy airstrip behind the barn. Slowly, he taxied to a small hangar. Opening the door of the aircraft, he stepped out into the sunshine, his wide shoulders barely fitting through the exit.

Jake looked down and frowned at the small box wrapped in brown paper in his hand as he walked toward a black and chrome twin-cylinder Norton parked beside the hangar. He saw the herd of horses, now quietly grazing again in the meadow nearby. In the distance to the west, the colors had changed on the snow-capped glacier on Mount Hood as the sun rose slowly overhead.

Heaven, he thought to himself with a sigh.

He stuffed the package through his belt. Just as he was about to get on his bike, he stopped when he heard the sound of a horse's hooves. Charlie Smith, a sandy-haired man with a handlebar moustache, rode up on a marbled Appaloosa.

Charlie was Jake's foreman. He'd been at the Diamond H since be- fore Jake was born, when Dan inherited the ranch after Joseph Hamilton died.

"Hey, Jake," the older man called as he dismounted.

"Charlie." Jake could see the muck on Charlie's boots from working in the barn.

"Did you get Dan's package?" Charlie asked, his eyes squinting against the sun. The older man took out his handkerchief and wiped his brow and neck.

"Yeah." Jake glanced up toward the high hills, still covered in snow. "I saw Larry riding up in the west pasture," he said to change the subject. "He shouldn't be up there by himself."

"I sent him out to look for those stray cattle you said you'd seen from the air." Charlie spat chewed tobacco onto the ground near his own boot. "He'll be alright."

"But, he's only eighteen. What about the cougar reports?" Jake asked.

"Heard that someone shot him. Larry's going to stay in the mountain cabin overnight. Probably won't be back till Friday, knowing him. He's earned it, don't you think?"

"Still, maybe I should fly up—" Jake was about to turn back to the plane, but Charlie stopped him with his hand.

"Dan wants to see you," Charlie said. "Pronto."

"Did he say why?"

"Nope." Charlie took his hand away and put it in his pocket. "He just said I was to come fetch you as soon as you landed."

Working beside this man all his life had taught Jake to look past the words and watch his eyes. He nodded and hiked his leg over the Norton's seat. With a wave to Charlie, he kicked the engine over and drove off in a cloud of dust.

As Jake neared the barn, the noise of the bike sent two geldings running and bucking toward the other side of the corral. He stopped in front of the house and turned off the engine.

Dan stood waiting on the porch. With a heavy sigh, Jake took off his Ray-Ban glasses and placed them in his shirt pocket as he walked up to Dan. He noticed that Dan was very thin, his clothes hung loosely on his tall frame now. Jake wondered why he hadn't seen this before. Life had gotten so busy in the recent months since Dan had stopped his treatments.

Dan's skin was ashen, making the dark circles under his green eyes seem as if they'd been painted on his face. Jake watched the older man's eyes follow his hand as he placed the package on the table next to the large swing. He hated to see Dan like this.

"What's up?" Jake asked, even though he thought he knew the answer. "Charlie said you wanted to see me."

"You sent my letter to Shannon, right?"

"Yeah. That was only a few days ago. Why the rush now…" Jake began, but stopped as he realized the impact of his words. He shook his head, then saw Dan double over in pain. Jake ran to help him into an Adirondack chair on the porch.

"Do you want your meds?" Jake asked as he glanced at the package, trying to keep his voice calm, while his heart raced.

"No…I'll be all right…in a minute."

Dan's breathing eventually came easier and he seemed to relax. Jake felt helpless. Dan had always been larger than life to Jake as he grew up.

"You sure you want to try this again?" he asked Dan. "We

haven't heard from her since she was little…God knows what she's like now."

Dan straightened in the chair and ran his hand through his thin hair with a wan smile. Jake could see that Dan was trying to pretend that his life hadn't changed drastically in the last year - his hair was starting to grow back after the chemo, but his eyelashes and eyebrows were still missing.

"I remember how she followed you around most of her young life here," Dan said to Jake. "You two grew up together…said you were going to marry her—"

"That was a long time ago," Jake snapped, shoving one hand in his jeans pocket while he stared at Dan.

"Wouldn't you want to do this…if she was yours?"

Jake looked at the ground. "She's not," he answered softly.

"She could be."

Jake heard the hope in Dan's voice, but he ignored it and didn't respond.

"Shannon has a right to know," Dan began. "And…I want her here."

Jake watched as Dan looked out over the land that'd been in the Hamilton family for generations. "I want to see her here - before it's too late."

***

It wasn't until late afternoon when Shannon walked out of the elevator of The Dalles Hotel in a dark silk suit and high heels. She'd gone through every piece of clothing she'd brought, trying to decide what to wear when she confronted her father for the first time. She'd settled on the navy blue skirt and jacket she'd worn when she'd graduated from college, in hopes it would bolster her confidence for what she had ahead of her.

Looking around, she was glad the lobby was empty. Shannon glanced at the piled copies of "The Oregonian" newspaper sitting on the counter. She picked one up, quickly scanned the headlines, then set it down, glad to see there wasn't anything about a recent murder in Dublin.

The bright sunlight blinded her for a moment as she stepped out of the hotel. Shading her eyes, she looked up and down the street. One end of the road climbed upward, the roadway splitting around a large stone monument standing dead in the center. One car drove around it, then continued up the steep hill. To the north, she saw the wide river and some men fishing from a rugged pier jutting out over the dark water.

Across from her was a large red brick building, which looked like it once had been a schoolhouse. A small, white steeple stood at the top that may have housed a bell at one time. Shannon smiled when she saw the building was now an art gallery.

The sun was beating down on her as she walked toward it. She was sorry now for the black tights, which made her legs itch in the heat, but in Ireland, she almost always wore them.

Once inside, she was thankful for the cool air. Shannon saw a collection of paintings of Mount Hood. One was almost a copy of the one she had in her apartment in Dublin.

One large oil painting of a Native American woman with long, dark, braided hair caught her eye. The woman's face was lined and weathered, but her striking, blue eyes captivated Shannon. She looked down to break the spell and noticed the artist had signed it with the initials 'GL'.

Shannon continued walking through the gallery and was surprised to see there were only a few sculptures on display. She wondered to herself how some of her pieces would look among this collection of birds and animals.

A tan, ash-blonde woman, with the posture of a dancer, came out of a backroom of the gallery with numerous letters and packages in her arms. Her long, colorfully-patterned skirt flowed around her legs. Shan- non smiled when she saw the woman's yellow cowboy boots.

"Hi," the blonde said, gently placing the mail onto the counter. "I'm Gina Long. Welcome to my gallery. May I help you?"

"Yes. Who painted this?" Shannon asked, pointing towards the oil of the woman.

"I did," Gina replied, her hand resting on her hip.

"It's very good."

"Thanks."

"Do you know this sculptor?" Shannon nodded to a bronze statue of a puffin nearby.

"That's Hank Whitebird's."

"I like his work."

"Yes, he's a favorite of mine. He lives in Joseph."

"I read in a brochure that there's a Whitebird Foundry there."

"That's Hank's."

Gina moved the mail to one side and leaned her elbows on the counter. Shannon noticed the woman's hazel eyes scanning down Shannon's suit and felt uncomfortably overdressed.

"Are you a sculptor?" Gina asked.

Shannon stared at Gina. "Yes, I am. Why do you ask?"

"Your hands."

Shannon looked down at her hands. "What about them?"

"They're rough, like the hands of a sculptor."

Shannon saw Gina's face change, as if a light seemed to have turned on inside of her mind.

"My god! I can't believe it," Gina gasped.

"What?" Shannon asked, looking behind her.

"Shannon O'Toole!"

In Ireland, Shannon was used to this kind of recognition, but was now surprised, considering where she was.

"In the flesh," Shannon said, smiling as she walked over to the counter.

Gina wiped the palm of her hand on her skirt and offered it to Shannon.

"How do you know me?" Shannon asked, her hand still tingling from Gina's strong grip.

Gina hesitated and began straightening some brochures on the counter. The silver and turquoise bracelets on her tanned arms jangled in the still room. She looked back at Shannon. "I'm an artist, Miss O'Toole," she finally said, shrugging one shoulder.

"Please, call me Shannon."

Gina sighed, shaking her head. "He's not going to believe it, Shannon."

"Who?"

Shannon saw a small package bearing the Diamond H logo and watched as Gina quickly slipped the package into her pocket. "Have you been to the ranch yet?"

Shannon looked up into Gina's eyes.

"Ranch?"

"The Diamond H."

"How do you know…"

Shannon's eyes followed Gina's as she looked at one of the paintings of Mount Hood, with a large red barn in the foreground. Suddenly, she knew why it had looked familiar. It was a view she now remembered from her father's house.

Then, Gina turned back to Shannon. "I know Dan Hamilton. We've been…friends for a long time."

"Can you tell me where I can find him? I don't remember the way."

"Sure. Do you have a car?"

"Yes."

"Then, just take the road in front of this building through town till you come to a 'T'. Turn right, and stay on that road until you see the sign for Dufur."

"But, how will I find his ranch?"

"Stop at the Log Cabin in Dufur. Gladys is a waitress there. She'll give you the directions to the ranch."

"Gladys. Okay, thanks."

Shannon started to turn toward the door.

"Shannon," Gina called. "You're going to want to take those tights off. It's a scorcher today."

Shannon stopped and looked down at her dark-covered legs.

"How long are you planning on staying in the area?" Gina asked.

Shannon squinted at the bright sunshine outside the window, then turned back to Gina.

"I don't know yet."

***

Shannon drove out of The Dalles and turned toward Dufur. The rolling fields were covered with large bales of golden hay, stacked eight high. In some areas, tall grasses waited to be harvested, which had been swirled and flattened by the winds, creating nature's art on the hillsides. Rows of irrigation systems shot streams of water into the air, creating arches of color, painted by the man-made raindrops. When Shannon saw the snowy peak of Mount Hood and the blue hills of the mountain range in the distance, excitement began to rise inside of her. Then, she was filled with dread as she remembered why she'd come.

The air conditioner was on in the car, but she was getting warm. As she drove, she began to tug at her tights while trying to keep the car from swerving, even though the last car she'd passed was two miles ago. She swore when she poked a fingernail through the material in one leg. Finally, she was free of them and stuffed the heavy stockings under the seat.

Shannon thought about the ranch for a moment and suddenly remembered the face of a short Spanish woman who'd lived there. Maria was more like a mother to Shannon than her own, and wondered now if she was still there.

At the Dufur sign, Shannon turned and drove along the main street of the sleepy town. She passed a sign that marked this road as part of "The Oregon Trail."

An older couple walked hand in hand. The man waved to a mechanic in overalls, who stood in front of a garage in need of paint. The houses were old and close together.

She slowed her car as she came to a small log cabin, but then continued when she noticed that it was a museum. After passing a country store, she saw the sign for the "Log Cabin Restaurant & Bar."

Shannon parked in the gravel area in front of the building, next to a shiny motorcycle. She got out and saw that the road continued out of Dufur toward the mountains. Across the road was a lovely, old, Victorian- style building that at one time had been a hotel, the faded sign still in the lawn.

She walked to the red door of the restaurant. Just as she reached for the knob, the door opened and she ran into what felt like a brick wall. She looked up and saw a man with dark hair. The sun on his white cowboy shirt blinded her for a moment.

"Oh, excuse me," she said shyly.

The man stared at Shannon. Then, he slowly smiled, a toothpick dangling between his teeth. He had a black Stetson hat in one hand.

"No, Ma'am," he said in a soft voice. "Pardon me." Then, he looked over at the silver Mercedes she'd arrived in. "You're not from around here, are you?" He smiled, lazily placing his hat on his head.

Shannon was getting tired of that question.

"No, I'm not," she said defiantly, her hand on her hip.

The man tipped his hat to her. "If you'll excuse me," he said, then walked to the motorcycle.

Shannon watched him, surprised his soft, leather belt in his worn, tight jeans didn't have a big buckle like the ones she'd seen in the movies. He climbed onto the bike and put on his sunglasses, no longer smiling.

She turned and went into the restaurant, which was dark inside, after the bright sunlight. Shannon took a moment to let her eyes adjust, as a woman's voice on the juke box sang about the man that got away.

The only person inside was an older man, sitting on a bar stool, sipping a tall beer. His shoulders were broad, and his hair and beard were a yellow-gray. His beard was braided down to his chest, which reminded Shannon of pictures of a Viking she'd seen once.

She looked around the large room, where neon signs and posters advertised various beers and whiskeys. Above the signs hung numerous mounted animal heads. Shannon stared at a jack rabbit, with antlers.

Just then, a door opened next to the bar and a short skinny woman walked out, carrying a plate of food. A tempting smell of hamburgers and French fries followed her. The woman's body looked like she was thirty years old, but her dark, tanned skin and albino white hair, bleached from too many hours in the hot sun, made her look more like sixty.

"Here you go, Bobby Joe," the woman said, placing the plate in front of the man. The man gave the woman a big, almost toothless grin.

Shannon noticed that the woman's nails were short and broken, with chipped pink polish on them.

"What can I get you, honey?" the woman asked her.

"Are you Gladys?"

"Yeah."

"I'm looking for the Diamond H Ranch."

"You could follow Jake," Gladys said. "He's going there."

"Jake?"

"He's D.J. Hamilton's right-hand man," the man called Bobby Joe said. "Some say D.J. thinks of Jake McLeod as his son."

"Honey, he's that big hunk of man you just ran into," Gladys added, nodding toward the door. She crossed her arms over her small breasts and placed one chipped fingernail near her lips, a wistful look in her eye.

The sound of a motorcycle starting up was heard over the music. Then, it roared away.

"Thanks," Shannon yelled over her shoulder as she bolted for the door.

She got into her car and raced after Jake. Mount Hood loomed ahead as she followed the speeding motorcycle through the vast valley.

Why didn't I recognize him? she wondered. She always thought she would. Then, Bobby Joe's words came back to her and she began to fume inside. "So, D.J. thinks Jake is his son?" she said out loud. "We'll see about that!"

Farmland and open ranges were on both sides of her. Then, groves of tall Ponderosa pine lined the road as her car climbed up to the crest of the canyon. In a flash of memory, she knew she was in the Hessian Canyon.

Shannon watched as Jake turned onto the road leading into the Diamond H Ranch. Her heart raced as she turned and followed him toward the front of the big house. As she parked the sleek Mercedes next to his bike, she pushed the button to lower her car window.

"Damn!" she heard Jake yell as he walked onto the porch and opened the door. "Dan, you'd better get out here," he called into the house. "Shannon's here."

Jake sat on the railing of the porch and crossed his arms. She stepped from her rental car, her heels digging into the gravel, aware that Jake was watching her from behind his sunglasses. Shannon looked down and saw that her skirt was rising up, revealing her long legs. She smoothed it back down and straightened up, standing by her car.

It hasn't changed much, she thought as she looked up at the house. She was surprised it wasn't as large as she remembered it. But, then, she'd only been eight when she'd left.

A large, majestic oak tree stood to the left of the log home. An old, wooden swing hung from one branch of the tree. It was the tree she'd sculpted that now hung over her bed in Dublin. She'd created that sculpture from one of the few photos she'd found at her grandparents' cottage.

Suddenly, Shannon recalled a moment in time when she was around four years old, and her father was pushing her in the new swing he'd hung in that tree, while a large dog ran barking around them.

Just then, a loud bark brought Shannon back from her memory. She saw a big dog running toward her, which looked like a cross between a Great Pyrenees and Mastiff. Standing on all fours, its head came up to Shannon's waist. The dog stopped a few feet away from her, sat down, and cocked its head.

Shannon smiled at the dog's big, laughing eyes.

"Misty?" Shannon said to the dog and held out her hand.

The dog barked softly, went to Shannon and sat, her tail sweeping the dust on the ground. Shannon stroked the large, silky black head.

"That's Jolly," Jake said from the porch, "Misty's daughter."

Shannon looked up at Jake. She couldn't see his eyes, but saw that his jaw was tight and he looked like a soldier on guard. She also noticed that her palms were sweating. This was a moment she'd thought of for a long time, but now wondered if she'd made the right decision.

"Oh," was all she could think to say.

Just then, an older man walked out onto the porch. He pulled himself taller, straightened his shirt, and walked out to where Shannon stood, his weathered face breaking into a smile.

"Shannon. Gina called to tell me…" Dan stopped and stared at her. "You're the image of your mother."

"D.J.?" Shannon asked, not believing her eyes. He was half the man she'd remembered, and his skin had a paleness beneath the tan. She'd always thought of him as a tower of strength.

Shannon saw her father wince at her curtness, but he continued to smile. "In the flesh. How long can you stay?"

He reached out a hand to touch her, but she stepped away. When she'd first seen him, she felt like a scared rabbit, about to run at the first movement. But, now, she pulled on her anger.

"That all depends."

Shannon looked into her father's face, trying to see the man she'd known and loved as a child, but only saw the man she'd come to hate over the years.

"Do you need help with your bags?" her father asked, breaking the uncomfortable silence.

"No, I left them at the hotel in The Dalles."

Shannon felt a small amount of satisfaction when she saw the hurt in his eyes - the same color as hers.

"You're welcome to stay here, you know that," Dan said.

"I prefer the hotel," she said tersely, taking another step back. Behind her father, she saw Jake abruptly remove his sunglasses.

Dan was silent for a moment. He looked at Jake, but neither man moved. Jolly lumbered off toward the barn.

"Come on into the house," Dan finally said to her. "It's too hot out here." He turned and walked toward the house.

Shannon followed Dan. She stopped at the top step and looked over at Jake and her father, now standing together on the porch. Dan placed his arm around Jake's shoulder in a warm, familiar manner.

"Do you remember Jake?" he asked.

She hated the closeness between her father and Jake and felt uncomfortable under Jake's dark-eyed stare.

"Yes."

"We bumped into each other down at the Log Cabin," Jake said.

She watched as he looked down at her high heels, then back into her eyes.

"It's been a long time," he added. "Guess I can't call you 'Kid' any- more, huh?" Then, his face changed, growing more sullen. He turned and walked down the stairs.

"Where're you going?" Dan called to Jake.

"I've got work to do. Besides," Jake looked at Shannon again, "you've got a lot to catch up on."

Shannon watched Jake walk toward the corral, where a tall, roan Appaloosa stallion stood waiting. He mounted the horse with ease and rode toward the hills in the distance.

Finally, she turned and followed her father into the house.

***

The sky in the western horizon was still light behind Mount Hood. Larry hated coming up here alone, but he knew it was the only way. He was glad the cougar alert was over, but that didn't stop his jittery feeling.

He twirled his rope along his side, leading the six cattle he'd found in a canyon nearby.

Jake was right, Larry thought to himself. *These young Angus wouldn't have survived here alone.* He looked up at the snow level on the mountain, which was already lower than the same time the year before.

"Come on, you rascals," Larry said to the cattle ahead. "I'm getting hungry."

The soft, yellow light of the cabin and smoke from the chimney were a welcome sight. *Just a few more yards*, he thought.

His horse whinnied, and the cattle took off running ahead. Larry swore and kicked his horse into a gallop until he caught up with them.

He didn't see the pair of golden eyes watching as he led the strays into the small corral by the cabin and dismounted to shut the gate.

"Whoa, Raindance," Larry said to his gelding, holding onto the reins as the horse darted around him, his head back, eyes rolling, and ears flat.

"What's gotten into you?"

Nervously, Larry looked around, but didn't see anything until the big mountain lion leaped from the boulder nearby. As Larry fell to the ground, his horse shied and ran away.

Larry's pistol exploded in the dusky light.

CHAPTER TEN

The smell of the large, golden logs of the ranch house brought back a flood of memories to Shannon. At the end of the entry was the wide staircase that led to the second floor. Overhead, she saw the familiar balcony that wrapped around the upper level to the bedrooms. Suddenly, she thought of how she had helped decorate it with small twinkle lights at Christmas. She finally felt she was home.

Looking to the left, she saw the kitchen and dining room, where she'd spent most of her time here as a young child. She hoped to see Maria in the kitchen, but was disappointed.

Shannon turned and followed her father into the den. She couldn't say whether the room had changed much or not. She remembered very little about it, not having spent much time there before. The stone fireplace was all that she recalled. Her mother had told her that this was a room for grownups.

She stopped in the center of the room and stared up at a large oil painting of her mother, which hung above the mantle over the enormous fireplace.

"You still have this?" Shannon asked, indicating the painting.

"Yes."

Shannon turned to her father. She had come to confront this man who had abandoned her, but now she saw pain in his eyes as he looked at the painting.

"Why?" she asked.

"I didn't have any reason to take it down."

Confused, Shannon turned her back to her father. She looked down at the mantle and saw a photo of herself when she was small, wearing a white Stetson, a yellow summer dress, and red cowboy boots, walking down a dusty lane with a black puppy. She smiled.

"How long has Misty been gone?" she asked, even though she

thought she knew the obvious answer.

"Quite a few years now."

Shannon looked out of the vast, prow window that faced Mount Hood. The evening light reminded Shannon of her painting in her apartment, and she knew she had stood in this exact same spot the day she left, when this image was imbedded in her memory.

She walked around the room. "Is Maria still here?"

"Oh, yes. She and Charlie are institutions, they'll never leave on their own."

Dan motioned to the deep maroon, leather couch. "Why don't you have a seat?"

Shannon crossed her arms and continued to stand. She then saw a small photo of Gina sitting next to a deep leather chair that looked like it was used daily. She looked sharply at her father.

"How was your flight?" Dan asked in a lighter voice.

"Fine."

Walking away from him, she noticed a glass case with trophies and ribbons. As she got closer, she saw numerous photos and articles about Jake and a horse named Thunder, winning awards for classes such as 'Top Cutting Horse,' and 'Senior Reining.'

Just then, a large cuckoo clock chimed, the small, blue bird peeking out of its window, making Shannon jump. She walked to the clock and watched until the bird disappeared.

"I used to sneak in here to watch that bird," she said in a small voice.

"I'm glad you came," her father said softly behind her.

Shannon clenched her fists and wheeled around. "Why am I here?"

Dan sighed and sat down in the big chair. "I can't answer that for you, but I needed to see you."

"What for?" Shannon knew she wasn't making this easy on him, but she had a world of hurt stored inside of her - so many unanswered questions.

"It's complicated…please sit down."

Shannon silently stood her ground. She watched her father, her jaw set tightly, then nodded toward Gina's photo.

"I met Gina Long at the gallery in The Dalles before I came here today." She watched her father closely for his reaction.

He looked at the photo and smiled. When he looked back at Shannon, his smile faded. Shannon knew it was probably because of her icy stare, but she couldn't help herself.

"Gina's a good friend of mine."

"That's what she said."

Shannon paced the room. Then, she stopped and stood in front of her father. "What was so important that you finally felt compelled to contact me. Why now, after all these years of silence?"

Dan looked confused and said, "But, I've sent you hundreds of letters."

"What?" Shannon yelled in surprise. "I didn't get anything from you, until now."

She watched as her father looked up at her mother's portrait. He stared at it for a moment, then sighed heavily. Placing his hands in his pockets, he smiled and said, "You're here now."

"Now that I am, what was so important?" she asked angrily.

Dan stared at the floor and a look of sadness came over his face. Then, his eyes returned to hers.

"I don't know how to tell you this…I, huh,—"

The sound of footsteps running into the house interrupted Dan. An older man with a large moustache came running into the den.

"Dan, come quick! Larry's horse just came back without his rider—" Charlie stopped when he saw Shannon. "Oh,…I didn't know…," he stammered.

"Charlie?" Shannon said, suddenly remembering.

"Hey, Shannon. You've gotten taller." Charlie quickly looked back at Dan. "Sorry, Dan, but we'd better hurry, we're losing light."

Charlie ran from the house.

"Shannon, I've got to go…" Dan began, then, turned and left the room.

"Who's Larry?" she called after Dan, but was too late. She ran to catch up with the men, finding it difficult in her high heels.

In the dusky light, an excited horse pranced in front of the barn, stir- ring up dust, while Jake held the reins. Jolly circled the two, barking excitedly.

"Whoa, fella. You're all right now," Jake said soothingly to the animal.

"What the hell happened?" Dan asked Jake.

"I don't know. Raindance came riding in here like a ghost was after him. Charlie sent Larry up earlier to find some strays I'd seen from the air."

"We'd better go find him before it gets much darker. Charlie, get our horses."

Jake tied Raindance to the corral and hurried after Charlie into the barn.

Dan turned to Shannon. "We'll have to talk more later. I—" he began, then stopped.

"I can see that. What do I do now?"

"You can wait in the house, if you'd like. I don't know how long this'll take." Dan looked like there was more he wanted to say. Instead, he began to reach out his hand to touch her face, but then dropped it to his side.

Shannon stood watching a little sadly. Suddenly, she felt very small and wondered what his touch would have felt like after all this time.

Charlie and Jake returned with the saddled horses. Shannon and Jolly stood together, watching all three men mount and ride off in a cloud of dust, Jake leading the riderless horse behind him.

Shannon walked back into the house, wiping the dust off her skirt. She took off her shoes at the door and walked back into the den in her bare feet.

She looked up at the painting over the fireplace, and thought about her father's words: '*I've written you hundreds of letters…*'

Then, her mother's words flooded back to her:

'*D.J. Hamilton didn't want anything to do with either of us…*'

The expression on Shannon's face changed as she began to under- stand the role her mother must have played in keeping her father from contacting her. Then, she thought of the pain she'd seen in her father's eyes. Shannon wrapped her arms around herself and looked up at her mother's portrait, tears welling in her eyes.

"Lupita!" a voice yelled behind her. Shannon quickly wiped her eyes and turned at the familiar greeting.

Maria was now a short, round woman in her late fifties, with salt and pepper hair pulled up in a bun at the nape of her neck. She stood with her arms stretched wide, which Shannon ran into.

"Oh, Maria, I've missed you." Memories of hours in the kitchen, sneaking treats for Molly and herself, flooded through her mind.

"Chiconita, my little one. It is so good to hold you again." Maria softly pinched one of Shannon's cheeks in affection. "But, I wanted to wait until your father..." Maria took Shannon by the shoulders and held her. "Let me look at you, all growed up."

Shannon looked shyly down at her feet. "Where are your shoes?" Maria asked.

"I took them off—"

"You always went around here barefoot. Your mother hated it."

"I know," Shannon said with a smile, feeling now as if she'd never left. Suddenly, she wished she was eight years old and could start her life all over again.

"I heard the commotion and came to see what all the fuss was about," Maria said, then raised her arms in a gesture of bewilderment. "I guess I'm too late."

"Da...I mean D.J. and the other men rode off to find someone called Larry. His horse came in without him."

Maria nodded her head, and began to wring her hands in front of her nervously. "Larry is one of our new hands," she explained. "Aiya! This is bad. I hope they find that young man in time. Remember, Lupita, there are still bears and cougars in the mountains."

"Do you think they'll be back soon?" Shannon asked, suddenly frightened.

Maria looked at Shannon, then her face softened. "You were so young when you left. It could be hours before they return. It all depends on where Larry is and what condition they will find him in." Maria crossed herself. "God, help them."

Shannon looked around her, wondering what she should do. She was relieved when Maria slipped her arm around her and said, "Come, I will make us some coffee while we wait. You do drink coffee, no?"

The large, bright kitchen had copper pots hanging on one wall above a gas stove. A well-used chopping block stood next to the stove. Shannon walked over and sat down at the long table that was covered with a red-checkered cloth.

Maria looked at Shannon. "How much do you remember?"

"I remember this room, some of the house. I used to have to sneak in here to see you."

"I'm not surprised. Your mother always tried to keep you away from me. She said I was…"

"What?"

"I don't like to speak badly of people. How do you like your coffee?"

"With cream, please."

"My Charlie, he is now the foreman here at the ranch."

Shannon watched as Maria took heavy, white porcelain cups from the cabinet. She noticed her hands were bent with arthritis.

"It is good that you are here," Maria continued. "Mr. Dan needs you now."

"Why?"

Maria stared at Shannon until a look of revelation came over her face. "Oh, he has not told you," she said. "Then, I cannot say." Maria turned and silently busied herself with making the coffee.

After a long silence, Maria asked, "Would you like to go to your room?"

Shannon's temper began to simmer again. She stood up and said, "No, Maria. I want you to tell me - tell me now why my father sent for me."

"I…I can't. It's not my place."

Shannon's body began to shake. "On second thought," she said, "I'm going back to my hotel. Tell D.J. I'll see him tomorrow."

As she ran from the kitchen, Shannon heard Maria call to her, but ignored her.

At the open front door, Maria placed her hands on her wide hips and shook her head in disapproval as she watched Shannon drive away.

"I always thought that girl would not turn out like her mother," she said out loud. "Maybe I was wrong."

***

Ireland

Maggie went to her bedroom and opened her closet door. She pushed aside the Chiffon dress she'd worn recently. Fingering through various colored negligees, she chose a long, black lacy one. Slipping the silky material over her skin, she sighed.

"I was made to wear silk," she said to her reflection in the mirror.

Just then, there was a knock at her door.

She quickly threw on the matching robe and walked into her small living room, tying the sheer material just below her full breasts.

Maggie smiled when she saw her visitor.

"What're you doing here?" she asked, turning away to allow him to enter. "You never come to my place. I was going to call. There's something I want to talk to you about—"

As the door closed, the man grabbed her roughly from behind. He never said a word. She began to struggle, feigning fear of his strength. She knew it was what he needed to become more aroused.

He dragged her to the bedroom and threw her on the bed, tearing at her negligee. He grabbed her hands, then tied them to her metal head- board with a leather strap.

"That's different," she sighed, getting excited herself over the change in his routine.

Hysterically, he began pounding his fists into her body in places where it wouldn't show. She began to cry out, as she'd done before. It was what was expected of her. But, this time, his blows were stronger, more powerful. She struggled harder in an attempt to stop the game, but he slapped her hard across her face with the back of his hand and stuffed pieces of the torn negligee into her mouth.

Her eyes widened in fear as she saw him pull a thick cord out of his pocket. She struggled and bucked her body in an attempt to get him off of her, but he was too strong. He wrapped the cord around her neck and pulled it tight, cutting off her air. While her body convulsed as she fought to live, he violently forced himself into her. Just as he climaxed, he cried out Shannon's name.

Maggie fell into darkness.

CHAPTER ELEVEN

Oregon

Jake walked toward the barn with an empty wheelbarrow, the sweat streaming down his back under his shirt. He stopped outside the wide doorway to wipe his brow with a red handkerchief. Shading his eyes, he looked up at the high sun in the cloudless sky and shook his head, then rolled the wheelbarrow into the barn. It'd been a long dry harvest, and he was ready for a change.

Just as Charlie tossed new straw into an empty stall, Dan led a tall white mare to the center aisle.

"Charlie, saddle her up," Dan said to the older man. "I want her ready when Shannon gets here."

"You got it, Boss."

Jake watched as Charlie tethered the mare outside the tack room. "What makes you think she's coming back?" he asked Dan.

"She'll be here," Dan replied. He looked around the barn. "We're finished for now. Let's go outside."

Dan and Jake walked together toward the corral. The slight breeze was refreshing.

"I wish you hadn't gone with us yesterday," Jake said after a while. "Charlie and I could've handled it."

"Stop treating me like an old woman. I was the one who found Larry, wasn't I?"

Jake smiled and nodded. "You always did have a nose like a blood- hound. It's a good thing Larry only broke his leg when he fell into that ravine or we would've had a heck of a time getting him down off the mountain. The cougar that Charlie'd heard about must've only been wounded. Larry finished the job before he fell."

"It was lucky you spotted her mate when you did," Dan said. "He was about ready to jump, meaner than hell. Did my heart good to see your aim hasn't faltered." Dan leaned against the fence and looked out toward the pasture.

"Larry's settled now, but we're short a hand."

Jake watched as Charlie led the saddled mare from the barn. "We'll manage."

"I heard a rumor in town this morning about a new fellow looking for work," Charlie said as Jake opened the corral gate. "Just a thought."

The sound of wheels on gravel could be heard in the distance, and the three men turned to watch Shannon's car approach the ranch house.

"She's back," Jake sighed, then closed the gate. He saw the change in Dan's face. "You look better than you have in a long time, in spite of the long ride yesterday. Your color's good, and you're actually smiling."

"I've waited a long time for this," Dan said, taking his leather gloves off and shoving them into his back pocket.

Jake nodded, but was skeptical. Then, he turned and watched as Charlie tied the mare to the corral fence.

"She sure is a pretty thing," Charlie said.

"The girl or the horse?" Jake asked, looking Shannon's way.

"Both," Charlie beamed, then walked out of the corral.

Dan waved to his daughter as she got out of the car. "I hope Shannon likes her surprise."

Jake grinned when he saw the camera in her hand and lit a cigarette. "I'll bet she doesn't even remember which side of a horse to mount on," he said through the smoke.

"Go easy on her, okay?" Dan asked. "She's not like her mother."

"How do you know?" Jake snapped. "Maybe she's just here to see what she can get."

"Your anger is showing, son," Dan warned.

Jake threw down his cigarette and ground it out with the heel of his boot. He looked at Dan. "You may be able to forgive so easily, but I can't. I know what their leaving did to you." He also knew what it had done to him.

Dan nodded sadly. He cocked a booted foot onto the bottom rail of the fence and looked back at the mare.

"You don't know her," Dan said.

"Neither do you."

Shannon walked toward the corral, wearing jeans and a white shirt, the Nikon 35mm slung around her neck. Jake smiled to himself when he saw her red cowboy boots and thought of the little girl he used to know. *At least there's something of her past she hasn't forgotten*, he thought.

"Hi. How's Larry?" Shannon asked her father, fingering the leather strap on the camera.

Jake saw Dan's sideways glance and shrugged.

"Just a broken leg," Dan said. "He'll be hobbling around in a cast for awhile." He paused, then added, "I thought you were going to wait here for us to come home."

Shannon looked away. "This isn't my home. Besides, jet lag was catching up with me."

"What's the camera for?" Jake asked. He'd seen what Shannon's comment had done to Dan.

"Taking photos - for my work." Shannon looked at the mare in the coral. "What a beautiful horse."

Dan turned toward the white horse. "Shannon, this is Skye. I named her after your first pony. She's a three-year-old Appaloosa, out of one of our finest breeding mares. I'd like you to have her, sort of a 'Welcome Home' present."

Jake was startled to see the quick anger leap into Shannon's eyes. She stood with her arms crossed in front of her and looked between her father and the horse, her shoulders and jaw tense.

"Do you think you can buy me with presents, too?" she snapped.

The men stared in shock at Shannon's outburst.

Charlie quietly walked back into the barn, fingering his moustache.

Jake stepped in closer to Dan, pulling on his sunglasses. The air was thick with silence.

Finally, Dan smiled and walked to Shannon. He placed his hand on her arm, but Shannon pulled away.

"Shannon, I didn't mean anything by this," he said softly. "I'm sorry if it seemed that way."

Shannon stood shaking. "I thought it'd be different here, but you're just like my mother, always giving me things, thinking that'll get me to do something for you." Shannon's eyes bore into her father. "What do YOU want from me?"

"Nothing. I...I just thought you might like a horse of your own...to ride...while you're here." Once again, Dan gently placed his hand on her shoulder. "I'd like to show you around the ranch."

Shannon saw the look on her father's face and her shoulders began to relax. "I'm sorry. I'm just used to people using me this way...I didn't mean to..."

"It's all right. I understand." Dan smiled. "She used to do that to me, too, remember?"

"Not really. There's a lot I've lost."

Dan slowly opened the gate to the corral and motioned for Shannon to follow him as he stepped inside.

Shannon smiled awkwardly at her father and walked up to the mare, holding out her hand. The horse slowly sniffed the air, then placed her soft muzzle into Shannon's hand in search of a treat. Shannon's face softened.

"Sorry, Skye," she said. "I don't have anything for you, but next time, I'll bring you a carrot. Okay?"

Shannon patted the mare's neck, then ran her hand over the spotted coat. She looked at her father. "I did some studies on the Appaloosa in art school."

"She's a roan, with a leopard pattern over her base," Jake said from the fence. "Her coat will change as she gets older."

Shannon noticed a collection of spots on the horse's flank. "What are these markings?"

"Some call it a hand print, because it resembles a man's hand. They're rare," Jake said stiffly. She couldn't see the anger in his eyes, hidden be- hind the dark lenses.

Nervously, she turned away. "When can I take Skye for a ride?" she asked her father.

"How about right now?" Dan said, then yelled toward the barn. "Charlie, would you saddle The General?"

"Sure thing," Charlie's voice said from inside the building.

"Do you think you're up to it?" Jake said to Dan.

Shannon caught the warning look her father gave him.

"Do you want to come along?" Dan asked Jake.

Jake shook his head and looked at Shannon. "Naw, I've got better things to do."

She caught the sarcasm in Jake's voice and was confused.

Charlie came out, leading a tall Appaloosa gelding with a frost coat - white speckling, on a black background. "Here you are," he said to Dan.

Dan took the rein of his horse, and Charlie quickly retreated into the barn again with Jake behind him. Then, Jake returned with his horse, a blue roan stallion, with a white blanket over his hips. He mounted, tipped his hat toward Shannon, then rode away.

Shannon watched Jake gallop over the nearby hill. "Jake always was a loner, wasn't he?"

"He's turned into a fine young man," Dan replied, "just sometimes set in his ways. I think it's the Nez Percé in him."

"You two seem very close," Shannon said, watching her father. She didn't like the green serpent of jealousy that was snaking up her spine.

Dan looked toward Jake and nodded. "I couldn't have run this ranch without him."

Shannon's eyes followed Jake, her hands on her hips.

"Are you ready?" Dan asked, smiling.

"Yes."

Shannon took Skye's reins in her left hand, placed her foot in the stirrup, and pulled herself into the large saddle. She was used to a smaller English saddle, but would have to make do. Skye reared for a moment, but Shannon calmed her. She gently nudged the horse into a trot toward the gate, posting at every other step of the horse.

"Where'd you learn to ride like that?" Dan asked.

"Boarding school."

A shadow fell over her father's face. At first, she was glad to see the hurt in his eyes, but then he smiled. She tried to remind herself why she was here. Her father mounted his horse, then turned westward and led the way. She looked out at the meadow and saw Jake watching them.

The range was vast, with pine trees climbing up the hillsides. The soil was dotted with small clumps of grasses and sagebrush. Dried thistle rustled in the soft, warm breeze. Feeling the burning sun overhead, Shan- non sighed as a haze of heat rippled across the land. In Dublin, she was always cold, running into the sunshine for warmth. Now she knew why. She was home, where she was born.

The sound of a small stream gurgling along the pasture grew louder as they approached. Lush, green brush and small purple flowers, with faces like daisies, grew near the banks in an otherwise dry land.

"What a glorious day!" Shannon exclaimed, bringing her camera to her eye and snapping a picture of a patch of black-eyed susans flourishing near the water's edge. "Is it always like this? I can't remember."

"Most of the time," Dan said, "until winter comes around."

"I remember the Christmas when we got Misty at the animal shelter. She was so adorable."

"Did you have any pets in Ireland?"

"No. Mother thought they carried diseases."

Dan shook his head as he rode on in silence.

Shannon loved the feel of her mare under her, the gentle rocking of her body as the horse stepped along the path. At times, Skye would take a double step when she maneuvered around a branch or rock, causing Shannon to tighten her thighs against the larger saddle. A herd of Appaloosa stood grazing in a fenced range to the west. She pulled Skye up and looked at her father.

"How many horses do you have?"

"We keep around thirty head on the ranch, selling the young foals each year, after they're trained." Dan led the way further down the worn path.

Skye broke into a slow trot to catch up to her father's horse.

"Who trains them?" Shannon asked when they were closer.

"Jake."

"You didn't always have Appaloosa, right?"

"No. It was Jake's idea, and a good one, at that. The Nez Percé have always been great horsemen, and the Appaloosa was the best horse suit- ed for their needs."

"In school, I learned that spotted horses were painted in Chinese art. There are cave drawings dating back thousands of years ago. I even sculpted one once. Aren't Appaloosa supposedly easy to train?"

"Oh, yeah," Dan said, patting the neck of his tall mount.

"They're very intelligent, and they love to please. You should ask Jake more about it sometime."

They rode in silence for a while. Shannon heard a piercing cry and looked up. Two red-tailed hawks soared overhead, one circling the other. She knew they were too far away to capture on film.

The path turned west at a fence line. A coil of rusted barbed wire hung on a corner post, which was anchored with a large pile of rocks at the base.

In the far distance, Shannon noticed dark clouds hanging low in the foothills toward Mount Hood. She then saw a cabin. "Is that still used?" she asked, pointing to it.

Dan followed her glance and smiled. "Yes, sometimes. We found Larry near there last night. Once, a long time ago, Jake ran away. I found him hiding in that cabin."

"Why did he run away?"

"It was after his father died."

Shannon ran her fingers through Skye's mane as they slowed their horses to a walk.

"You're becoming quite a famous sculptor," Dan said. "Gina shows me photos of your work in magazines and articles about you in the New York Times."

Shannon looked at her father, waiting, holding her breath.

"You're very good," he added. "I'm proud of you, Shannon, of... Well, I just wanted you to know I like how you turned out."

Shannon sighed, staring at her father. She wasn't used to praise. She looked down at her hands, tears welling in her eyes. She thought of the criticism she'd received from her mother over the years. It didn't matter what Shannon was doing – she could never please her mother.

She looked to the snow-capped mountain in the distance, then back to the man she'd missed in her life.

"Thank you," she said as she fought to push the tears back. "You've no idea how much that means to me."

Skye shied, and Shannon's left foot flew out of her stirrup. As she regained control, a movement caught her eye as a small rabbit scurried for cover. She laughed and scolded Skye for being scared of such a little thing.

"I noticed that you use animals in your work," Dan said, his glance following hers as the rabbit disappeared under a bush.

"I've always liked using nature for my models," she said. "Mother hates it."

"Good choice," Dan said, smiling. Then, he led the way to a shaded area. "Let's stop awhile and let the horses rest," her father said.

Shannon looked around her and could see the house and barn from there. Jake was nowhere in sight.

They dismounted and walked to a large rock under a tall pine tree. She touched the red bark, expecting it to feel wet because of the vibrant color, but was surprised to find it dry. She sat down on a flat edge of the rock, while Dan leaned against the tree. A large blue bird darted between them.

"What was that?" she asked in surprise.

"Stellar Jay. They're a nuisance."

Dan took off his hat and wiped the beads of sweat from the back of his neck with his handkerchief. Shannon saw his hands shake.

She had the feeling they were being watched. Looking around her, she saw a man sitting on his horse far off in the distance, shaded by a large boulder. Looking more closely, she could make out the color of the horse and knew it was Jake. At first, she was alarmed, but then a comforting peace washed over her. She felt safe.

"It's amazing what I'm starting to remember about the ranch," she said, looking toward Jake. "I've lived all over Ireland and some of Europe. But, I love it here the most."

"Good…It's important," Dan said.

"Why?"

"Nothing…I'm just happy you're back."

Shannon was quiet for a moment, then said, "Tell me about when I lived here before - when I was little. Mother refuses to talk about any of it."

"You were fearless. I think you would have stood up to a rattle snake, if it had crossed your path."

Shannon looked at her father in surprise. That wasn't how she thought of herself now.

"When I gave you your first pony, I thought you'd name him Snow- flake, since that was the pattern on his coat. But, you had your own ideas. You jumped right on him. I didn't have to teach you how to ride. You did that all on your own."

"I remember the pony, but not much else. I never forgot Jake..." Shannon's voice trailed off as she looked in the distance. "How did you and Mother meet?"

"You know this story."

"That was a long time ago."

Shannon watched as her father looked down at his hands, then back up at her.

"Before the Appaloosa, Jake's father and I were looking for new stock. We wanted a horse that was sure-footed in these hills. I'd heard about the Connemara ponies in Western Ireland. So, I went there to get a look at them."

"Did you buy any?"

"No. Your grandfather talked me out of them. He was right. The Appaloosa are more suited to this area."

"Oh. So, that was when you met Mother?" she asked.

"No. After leaving Clifden, I went back to Dublin. As I was checking into the Gresham Hotel, I saw Sarah. She captured me with her eyes, and I knew she was the woman I would marry."

"But, I thought she was in Shannon, because of the new airport."

"No. She told me that many of the country girls went to Dublin for work. She said it was better pay, so they could help their families."

Shannon thought of what little her grandparents had and knew that her mother had done nothing for them. She vowed now to change that.

"Your mother used to say, 'The lights of Dublin were always on.' I think she preferred the city to her home in Clifden...and, here, at the ranch."

"She still does."

Shannon folded her arms around herself as she thought of her mother, a chill running through her. "I was hurt when you never tried to find me...in Ireland, I mean."

Dan looked at Shannon in surprise.

"I did try. I went to your grandparents' house, shortly after you left. But, you were gone by then. Your mother said you didn't want to see me...It was Liam who recently gave me the gallery address—"

"You came to Clifden?" Shannon broke in. "I...I thought—"

Shannon stopped when she saw her father wince, as if from a sharp pain. His skin had a gray tint and his forehead was beaded with sweat.

"Are you all right?" she asked.

Dan sat down on a smaller rock nearby, trying to catch his breath.

"I...I think so." He smiled weakly at Shannon. "Don't worry so much—"

Suddenly, Jake rode up and quickly dismounted. He ran over to Dan and put his hand on his shoulder. "You okay, old man?"

"Sure." Dan said, "And don't call me 'old man'."

Shannon watched her father attempting to sit straighter. She went to help him.

"Stop fussing, both of you!" Dan yelled. "I just got too much sun, that's all."

Shannon looked at Jake, then at her father.

"Is there anything you want me to do?" Jake finally asked.

Dan was quiet for a moment. She could see his breath leveling out. Then, he looked between her and Jake and tried to smile.

"I'm going back to the house," Dan said, rising, placing his hat back onto his glistening hair. "Jake, why don't you finish the ride with Shan- non? We haven't been over to the pond yet."

"I don't have to—" Shannon began.

"Nonsense," her father interrupted. "Now, you go along with Jake. The General will take me back to the barn. He never misses a meal."

Dan carefully mounted his horse, then turned back to Jake and Shannon.

"I'll see you two later. Take your time and get to know each other again."

Dan smiled, then slowly rode back toward the ranch house. The two watched until he was near the corral.

"What's he planning?" Shannon asked Jake. She saw her father walk into the house.

"I have no idea what you're talking about. Let's go." Jake said impatiently, as he mounted his horse and turned toward the west.

"Damn!" Shannon exclaimed. She jumped onto Skye and followed Jake.

***

Ireland

The pretty blonde waitress brought Neville's order of fish and chips and Michael his stew.

"Enjoy your lunch," she said, then returned quickly to the kitchen.

Michael looked around the pub. He'd been in McDonagh's a few times before, but recently, it had become his favorite. "You should come here some night to hear the singing," he said, taking his first bite of the heavenly stew. "There's one brown-eyed beauty I'd like to meet some- day, but I'm too...I...haven't found the right...moment."

Neville looked at Michael. "You weren't going to try to tell me that you're too shy, now were ya?"

Michael kept his head down and took another bite. Taking a long sip of soda, he turned to Neville. "What did you learn about Nikki Conroy's alleged boyfriend?"

"I didn't want to say anythin' at the morgue, but what's Nikki got to do with the money-laundering case we've been assigned to?"

"I'm beginning to think," Michael said, leaning closer to Neville, "that our case and the murders are somehow related. Nikki worked at the Pearse Gallery."

Neville stopped mid-bite, then slowly laid down his piece of fish. "Right." He wiped his hands on his napkin and said softly, "Nikki lived on the south side of the Liffy."

Michael whistled softly. "That must've cost her a bundle!"

"Exactly. I overheard Whelan saying her place was cleaned out. Nothin' was left behind. But, she hadn't cancelled her lease. The Technical Bureau's report showed no prints were found - not even Nikki's. After I dropped the Conroys off, I went by there."

"Someone was making sure there was no trail left," Michael said. "Did you get an interview with any of her neighbors? Didn't anyone see all of the activity when her things were removed?"

"Yes and no. Yes, I talked to them, and no, no one seen anythin'. I checked the moving companies, but the name on the paperwork was false and cash had been paid. One of her neighbors did say Nikki never had visitors, but that she went out often - late at night."

"Did she have a car?" Michael asked.

"No. They said she used the public transpo whenever she went out."

"Well, it seems I'm not the only one interested in these murders," Michael said, smiling.

Neville took a few bites of his fish. He avoided looking at Michael. Then, he said, "This morning, I asked me Maggie if she knew anything about it."

Michael's smile faded. "And?"

"I'm worried about her," Neville said as he sprinkled salt on his chips.

"What do you mean?"

He stopped and looked around as he wiped his hands on his napkin again. Leaning closer to Michael, he said, "Well, when I was in her new apartment, I noticed some things."

"What things?"

"Things that cost a lot of money."

"Did you ask her about it?" Michael asked, leaning back in his chair. He was trying to decide if he should mention the bruise he'd seen on Maggie, but figured if Neville had seen Maggie this morning, he probably also noticed it.

"Aye. She said it was from the money she was making at her new job." Neville was silent for awhile. "I'm not sure she makes that kind of money there."

Michael was silent for a moment. "I went to the Pearse Gallery. It looks like the sculptor, Shannon O'Toole, has left for the U.S."

Neville nodded and started to take another bite, but dropped the fish onto his plate.

Choosing his words carefully, Michael continued. "I couldn't get any more information out of Aherne. The owners were there, the Pearse's, but they refused to talk to me. They're all being evasive for some reason."

"Do you think they might leave?"

"Aherne talked about an art tour for O'Toole, but I said he'd need to cancel it."

Michael's cell phone rang.

"O'Sullivan."

"Detective, your superior gave me your phone number. I think we need to meet."

"Who is this?"

"The Special Agent for the IRS."

"Oh, right. I'll be at my office in thirty minutes."

Michael closed his phone and looked at Neville.

"That was the American bloke. Funny, I never would've expected an Irish lilt in the man's voice."

***

The man entered the apartment, carrying a brown shopping bag. He walked to a door next to where Shannon's statue stood in the soft light and unlocked it. Before entering the room, he reached over to the statue and straightened it on the pedestal.

He walked into the dark room and turned on a light, then lit some candles sitting on a small table nearby that was covered in a lemon Chiffon material. He looked up at a photo that hung on the wall of an older woman with red hair. She stood next to a dark-headed boy, her arms possessively wrapped around him. The boy seemed to be trying to pull away. Pinned next to the photo were two yellowed newspaper articles about this same woman. One praised her as the star in a Dublin play, posed with her hand on her hip, smiling at the camera. The other reported when her body was found, strangled and naked in a bay in Western Ire- land. At the end of the article was written: "She leaves behind a grieving son."

Around the large room stood nine mannequins, each under a spotlight. Eight were dressed in various colored Chiffon dresses, the head- less forms eerily posed in the same seductive stance as the actress in the newspaper article. On the wall above each mannequin, a photo of a woman's face was pinned where the head should be.

He walked to the naked mannequin and set the bag down. Carefully, he placed Maggie's dress on the naked form, smoothing out the wispy orange material.

Stepping back to check his work, he pulled a photo from his shirt pocket. He walked to the wall and pasted Maggie's photo next to the last woman's.

He stood for several minutes and stared into Maggie's image. Waiting. Waiting for some sort of sign. Eventually, he gave up and slowly left the room.

In a moment, he returned with another naked mannequin and set it down next to Maggie's. He walked to the table and stared at the photo of the actress.

"Will I ever be rid of you?" he yelled at the woman in the photo.

Receiving no answer, he blew out the candles, turned out the light, and closed the door. The sound of a key locking the door echoed in the dark room.

CHAPTER TWELVE

Oregon

A one-acre pond sat nestled in the canyon meadow, a large gnarly Juniper tree stood near the bank. The sun was low in the western sky as Jake and Shannon sat on a small dock that extended out over the water's edge, their horses grazing nearby. Jake held a handful of flat rocks.

Shannon watched as Jake threw a stone sideways across the water. It skimmed the surface like the wind-surfers she'd seen on the Columbia River, then disappeared into the dark water. His body was lean with muscle, nothing like the skinny boy she remembered.

"You've changed," she said finally to break the silence.

"You knew me a long time ago," Jake snapped. He fired more rocks across the water in quick succession.

"You don't like me very much, do you?" she asked.

"What makes you say that?" Jake threw the last rock across the surface, it bounced four times before plunging into the water.

"You've got a big chip on your shoulder about something."

Jake stood and turned away. Shannon looked at Mount Hood in the distance. The lowering light was turning the snow cap a soft shade of coral.

"I just want to know why you're here, now, after all this time."

"Because…" she began, then stopped when she saw the fire in his eyes. She straightened her shoulders and said, "My dad invited me."

"He's done that a hundred times before." Jake grabbed her arms and pulled her to her feet. "Why now?"

Their faces were inches apart. She could feel his breath on her cheek. "I never knew," she said, her voice quivering. "His last letter was the first one I ever received."

Jake looked at her in disbelief, then let her go and looked away. She knew he must have seen the sadness in her eyes, and she could see he was fighting with his anger. His hand shook as he lit a cigarette.

She struggled to breathe, still feeling the sting of his strong hands and the closeness of his body. She rubbed her arms gently.

"That's a nasty habit," she said, nodding toward his cigarette in an at- tempt to change the subject. She was surprised that he took one last puff, then crushed the cigarette out.

"I'm sorry if I hurt you. I didn't mean...," Jake began, then stopped and sat back down on the dock.

"I know," she said, sitting next to him.

They sat in silence for awhile, watching the soft wind causing ripples across the water's surface.

"I heard about your father," Shannon said to break the silence.

"He died when I was twelve, not long after you left."

"How?"

"His horse threw him. Broke his neck."

"I'm sorry," she said, touching his arm. She felt a jolt run up her arm and pulled her hand back.

Jake sat quietly, staring at the pond. Shannon saw the reflection of the sky on the water's surface.

"I remember you lost your mother when you were very young," Shannon added. "She used to tell us stories about her people. My favorite was the one about her ancestors at the Lapwai missionary."

"You remember more than I thought you would."

"There's a lot I've forgotten," she said sadly. "I know what it's like to live without your parents," she added, crossing her arms on her knees and resting her head on her arms.

"What do you know about it? You always had your mother."

Shannon shook her head. "Not always. In Ireland, she left me with my grandparents in Clifden. After awhile, I was happy there." She looked around her and smiled. "Granda and Granma would like it here."

Shannon was aware of Jake's eyes, silently watching her. She swallowed and continued. "Later, my mother re-married. That was when I was sent to boarding schools in Ireland and Europe. I hated them - until I met Brid."

"Brid?" Jake asked.

"She's my best friend."

The soft, warm breeze passed over them as it whispered through the leaves overhead, and she remembered that Jake had once been her best friend.

"Wasn't there anyone left in your family, after your parents were gone?" Shannon asked.

"I have an uncle…"

"Why didn't you go to live with him?"

"This is my home."

Shannon was silent. *What is a home?* she wondered. *Certainly not my apartment in Dublin.*

"Dan told me I could stay," Jake continued. "He sent me to Oregon State to study Ag-Economics."

Shannon looked away, her jealousy growing inside.

"Life on a ranch is changing." Jake continued. "Everything is becoming more automated. When I graduated, Dan bought a little Cessna, and I got a pilot's license."

Shannon looked out over her father's land, while a breathlessly beautiful sunset shaded the meadow with a soft hue that brought all the colors to life.

"How long have you lived in Dublin?" he asked.

"Ten years."

"Don't you miss the hustle of the city, being out here?"

"Not really." She'd heard the sarcasm in his voice but decided to ignore it.

Jake picked up another rock and lobbed it into the water. They watched the rings slowly expand as the water rippled.

"You won't last a week out here," he said bitterly.

"What do you mean?"

Jake didn't answer.

Shannon looked down at the water, the mountain reflected on the now smooth surface. Just then, two white swans slowly descended from the sky onto the water, folding their large wings behind them as they swam together. They made a high-pitched cooing sound.

"Oh!" she whispered, "It's like 'The Children of Lir'."

"What?"

"It's an old Irish tale of children who were turned into white swans by an evil step-mother. The people of Lir came to listen to the songs of the swan children."

"What happened to them?"

"One day, St. Patrick came to the island where the children were and built a chapel. He rang the chapel's bell three times and the spell was broken. However, the children were now old and withered. It's a sad story."

"The Nez Percé believe in various spirits of nature, and the swan is one of them. We each have an individual protective spirit. When Christianity was introduced to them, they learned that all cultures and religions seem to be seeking the same thing - a way of explaining their world to make some sense of it."

"Your spirit is the horse, right?"

Jake looked sharply at Shannon. "Yes."

Shannon squirmed under his stare; his brown eyes seemed to penetrate into her soul, like the eyes of the Red-Tailed Hawks she'd seen as a child. That was one of the things about him that she'd been drawn to when she was young, but now they made her nervous.

"Do you remember your spirit?" he asked softly.

"The swan."

They sat quietly for a moment, watching the birds. Shannon liked sharing the silence with Jake. At her art shows, she hated the expected small talk with the customers. She preferred the solitude of her studio. But, here, she was surprised she now found comfort with Jake at her side.

"Sometimes, I feel like one of those children," Shannon said softly, as she took out a small pad and pencil from her shirt pocket and began to sketch the birds as they swam effortlessly across the water.

"Why?"

"The wicked witch reminds me of my step-father. He was the reason I went to those boarding schools. But, then, when I was eighteen, he surprised me and brought me back to Dublin. He paid a lot of money for my art school. I didn't like the short time I lived with my mother, I could never relax there. He was always watching me."

One of the swans reared its body further out of the water and flapped its wings. Shannon frantically captured the expanded wing on the pad. Then, a hawk cried overhead, startling the swans, and they flew away.

"You're good," Jake said finally, nodding toward her sketches.

She looked at him in surprise. "Thanks," she said shyly, making a few notes on the side of the sketched wing.

"Why didn't you use your camera?"

"The swans were too close. The shutter noise would have scared them off. I wanted to capture their beauty."

"What made you choose sculpting?" Jake asked.

"I first learned from my grandfather in Clifden, he taught me how to use Irish clay. He said the Irish are connected to the land, and working the land with your hands is a way to keep that link. That's why I like to use nature for subjects."

"I remember those first awful mud pies you made here at the pond's edge. You were really bad then," Jake said, laughing for the first time.

Shannon stared at his dimples when he smiled. She noticed that the one on his left cheek was deeper than the other and that he now had a scar just above his lip.

"My mother hated it when I came home dirty." Shannon smiled and placed her notepad back into her pocket. "I loved it!"

Shannon hugged her knees, and looked out over the pond. "You kissed me once here, remember?"

"Yeah. But, things change."

Jake stood up. He pulled out a cigarette and was about to light it when he saw Shannon's face.

"We'd better go," he said, putting the cigarette back into his pocket. "It'll be getting dark soon."

He reached out his hand to help Shannon up. When she stood next to him, he quickly released her and walked to his horse.

A little disappointed, Shannon walked to Skye and began to mount, aware that Jake was watching. Skye danced in a circle, and Shannon swore as she hobbled around with only one foot in the wide stirrup. I know how to do this, she thought as she managed to calm Sky and pull herself up in the saddle. She let Skye trot a small way from the pond, then posted as she brought her back to where Jake stood.

"Who taught you to ride that way?" Jake asked, smiling.

"Mrs. McCabe, at one of my boarding schools."

"English saddle, huh?"

"Yes," Shannon said, unaware that she had thrust her nose in the air. "She was determined to break me of my wild Western riding style of my youth. I rode an Irish Hunter, used for jumping. Mine was an Irish Draught horse that was bred with a Thoroughbred for speed."

"Well, that explains it."

"Explains what?"

"You ride like you've got a board up your back."

"What's that supposed to mean?" Shannon asked, straightening up in her seat even more.

"The relationship between you and your horse needs nurturing, just as everything in life. I know that you've only known Skye for a short while, but let me show you something."

Jake walked up to Skye and stroked her neck. "Let go of the reins and close your eyes."

Shannon's eyes grew wide, then she sighed and followed his suggestion.

"Now, take a deep breath and relax your body." He waited, then added softly, "Sit back in the saddle, slightly rounding your back. Feel the horse breathing beneath you."

Jake was silent for awhile. Shannon knew he was watching her, so she tried not to peer at him. His voice was soothing, and she felt her body relax and her breath slowing.

"Now, keep that point of center in your seat and lean forward slightly."

Shannon was surprised to see Skye take a step forward.

"Praise her, even for that small step."

"Good girl, Skye," Shannon said, rubbing the horse's neck. Then, she looked down at Jake, his hand on her shin. "It felt like when I start to work in my studio, I get into that same Zen sort of center."

"Horses love to please and can detect the slightest change in your center, which tells them what you want them to do. It all works if you just learn to listen, both of you."

"Thank you," she said shyly. "Will you teach me more sometime?"

"We'll see."

Suddenly, just as the sun dipped behind the mountain, Shannon felt young again and the world she knew had slipped away.

"Race you back," she yelled to Jake as she kicked Skye into a gallop toward the corral.

She looked back and saw Jake mount Thunder and come charging after her, a smile beaming across his face.

***

Ireland

A mist hung low at the small airstrip outside of Dublin, shrouding the ground with a moving fog. The two men in white shirts looked as if they walked without legs, carrying a large crate stamped with Paris on its side. Another crew followed with an even larger crate with no stamp on it.

William stood in the silence next to the long, sleek jet. He watched as the men loaded the crates into the jet's cargo hold. When they had finished and walked away, he turned and went up the plane's steps.

Sarah was already sitting in the soft, white leather seat, checking her makeup in a small mirror. Thomas was mixing a drink at the bar in the back. William and Sarah joined him.

"Make one of those for me," William said.

"I'm delighted that we decided to take some of Shannon's work to the Paris gallery," Sarah said, "even though my daughter won't be there. It's the least we can do."

"Yes," William smiled. "I thought you would agree." He handed his wife a drink and watched her as she slowly walked back to her seat. Sarah no longer excited him, in spite of her shortcomings.

"We've already lost two days since Shannon left—" Thomas began nervously.

"Relax," William cut in. "My friend in Portland needed time for the publicity. We'll just have to be patient. Besides, we know where Shannon is."

"In that case, will we have time to stop in New York?" Sarah asked.

William winked at Thomas. "After Paris, we'll be making an extra stop in the States, but it won't be New York."

"I need to talk to you," Thomas said to William in a low voice. "That Matisse…I didn't like the signature…the paper was all wrong—"

"Enough!" William looked up at his wife, who was now applying lipstick. He leaned in toward Thomas and lowered his voice. "It's not your job to question what leaves my gallery, just to make sure that my orders are carried out."

CHAPTER THIRTEEN

Oregon

The soft yellow glow of light through the windows of the ranch house was welcoming, but Shannon took a deep breath before she walked in. She saw the fire was lit and was thankful for the warmth in the room. She'd forgotten how quickly the temperature outside changed once the sun went down.

She couldn't deny the rush of joy she'd felt when she'd raced Jake back to the barn. He'd offered to take care of the horses, but she'd insisted on grooming Skye herself. She knew it was a way of avoiding the reason she'd come to Oregon, but now it was time. Slowly, she walked over to the long couch and sat across from her father.

Dan shook his head, as if he was coming out of a dream, then he smiled at her.

"Hi," Shannon said a little breathlessly, putting her hands to her face and feeling the warmth.

"How was the ride?"

"Great! I beat Jake back..." She stopped when she saw the ashen color of Dan's face. She went to him and took one hand in hers, then finally asked, "Now, will you please tell me what's wrong?"

Dan sighed heavily, took both of Shannon's hands in his, and leaned forward, his elbows on his knees. He was silent for a moment, staring at her face. She wondered what he saw there. She knelt down next to him and waited, holding her breath.

"Shannon, love..." Dan stopped and placed his hand on her cheek. "I'm dying."

She sat back on the heels of her boots and stared at her father. It felt like a fist had grabbed her heart and she could hardly breathe.

"I hate to just blurt it out like that," Dan began. "I've been sitting here, trying to find a better way…there just wasn't any."

"No," Shannon cried, trying to erase the truth.

"I've got cancer."

Shannon continued to stare at her father, a face she had longed to see for years. Now, she was going to lose him again. Tears welled in her eyes as her mind searched for words, but none would come. The word 'cancer' circled in her head. Brid's mother had died of breast cancer a few years ago. Shannon shivered at the thought of the pain and long struggle.

"What kind?"

"Pancreatic…Doc says I only have a short time left."

Shannon looked around the room, which seemed to have suddenly turned dark. "How long?"

"Maybe a month."

"There are treatments," she began. "We could—"

"I'm not going there…not anymore," Dan said softly.

"But, why?" she yelled, the hot stream of tears began now, creating ribbons through the dust on her face. Her body shook with fear. "You can't give up…we've got to fight it. There's got to be more we can do—"

"I have…that's no way to live. I want to live it my way now."

"I've read about some new things they're—"

"Shannon, I've made my choice."

The finality of his words stopped her, and she knew she had to respect his decision. Placing her head on his knee, she let the tears fall, while her father stroked her hair.

A log on the fire fell and sparks rose up the chimney. The silence that remained brought them closer together.

"I wish I'd known sooner," she said after awhile.

"I wrote to you six months ago, when I first found out." Dan looked up at the painting of his ex-wife and sighed. "Now, I see you never received my letter - just like all the others. All that time we've lost…"

Shannon rose up and hugged her father. In that split second, she knew what she had to do.

"I'm here now," she said. "I'll go get my things tonight and bring them here, if that's okay with you. I won't leave, Da, 'til you want me to."

Dan's face transformed, no longer so pale and tired. Tears threatened to spill over in his eyes, but Shannon could see him struggling to hold them back.

"Oh, baby. You have no idea what that means to me. I've waited all these years to hear you call me 'Da' again. I know it was your mother's idea from the beginning, but I liked it. This is your home. You can stay here forever."

***

Later, the door to Shannon's bedroom was open, the room softly lit by a small lamp on a table between two single beds. Her opened suitcase lay on the bed next to the door. Shannon looked around her old room, still filled with forgotten toys in a wooden box and a shelf of well-loved dolls and stuffed animals on one wall. The logs burning in the fireplace crackled.

Shannon held her cell phone to her ear and paced the room. "Just send them Express, Brid," she said into the phone. "Promise you won't tell Mother or Thomas?"

"OK," she heard Brid's voice say, the noise of the Dublin pub in the background. "But, why do you need your other tools and stuff?"

Shannon paused when she heard footsteps in the hallway. Jake walked to her door and stopped. She held her breath as he eyed her lug- gage in the room. Then, without saying a word, he walked down the hall. She heard a door close.

"Shannon?" Brid's voice said in her ear.

Nervously, Shannon walked over and closed her door, surprised that Jake's room was so close to her own. "Sorry, Brid. Jake just walked by…"

"Oh, what's he like?"

"Different." Shannon walked to her suitcase and took out her red boots, clutching them to her chest.

"So, tell me why you want me to do this?"

"I…I need to work," Shannon said impatiently into her phone. She set her boots down, then put her hand to her hair and pushed it behind her shoulder.

"Work?"

"Include any unfinished pieces you find in my studio."

"But, I don't get it," Brid said. "You were only going there to—"

"Things have changed here." Shannon looked at her closed door, then said, "I'll pay you back."

"Don't worry about it," Brid said. "You know your mother's pulling out her hair over here."

"I'm sure she is—"

"Oh, there's something I have to tell you."

"What?" Shannon frowned. She could hear the panic now in her friend's voice.

"Uh, it was Nikki Conway's body that was discovered by a runner in North Park…she'd been strangled."

Shannon slowly sank down onto the bed, thinking back to the last time she'd seen Nikki at the gallery.

"There's more," Brid continued. "I met Maggie Murphy in the hall the night after you left and took her to my room. She was pretty beaten up, but for sure it wasn't from a fall this time."

"What the devil's going on back there?"

"I don't know. Maggie says she's fine, but I know she's lying. This is all too scary."

"Did she say who did that to her?"

"No, she refused to tell me. But, she did tell me one thing…"

"What?"

"Remember your statue that was stolen? The nude?"

"Yes," Shannon said, waiting.

"Maggie told me she'd seen it. I know she didn't mean to…it just slipped out."

"You mean, the guy that pounded on her stole my statue?" Goose bumps climbed up Shannon's arms. Now, she was frightened.

"Yes."

"But, who is he?"

"She only talked about how this creep's going to pay for her career. Then, she clammed up after she'd let that bit about the statue slip."

Shannon was quiet for a moment. Thoughts circled through her mind as she held herself with her free arm.

"When are you coming back?" Brid asked, bringing Shannon back to her reality in Dufur, Oregon. She looked around her room of familiar things, and tears started to flow down her face.

"I don't know. A month - maybe longer."

Shannon took a deep breath. If she said the words, would it make it any more real?

"My Da's dying…"

"What?"

"He's in my life again…but, only for a little while."

"What're you talking about?"

"He has cancer. He refuses the treatments, he's not going to fight."

"Brid," Shannon heard Brid's brother's voice say over the phone. "It's time we sing again."

"I've gotta go," Brid said after a moment. Shannon knew she was thinking of her mother. "I'll call you tomorrow."

Brid hung up.

Shannon sat on her bed and wondered what life could have been like with siblings. She'd always been jealous of Brid. Now, when she needed someone the most, she had no one to share her fear with.

CHAPTER FOURTEEN

Ireland

There was standing room only as a couple opened the door to Mc- Donagh's Pub. Brid's lovely alto voice lilted across the softly-lit room.

"Just give me your hand," Brid sang, "Tabhair dom do lámh...."

Her brother, Jack, strummed the eight-string bouzouki, a long-necked instrument that was like a mandolin.

Brid's parents had owned the pub since she was a little girl, and every family member worked to keep the establishment going. Jack was an architect by day, a musician by night. Her two sisters, Erin and Mary Caroline, kept the stoves in the kitchen busy with food orders, the aromas of Irish stew, fish and chips, and Guinness-and-beef casserole wafting from the back of the pub. Sean, her eldest brother, tended the bar.

As she sang, Brid looked around the crowded room she loved so much. A German couple smiled at her, their cheeks rosy from the warm fire in the large stone hearth beside them. She saw her father working the room, greeting the regulars who had become friends over the years and getting to know the newcomers. Mick McDonagh was a large, yet gentle man. At two-hundred-eighty pounds, her uncle had once said, 'he makes the beer vats look small!'

When her song came to an end, she saw a tall dark man with wide shoulders watching her from one corner. His hazel eyes captured hers for a moment before she turned away. Recently, she'd seen him in the pub before, but they'd never spoken.

She noticed some of the regulars began ordering numerous pints of Guinness, just before 'last call.' Technically, the pubs across the city would close in a few minutes, but the locals knew that they could stay, providing they already had their drinks lined up in front of them when the doors were locked. Brid's voice carried the last note. Then, silence.

Applause erupted. Brid and Jack smiled at each other, then thanked their audience.

"Let's do a jig," Jack said to Brid and she nodded in agreement. She looked over at Sean and tipped her head toward the kitchen door. Sean understood the signal she gave and called into the kitchen. In a moment, her sister, Mary Caroline, came out and walked over to the dais, her blonde hair glowing in the lights over the platform.

"This'll be the last one for me," Brid said, picking up a small whistle. She glanced once again at the tall man and her face reddened to see him still staring at her.

"And, where'll you be off to then?" Mary Caroline asked.

Without answering, Brid blew into the whistle and began a tune that was a variation of one from the mid-eighteen hundred's. The two-headed tipper in Jack's hand danced over the bodhran, while Mary Caroline played the melody on her fiddle. Feet began to tap around the pub and a few people danced in what small space they had left to them over by the dart boards.

Brid wasn't sure how she was going to tell her family why she would be leaving early tonight. Shannon's call had shaken her more than she'd thought. Memories of her mother just wouldn't let her be. She wondered what she would do if anything ever happened to anyone else in her family, she loved them all so much.

As the crowd roared when they finished, Brid saw her chance and stepped from the dais. She walked to the deeply polished bar where Sean was pouring two pints of Guinness. She watched as the dark liquid filled the bottoms of the glasses, followed by the creamy foam that slowly rose to the top.

"Ah, Sean," Brid sighed, "you always did have a hand to pour a perfect Arthur. 'Tis your talent!"

"Just wait till you try some of my new brew," Sean winked at his sister. "To be sure, Arthur Guinness won't have anything over me then."

Jack came up next to Brid as Mary Caroline disappeared through the kitchen door. "Don't let Da hear you talkin' like that," Jack cautioned, looking around the room.

Brid saw her father talking to the German couple. She overheard him saying, "Me daughters still use the recipes of me wife, Breeda, God rest her soul. She passed on two years now. But, all me children," he said, raising his voice so they would hear, "they keep you fed and entertained and yer glass full. So, enjoy yer stay in Ireland."

Jack turned back to his brother. "Just because you went to that fancy brewing school in New York, Sean, doesn't mean you're gonna change Da's mind. You know how he hates change." He took one of the pints and downed half of it.

"Hey," Sean yelled at Jack, who was wiping the creamy foam from his upper lip. "That jar was for a customer."

"Not anymore," Jack smiled, then finished the drink. He leaned in close to Sean and added, "You'd better be watching old McGuffy over there. He's pretty bolloxed by now."

Brid looked at the end of the bar and saw a sweet old man who spent most of his evenings at their pub. Brady McGuffy usually had to be escorted home by one of her brothers, but he was like family to all of them. He'd been coming to the pub since Brid was young.

"Come on Brid, let's give 'em another song," Jack said, nodding to the content crowd.

"You'll have to do a solo or get Mary Caroline to join you. I've got something I need to do—"

"What's more important? Where can you be going at this time of night? Got a new boyfriend?" Jack never let her answer a question before asking her another. She was used to his grilling, especially when she'd started dating back in school. She feared she'd never grow out of his protection.

"I've got to pack some of Shannon's things to send to her in Oregon."

"What's she doin' in Oregon?" Sean asked. "When I was in New York, I read that they're buildin' a lot of new brew pubs out west now."

Brid could see the stars in her brother's eyes and shook her head. "Shannon's going to be staying with her Da for a while," Brid said. "She's not sure how long."

"American brew pubs?" Brid's father yelled from behind her. "I thought we settled all of this nonsense yer been talkin' 'bout."

Brid turned and looked into her father's eyes, feeling the love swell inside of her.

"If you'll but listen, it's time we start brewing our own beer," Sean began, his chin jutting out. "'Micro-brewing' they call it in the U.S."

"I'll be havin' nothin' to do with any 'micro-brewin' in me pub," Mick roared, his voice bellowing over the crowd.

There was a hush over the entire pub for a moment.

"Guinness has been good enough for me father and me father before him," Mick boomed.

Everyone laughed and went back to their drinking and talking.

Brid's father turned to his children. "Now, Briddy, yer'll not be goin' to Oregon yerself, will yer now?"

"I…I'm sending Shannon some of her things," Brid began, then be- came quiet and looked down at her feet. She hadn't made up her mind about going there just yet. Looking back up at her father's worried face, she continued. "Her Da is dying."

"I'm sorry to hear that," Mick said, placing his arm around Brid's shoulders and giving her a hug. "I always liked Daniel Hamilton, ever since I met him on his first trip to the island. He'd come here to buy horses and left with a wife. Never cared much for that new husband of Sarah O'Toole's."

"I agree," Sean said from behind the bar.

"I love you all," Brid said. "But, I have to run. See you in the morning."

She kissed her father on the cheek, waved to Jack and Sean, then walked out into the night, leaving the men in her life to argue out the future of their pub.

***

Paris

It was raining outside the almost empty cafe, and the people were getting drenched as they ran across the avenue that led to the Sacre-Coeur Basilica.

But, the man who sat at a table near the back of the dark cafe quietly sipped his coffee, not noticing the rain. His eyes watched only one thing, a young redheaded woman who sat alone at a table near the door. Her wet red silk dress clung to her slender body.

He knew it was too soon to think about another woman, but he was in Paris. He usually found the satisfaction he needed to give him more time between his victims. But, tonight, an urgency was driving him.

He'd followed this young woman for two days and knew that she lived alone. He was too edgy to think of anything else.

His shoulders tensed when he saw her wave to the waiter. Quickly, he pulled a few Euro from his black coat pocket and placed it on his table.

The woman stood now outside the door, opening her red umbrella. As she started down the walkway, the man followed her. She turned down a small street, which seemed deserted. Walking to avoid the puddles, the woman continued to a small apartment building and went inside.

At her door, she fumbled and dropped her key.

The man quickly picked it up.

"Pardon, may I help you?" he asked.

"Oh, you speak English. What a relief. I've been in this city for a week now, but I can't get my head around this French..." The woman stopped. "Oh, I'm sorry...I didn't mean to be rude—"

The man slid the key into the lock and turned it slowly, smiling to the woman as he continued to hold the key.

Before the woman could say anything more, the man clasped his hand over her mouth and pushed her into the apartment. Just before the door closed, the light went out.

CHAPTER FIFTEEN

Oregon

Shannon sat in the small shed that she and Maria had quickly transformed into a studio. Looking up, she saw some of her unfinished pieces on the shelf near the window. Mount Hood was visible through the glass in the late afternoon light.

It's too easy to just sit and daydream with views like this, she thought to herself as she brought her gaze back into the room. The crates from Ireland now sat empty in the back of the studio. Shannon was thankful that it had only taken a short time to get them to her.

The rustic shed provided solitude, a place to work and think. It was crucial to her to keep busy during the times when her father had his own work to do. She refused to think about the future.

She stared at a large cone of hard clay mounted on a wooden base on the table in front of her, her sketches of the swans lay nearby. She thought of Jake at the pond and frowned. Yes, she was glad to see him again, after all this time. But, something had happened to him. When they were young, she could talk to him about anything. Now, she felt she needed to guard her words. *Does he have to be so damned cute?* she wondered.

Shannon looked back at the clay. She missed her modeling stand in her Dublin studio, but decided she'd make do with what she had at hand. In her studies, she'd learned that Rodin used to make some of his sculptures without using armatures, metal frameworks that supported the clay. He'd created cones of water clay that hardened when dried. Here, like the master, she would have to make her own armatures.

Studying the sketches, she walked to the shelf near the window where a heating pad lay. She checked the temperature gauge on the pad, then unfolded it to reveal the dark brown, warmed oil clay that lay inside, wrapped in plastic. A local sculptor in The Dalles had recommended the clay to her that morning, when he'd learned that Shannon didn't have a kiln in her new studio. He'd said the oil clay was never fired. Shannon was excited to see how the new texture would work for her project. The sculptor had warned her that it would cool and harden quickly, so she knew she had to work fast.

Cutting off a portion of the clay, she re-wrapped the rest and covered it with the pad to keep it warm. She sat down on a tall stool next to the table and began modeling the beginning form of the first swan, building up the clay onto the cone. At first, it looked like a large egg. But, slowly, the graceful body of the swan began to appear. She stood back and looked at the form, then at her sketches. Smiling to herself, she went to get more clay.

She began working on the long neck, stabilizing it with thick columns of clay to support the bends as she slowly built up to the head. Then, she went to work on the wings. A shadow darkened the window for a fleeting moment, but when she looked up, she saw only the blue sky.

Jake softly opened the door, glad that Shannon was intent on her work and didn't seem to notice him. He stepped in and leaned on the door jamb, watching her fingers fly over the form taking shape in front of her. He'd watched this process numerous times before, but never with such precision. Shannon's fingers shaped each small piece of clay to the desired form, sometimes frowning until she got it just right. Then, she'd mold it gently onto the bird's body.

He glanced around the room and saw ceramic statues and rubber molds of birds and animals in various forms standing on the shelves. The statue of a horse, rearing with hooves in the air, caught his eye and he smiled.

Next to the window, he saw an unfinished clay form that looked like the beginning of a bust. He recognized Dan's face, when he was a young and virile man.

He watched as Shannon went to the heating pad. When she unwrapped the clay, he said, "Clever idea."

Shannon jumped and dropped the pad on the floor, holding the clay in her hands as if it were made of gold.

"Damn!" she said.

Jake smiled when he saw her flushed face. He went to her and picked up the heating pad. As he handed it to her, he noticed that her hair glowed from the sunlight shining through the window behind her. He took a few steps back.

"I didn't hear you come in." She wrapped the clay into the pad and checked that it was still plugged in.

"What's all this?" Jake asked.

"I'm going to stay here and work - until..." She looked at the bust and stopped. "Just work."

Jake saw the change in Shannon's face.

"He told you," he said softly.

"Yes."

He walked around the room and stood near the bust.

"When did you start this?" he asked, nodding to the statue of the man he thought of as his father.

"A few months ago."

"Were you working from a photo of him?"

"No...from memory."

"Good memory."

When Shannon came over to where he stood, he placed his hand on her shoulder. Then, suddenly, he removed it. For a moment, he'd forgotten his anger and let himself remember when they were young and something inside of him had sparked. It was never sexual, much deeper than that - pure heart, more like a bonding of souls. It'd been a long time since he'd felt it. But, here it was again and it frightened him. He shoved his hands into his pockets.

"Why do you use O'Toole, instead of Hamilton, which is your birth name?"

"Because, at the time, the only people who'd ever cared for me were my grandparents. It wasn't because of my mother."

Jake thought about that for a moment, then said, "Well...let me know if you need anything."

Shannon looked at Jake with a quizzical expression.

"Well, if you're going to be hanging around here," he continued, "I figured the least I could do was be friendly."

"In that case, I heard there's a foundry in Joseph. I'm going to need to have some pieces bronzed, when I'm finished with them."

"I know the guy," Jake offered. "I could fly you there...if you want."

He felt like an idiot and was kicking himself for it.

"I don't want to be away too long..." she began.

"We'd only be gone a few hours."

"How come you're being so nice all of a sudden?" she asked, walking to the swan.

Jake looked down at his boots. He'd heard the sarcasm in her voice. His anger was surfacing again, and he tried to tamp it down. He looked around the room for a distraction, his eyes falling onto the clay swan. He watched as Shannon picked up another piece of clay, then tossed it back onto the table. He could see that the clay had dried out. She walked over to the heating pad and began to cut a small piece of warm clay.

"You know you should use a heater box, instead of that pad," he suggested.

Shannon turned on him. "What do you know about sculpting? I've been doing this for over ten years now. You're just a...a cowboy who mends fences and picks his teeth with the bones of small animals. The only thing cultured in your world here is yogurt!"

"And, you think your city culture entitles you to judge everyone else?" It felt good to be back behind his armor.

"You don't know anything about my life. At least my world is civilized, and...and we don't spit on the sidewalks."

"Civilized? You're world's a joke. It's not real," Jake yelled. He pointed to the mountain in the window. "This is real. You come here, thinking you can change everything. But, nothing's changed."

"You're dead wrong. Everything's changed," Shannon yelled back, her fists clinched.

Jake didn't answer.

"Why don't you like me?" Shannon asked slowly.

His eyes burrowed into hers, making her look away. "I don't trust you."

"Why?"

"It's history now, just leave it." Jake turned to walk out. He'd said too much already.

"Who put that chip on your shoulder?" Shannon asked before he got to the door.

He stopped and whirled around, his hands on his hips. "What chip?"

"That big, fat one that you're carrying around for some stupid reason."

"What do you care?" he said, then walked out, slamming the door.

Through the window, he saw Shannon pick up a hammer and smash the clay swan as tears streamed down her face.

"Damn," Jake cursed as he kicked his boot in the dirt, sending a swirl of dust into the air. He'd let his guard down and didn't like the fact that she could get under his skin so easily.

He looked up and saw Dan walk out onto the porch of the ranch house. Jake stopped, suddenly remembering what it was like to lose a father. He was going to have to go through it all over again. But, then, so was she.

Just as he was about to turn and go back into the studio, a flash of light caught his eye toward the entrance to the ranch. Jake stood with his hand shading his eyes. A man stood next to a blue sedan with what looked like binoculars held to his eyes.

"Who's that?" Dan called from the porch.

"I don't know, but I'm going to find out."

Just as Jake moved to get his horse, the man jumped into the car and peeled away from the ranch, spraying dirt and gravel behind him.

***

Ireland

The flashing lights in the next block caught Brid's eye as she neared her apartment building. It wasn't unusual for the Garda to come to a pub and remove an unhappy customer, but this was too close to her home.

She stopped when she saw the white van of the Garda Technical Bureau, an ambulance, and police cars parked at her front door. Men and women in blue uniforms bustled about in an attempt to keep the gathering crowd from the entrance.

Brid walked up to one policeman. "What's going on?"

"A young woman was found murdered on the third floor," the young officer replied.

"Oh, no!" Brid exclaimed. "Who was it?"

"I can't say, Miss. So, you'll be moving along now." He motioned for her to walk away from the barricade, but she stood her ground.

"I live on the second floor of this building. May I go home now? Is it safe to go in?"

"Yes, we've already searched the building. Just stay down on your own floor." The officer opened the barricade to allow Brid to pass through.

As she walked toward the front entrance, a team of Garda technicians in white suits passed her, carrying large containers. They were followed by ambulance attendants with a Gurney. Brid moved out of the way on the first landing and shuddered with relief as she watched them continue to the floor above her own. She hesitated, then decided to follow them. She'd lived in this building for six years and knew many of the tenants.

She stopped when she saw the officials turn into Maggie's apartment. She'd never seen it, but knew it was the one directly above her own. Looking through the open door, she was surprised to see the expensive furnishings that were out of place in this neighborhood.

Leaning in to get a better look, she watched as some of the technicians went down a hallway similar to her own and turned into what prob- ably was the bedroom, while others began dusting the living room for fingerprints. She noticed an older policeman sitting slumped in a large overstuffed chair, his face in his hands.

"What're you doing?" a deep voice said from behind her. She gasped and turned to see a tall, well-built man with dark hair and broad shoulders. She felt a flash of familiarity when she looked into his hazel eyes.

"I...I live here...on the floor below," she stammered, noticing that her palms were sweating. "I know Maggie. Is she...?"

"What's your name, Miss?"

"Bridget...Bridget McDonagh. Have we met before?"

"What's your apartment number?" the man asked as he wrote in a small notebook he'd pulled from his jacket pocket. She noticed his hands were large, with long fingers, like a piano player.

"Two-o-three."

He gazed up at her again. "That's next to Shannon O'Toole's

apartment, right?"

"Yes…Why?"

"I didn't get an answer there. Do you know where she is?"

"In the United States…with her father - in Oregon."

He nodded, as if he'd already known the answer. Brid's chin came up.

"Why do you want to know about Shannon?" she asked, suddenly concerned for her friend.

"It's police business," was all he said.

"May I ask who you are?" she demanded.

"Detective O'Sullivan," he said, pulling his ID from his tweed jacket. "I'm with the Criminal Investigation Unit."

He put away his badge and continued, "How long have you known Maggie Murphy?"

"She…moved in about a year ago."

"Have you seen anything or anyone strange around here in the past few weeks?"

"Only that…well, I'm not sure if…" Brid hesitated.

"Any information will help us find who did this to her."

"Well, she came home bruised and beaten a couple of times."

"Can you give me the dates?"

"Not really…the last time was just a few days ago. I took her to my place, but she wouldn't say who did it to her." She wondered if she should tell him about Shannon's statue.

"Do you know if she was seeing anyone - personally, I mean?"

"Not really, but it did seem obvious. He was a bleedin' git, though, beatin' on her that way."

"That's all for now," the detective said. "You must leave this area now and go back to your own apartment."

Brid turned to leave, but changed her mind. "There is one thing…" she began. "That night that Maggie came home beat up…she mentioned that she'd seen a statue of Shannon's that was stolen recently. She didn't say where it was or who had it."

Brid was surprised to see the detective smile as he noted this in his book.

"We know where to contact you, Miss McDonagh, if we need anything further," he said, then turned away, dismissing her.

His eyes were kind, but his manner was abrupt. Brid wasn't sure if she liked him or not. He'd left her standing in the hallway and entered Maggie's apartment. Brid watched as he walked to the older man and put his hand on his shoulder.

"Neville, I'll take you home," she heard him say.

"Me Maggie," the older man wailed. Brid realized he was Maggie's father. "I found her…," he said softly. "She was…" He covered his face again and sobbed.

Another officer came up to the two men and said, "What're you doing here, O'Sullivan? This isn't your business any longer. I thought you were on some money-laundering case."

"You know, Whelan, you're right. I just came to find Neville. We think our man has left for the U.S.," O'Sullivan said, catching Brid's eyes. She quickly stepped back into the hallway.

Just then, the attendants came out of the bedroom with Maggie's body on the Gurney. Brid turned and ran to her room.

Slamming her door, Brid paced back and forth, her arms crossed over her roiling stomach, not knowing whether to cry or vomit. She swallowed hard to clear the knot in her throat as tears began streaming down her cheeks.

Wiping her face with the back of her hands, she ran for her phone and dialed Shannon's cell phone number, then continued pacing the room.

"Pick up. Pick up," she said impatiently. "Damn," she swore as she heard the voice-mail message.

"Shannon…," she began, then stopped. She thought how it would sound if she just blurted about Maggie's death and quickly changed her mind.

"This is Brid. I've decided to come to Oregon." She cleared her throat. "I'll call you once I have my itinerary." She was about to hang up, then added, "Hope you're okay. Love you and take care."

As she pressed the end button, she froze, remembering now where she'd seen Detective O'Sullivan before - in her father's pub the other night. Her body trembled with fear.

Why had he been watching me? she wondered. He didn't look like someone she should be afraid of. He worked for the Garda, for God's sake. But, there was something about him she couldn't explain. She shook her head and turned toward her bedroom to pack.

"Oh, how'm I goin' to explain THIS to my family?" she moaned out loud.

***

Oregon

Dan walked into the barn and placed a thermos next to a bale of straw in the aisle way. He saw Skye tethered in the aisle, his daughter briskly brushing the mare's coat. It was a familiar sight and he sighed, knowing that he'd made the right decision in asking her to come. Even though he had Gina and Jake close to him, he'd always felt something was missing in his life. Now, he knew what that was - his own daughter.

He thought back of his own father and hoped he had done a better job with Shannon, even if it had only been for her early formative years. Joseph Hamilton drove Dan harder than any hand on the ranch, molding him into a replica of himself. His father was a respected man, but had few friends. Dan's mother was the one who showed him what was more important in life - family, love, and friendship.

"You're doing a fine job," he said softly so as not to make her jump.

"She's a fine horse." Shannon smiled slightly and Dan's heart melted. "Where's Jake?" she asked.

He could tell that something was bothering her. "He had some business in The Dalles. We're going to join him there tonight for dinner."

Dan was concerned about the stranger Jake had seen earlier. He'd sent Jake into town to find out who was new in the area. Everyone within miles of this place knew each other and would know if a stranger was around.

He looked at his daughter and his heart ached as he realized he'd missed watching her grow into the beautiful woman she'd become.

"Do you have a boyfriend in Ireland?" he asked.

"Not really."

"What do you mean?"

"Well, Mother keeps picking out the men in my life. She's so concerned that I'll ruin it if I'm left to make my own decisions."

"I'm sure she means well—"

"She's only thinking about HER status in the community."

Dan looked out the open doorway of the barn. Shannon looked so much like her mother, but he could see their differences. He remembered when Sarah first learned that all of his money was wrapped up in this land, she'd accused him of tricking her. She'd always wanted more. Yet, he would always brush his doubts aside when it came to Sarah.

"I don't believe—"

"You don't know her," Shannon shot back at him, then went back to brushing the mare, her strokes quick and forceful. Skye began to pull away from Shannon.

Dan took Shannon's hand and gently removed the brush, stroking softly on the mare's coat to soothe the horse.

"I know…" Dan said. "There's a lot I don't understand anymore. I can see you're angry, but you don't have to take it out on Skye." He stopped brushing and looked at Shannon. "What's got you in an uproar?"

"Well…it was something that Jake said earlier today."

Dan waited, watching his daughter. He was thrown by the curve ball she had just thrown him and wondered what her involvement was with these other men. His hopes were riding on these two young people in his life.

"When I asked Jake why he's so upset that I'm here, he got all hot and started yelling at me. He said he doesn't trust me. Why'd he do that?"

"Normally, I'd let Jake tell you…, but I doubt that he would. Shortly after you left, his father died."

"I know," Shannon said, looking away for a moment.

"Well, I told him that this was his home as long as he wanted it."

Dan handed the brush back to Shannon and sat down on a bale. He took a slow drink of water from the thermos sitting nearby. He'd seen the flash of jealousy in Shannon's eyes and was sorry for it.

"You two are pretty close."

"Yes." Dan didn't know what else to say.

"But, why's he so angry?" Shannon insisted.

"Grief. Loss."

"What's that got to do with me?"

"He didn't only lose his father." Dan saw the confusion in his daughter's face. This was going to be one of the hardest things he'd ever had to do.

"When your mother couldn't take living here anymore, she left, taking you with her. Jake saw how much that hurt me. Ever since then, he's been like a prize fighter waiting to enter the ring. He's sort of taken on the role of my defender."

The brush in Shannon's hand fell to the ground as if in slow motion, and she stared at him in disbelief. She blinked, then said in a small voice, "Mother told me that YOU sent us away."

Dan stood and went to his daughter, taking her shoulders in his hands.

"Why, in God's name, would I do that? You and your mother mean everything to me."

Tears welled in Shannon's eyes. "Oh, Da," she said as she wrapped her arms around him. "Why would she lie to me?"

Dan was silent for a moment, searching in his mind for an answer. "It was hard for her here. Maybe she felt she needed to...to protect herself."

When Shannon nodded and placed one of her hands on his, he said, "Your mother re-married, right?"

"Yes...His name is William Pearse. He owns the gallery in Dublin where I show my art."

"Do you like him?" Dan asked after a moment.

"He's all right, sometimes," she said with a shrug, picked up the brush, and softly resumed brushing Skye. "When I was young, I hardly ever saw him. After college, when my art was becoming popular, he started helping me. But, now, I just don't know him."

"What makes you feel like that?"

"I'm not sure, it's just a feeling."

Dan asked the one question he'd been waiting to know the answer to for years. "Is your mother happy?"

"I guess you could say that," Shannon paused. "You still love Mother, don't you, Da?"

Dan was silent for a moment.

"I never stopped."

CHAPTER SIXTEEN

Shannon was shocked to see that The Dalles had a restaurant with Mediterranean-style decor. A large mural stood behind elegantly-dressed people sitting at white-clothed tables in the dining room. She was glad she'd worn the short, black dress and had pulled her hair up with a large barrette.

Soft violin music filtered through the room. Looking around, she saw three men sitting at a polished bar in the next room, dressed in jeans and plaid flannel shirts, a stark contrast to where she now stood.

A tall man with a warm smile came to greet Shannon and Dan as they walked in. His dark hair curled around his head like some of the statues Shannon had admired during her travels to Italy.

"Dan, how are you?" the man said in broken English as he hugged her father.

"Never better." Dan placed his arm gently around Shannon's shoulders. "David, this is my daughter, Shannon."

David bowed with a flare and kissed Shannon's hand.

"I'm very pleased to see you again. My friend here has kept me in- formed about you."

"Thank you," Shannon said, glancing at her father.

"Do you remember David?" Dan asked Shannon. "He's originally from Naples. We were in high school together. He never lost his accent, though."

"I'm sorry, but I don't. How did you find your way to The Dalles?" Shannon asked.

"My family immigrated here to come to work in the orchards. Italian was always spoken at home," David said with a small shrug.

Another couple walked into the restaurant. "'Allo Mr. and Mrs. Waverly. I'll be right back."

David turned to Shannon, "This way, please," he said as he led the way into the bar. Shannon was surprised to see Jake sitting at a table with Gina Long.

"Shannon," Dan said, "I understand you and Gina know each other?"

"Yes."

"Hello again," Gina said, smiling. "I hope you don't mind my joining you."

"Not at all. Hello, Jake." Shannon found it very hard to stay calm. He looked extremely handsome in his black leather pants and white shirt.

"Shannon," was all Jake said, with a nod. He took a sip of his beer.

Earlier, as Shannon was getting dressed for dinner, she'd thought of what her father had said about Jake's anger - because of his loss. She'd wondered if Jake had been sad when she'd left, as well.

David held a chair out next to Jake for Shannon. She thanked him and sat down, then saw her father affectionately squeeze Gina's hand and kiss her forehead before he sat down next to her. Her father had told her that Gina was his friend, but Shannon wondered now just how close this friendship really was.

She was relieved when David handed her a menu. She pretended to look over the selections.

"Our steak," David said, kissing his fingertips, "it is the finest you'll ever find."

"Dan and I order it every time," Jake said, leaning toward her. "David's our best customer!"

"Then, I'll have steak," Shannon said, handing the menu back to David. "Rare," she added, looking over at Jake.

"Me, too," Gina said. "But, I'd like mine medium rare."

"I have a nice Chianti that has just arrived from Tuscany," David said. "It will go well with your steak, no?" He smiled and walked away.

"Shannon," Gina said, "I wanted to ask if you'd be interested in showing some of your work at my gallery...while you're here?"

Shannon thought for a moment, wondering how much time she really did have. Then, she saw her father and smiled.

"I might. I've set up a studio at the ranch, and I'm working on some new ideas."

David returned with an opened bottle, a symbol of a black rooster on the bottle's neck. He poured the dark red wine, the light overhead dancing on the liquid's surface as it swirled in the large, bulbous glass.

Just then, a small dark-haired woman dressed in black came out of the kitchen and called to him. "David, Georgio is giving me trouble with the desserts again. He's ruining my chocolate-raspberry torte." She retreated through the kitchen door.

David smiled at Shannon and shrugged. "My wife, Lily. She's from Austria," he said apologetically. "What can one do? *Divertirsi a*! Enjoy!" David bowed, then followed his wife.

Dan raised his glass. "A toast. To Shannon's homecoming."

The wine was warm going down Shannon's throat, but was dry and acidic. Jake whispered, "It gets better with food." He took another sip of beer.

Shannon smiled at him, but saw that his attention had turned to two women entering the restaurant. They sat next to the men at the bar. One woman was very young, wearing a short blue dress. Her blonde hair hung down her bare back.

Jake leaned over to Dan. "Isn't that Sherry Jensen?"

Dan turned to look at the two women.

"Yeah. I haven't seen her since she was fifteen."

"She's not fifteen anymore," Gina said slyly.

Jake smiled, staring at the young woman. "You've got that right."

Shannon rolled her eyes, watching Jake. She was too young when she'd left for Ireland to have him drool over her like that. Now, she wanted to know what it felt like to have him look at her like he was staring at the woman.

Gina saw Shannon's face and smiled. Then, she softly said, "We know everyone here. You'll get used to it. The problem is that you can't say or do anything around here without someone spreading it around."

Shannon smiled at Gina, then turned to look at the mural at the back of the dining room, an interesting collage of Michelangelo's magnificent statue of David at the Accademia Gallery in Florence, with a scene from the hills of Tuscany in the background. On the opposite side was a gondola in one of Venice's canals, and the white remains of the columns of a Roman temple were interposed at the top left. She sat on the edge of her chair in order to get a better view of the temple, but she knew it was a ruse. Her mind was really on the fact that she was surprised that she was actually upset by Jake's attention toward the young woman at the bar.

She was glad when the steaks arrived. Placing her napkin in her lap, she picked up her fork in her left hand and knife in her right, cutting into the meat. "Perfect," she sighed as the juice ran onto her plate. Her first bite was ecstasy, from the crunchy, charred surface to the tender and cool center. She closed her eyes and sighed.

When she opened them, she was surprised to see Jake smiling at her. "What?" she asked, looking around the table. Her father and Gina were also watching her.

"Told you so!" Jake said softly.

After the dinner plates were removed and dessert was being served, Jake placed his hand on Dan's arm. "What's the matter?"

Shannon looked up and saw her father's face was pallid as he placed his head in his shaking hands.

"Are you okay?" she asked her father, reaching out to him.

Dan looked at Shannon and then at Jake. "I'm suddenly very tired," he said. "I think I'll skip dessert." He smiled at Shannon and placed his hand on her cheek. She knew it was an attempt to reassure her, but she wasn't convinced.

"Jake, would you mind taking care of the check and get Shannon home? Gina can drive me back."

"No problem," Jake said.

When Dan and Gina got up to leave, he leaned down and kissed Shannon on the forehead. "See you back at the ranch, baby," Dan said.

Shannon watched as her father placed his arm around Gina's waist, and they walked out close together. She was actually glad that he had people like Gina and Jake to watch over him. Up until now, she'd been in denial about his illness. But, she knew she had to face reality and suddenly became very frightened. Life could be so unpredictable, yet so very precious.

***

The moon was full overhead when Shannon followed Jake out of the restaurant, her arms wrapped around herself. Without saying a word, Jake put his leather jacket around her shoulders. She welcomed the warmth, placing her arms inside the sleeves, but it didn't stop the fear inside of her.

She saw Jake's Norton backed up against the curb in front of the building, the chrome shining in the streetlight. He walked over to it and settled into the seat, then looked back at her.

"You came here on that?" she exclaimed.

She became uncomfortable when his eyes looked at her black dress, then down her long legs to her high heels. Jake smiled.

"Yep, it's a Commando. I had it custom built." He started the engine. "Get on," he said over the purring motor.

Shannon looked up and down the deserted street, hoping to see a taxi, but there were none. Shaking her head, she hiked up her skirt and got on behind him.

He twisted the throttle and slowly released the clutch. Shannon clung to Jake's waist as the bike roared to life. The street lights flashed over them like strobes as they left the city.

She saw the sign for Dufur, but Jake didn't turn. Instead, he took a road that led to a lookout point on the top of a hill. He turned off the engine and got off the bike, then held out his hand to Shannon.

"Why're we stopping here?" Shannon asked, climbing off the bike.

"It's the best view in town."

She looked out into the darkness and saw the lights of the city as it wound up the hillside. Turning east, she saw the brilliance of the flood- lights of a dam on the Columbia River, the rushing water escaping the gates. She walked to the edge of the hilltop and looked out over the dark water that she knew would eventually wind its way toward the ocean.

"Beautiful," she sighed.

Jake walked over to where Shannon stood. "It depends on how you define beauty. It was much different before the dam was built. There used to be a falls there, the Celilo Falls. That area was totally submerged when the dam started up."

"Weren't there also some families who had to move because of this?" Shannon asked, looking at the giant structure.

Jake nodded and lit a cigarette. "A lot of people lost some of their history for the sake of progress."

"I thought you were going to quit," she said, nodding at his cigarette.

He frowned and crushed it out under his boot. His dark eyes came back to hers.

"Did you know the woman who was recently murdered in Dublin?" he asked softly.

She was startled for a moment. *How did he know?* she wondered, then looked away. "Yes."

"How many does that make now?"

Shannon quickly turned to him again. "How do you—"

"There's such a thing as the Internet, way out here. We don't live in the boonies, you know."

"Does Da know?"

"Yes."

She wrapped her arms back around herself. "Nikki and I weren't very close, but she worked at the gallery where I show my work."

Jake shoved his hands in his pockets and kicked a rock over the edge. "That's too close."

"I know."

"At least you're safe here." Jake looked out over the water, then said, "What's it like, living in Ireland?"

Shannon thought for a moment. She knew he was trying to change the subject, and she was willing to let him.

"In some places, it's a lot like here - the green hills of the valley and mountains. People are warm and friendly, except there they have to know who you're related to and who you know before they'll invite you to share a pint." She remembered Gina's statement and added, "But, from what Gina said, maybe it's more like here than I thought."

Jake laughed, deep dimples cutting into his cheeks. She watched the moonlight dance over his hair.

"You have a great smile," she said. "You should wear it more often."

Jake shrugged and pulled out another cigarette. He stopped when he saw her watching him and put the pack back into his shirt pocket.

"I haven't felt this free in years," Shannon said, taking the barrette out of her hair so that it fell over her shoulders. For a fleeting moment, she wondered what it would feel like to have Jake's hands in her hair.

"What do you mean?"

"People are always telling me what to do. The only time I ever feel like myself is when I'm working in my studio."

"What people?"

"Mother, mostly. But, William, my step-father, and Thomas controls what happens to my work when I'm finished with it."

"Who's Thomas?" Jake asked.

"The manager of William's gallery in Dublin, where I show my work. He's the one my mother wants me to marry."

Jake looked away. Shannon could tell by his face that he wanted to know more, but he remained silent.

"Would you have some time to take me to the foundry in Joseph?" she asked. This time, she wanted to change the subject. "I've completed my latest project."

Jake seemed taken aback, but she watched as he collected himself. "What piece is it?" he asked.

"The bust of my father."

Jake was silent for a moment. "Maybe. I'll have to see, we're short a hand…"

Shannon set her jaw and looked straight ahead. "Never mind. I can drive there myself."

Jake laughed again. "Drive there? Are you crazy?"

Shannon crossed her arms and didn't respond.

"It'd take you hours to get there!" Jake finally said. "I could have you there much faster by plane."

She looked at Jake and smiled. "Okay."

"Come on, we'd better head back," Jake said.

They got onto the bike and rode to the highway leading away from the Columbia River.

On the ride to Dufur, Shannon held onto Jake again. Once they were on the distant road to the ranch, she began to let herself relax. The air was warmer now. All her thoughts of Ireland and her father's health vanished for just a moment, and she felt her muscles letting go. She reached up with one hand and removed her barrette, letting her hair whip out behind her.

Suddenly, Jake turned off the headlamp. The large moon was

now the only source of light. At first, Shannon tightened her hold again on Jake. Then, she slowly released her grip and began to lift her hands above her head, whooping with joy, feeling the wind in her hair.

Jake turned the light back on and revved the engine. Shannon wrapped her arms tightly around him, leaning into him again. She doubted if he could hear her over the roar of the engine, but the words began to bubble up from her heart.

"I love you, Jake McLeod," she yelled into the wind. "I always have."

CHAPTER SEVENTEEN

Ireland

Michael sat in his office, searching the media records on the Internet for other cases relating to money-laundering. When he found a similar case in London to the one he was working on, he noted the gallery and the investigating agent's name. Then, he pulled out his notebook and did a search for the name Greenburg, which is the one he'd seen on the crate at the Pearse Gallery. He was amazed at what he'd found. John Green- burg had businesses all over the world, including the London Gallery. He was a multi-millionaire with major International financial organizations backing him. He was an investigator's nightmare.

Just then, the phone rang.

"O'Sullivan."

"Michael, this is Flannery," the voice at the other end said. "I've got some new data on that latest murder victim."

"But—" Michael began, then stopped. He knew the examiner was aware that he'd been pulled from the serial-killer cases, but was glad he'd called him. "Is this the Conroy or Murphy case?"

"Both, actually. The weapon used on these two women was some type of wire."

"Finally, we have a link," Michael said excitedly. "Why didn't we see this before?"

"I don't know, maybe he's been using the same weapon and it's starting to break down or something. Criminals aren't very smart, usually. I'm not sure just what type of wire yet, but I'm still running some tests on the metal filings I found."

"Have you told Whelan and Graham yet?"

"Not yet. I wanted you to be the first to know."

"I appreciate it," Michael said. "Let me know when you've finished."

"Sure thing," Flannery said, then hung up.

Michael stared at the phone for a moment, still not ready to give up these cases just yet. He looked at his watch and saw that it was lunchtime.

He went to the door of his office and closed it. After retrieving an unofficial file from the middle drawer of his desk, he sorted the contents, glad now that he'd removed his personal notes about his own interpretations of the evidence before he'd handed over the killer files to Whelan.

Pulling out a new notepad, Michael methodically began writing a de- tailed outline, searching for a pattern - some signature that would help him to understand the killer more clearly. He added the new data about the killer's hair color, the common weapon, and the photos of the last two victims.

Michael rubbed his temples, tossed his pen onto his desk, and leaned back in his chair. He knew he was missing something, but just couldn't seem to put his finger on it.

He looked out the window to his left. Two young women in Garda uniform were walking toward the parking lot. Both were of the same height, with long, blonde hair. Michael thought they could have been twins.

At his elbow was the postcard, announcing Shannon O'Toole's art tour. Suddenly, he sat upright in his chair, his face white. There was a pattern. All the victims had been redheads, about the same age and height!

"Holy, shit," he swore as he picked up his phone and dialed the gallery number.

"Pearse Gallery's answering service. May I help you?" The voice was nasal and impersonal.

"This is Detective O'Sullivan of the Criminal Investigation Unit. I need to talk to Thomas Aherne right away."

"The gallery is closed for the next few weeks, Detective. Mr. Aherne will be checking in periodically for his messages. Would you like me to—"

"Where is Aherne?" Michael demanded.

"I'm sorry, but I cannot give out that information."

Michael took a deep breath to calm himself before speaking. "Look, Miss…"

"McBride."

"Miss McBride, I can have a warrant within minutes to get copies of your records. But, if you tell me now, you could be saving someone's life."

There was a pause, then the voice continued. "Mr. Aherne just called in from Rome. He's leaving for Portland, Oregon, to continue the art tour for Shannon O'Toole. He didn't give a return date."

"Thank you for your cooperation," Michael said, then hung up.

He looked down at a fax that he'd received from the IRS agent he was supposed to be working with. This man was slipperier than an eel and hard to get to know. Michael only dealt with him via his cell phone or a fax machine and had only seen him once on that day at the elevator. His fax had requested financial records from the Pearse Gallery, especially any in connection to a gallery in Seattle owned by John Greenburg. Michael wasn't surprised to find that there had been numerous transactions between the Dublin gallery and Greenburg.

He smiled as he dialed the number for the agent. It'd been days since he'd been able to talk with this guy, he kept getting his voice mail. Once again, the man's voice droned with the usual message.

Frustrated, Michael said into his cell phone, "This is O'Sullivan in Dublin. I've sent you the gallery records. Also, Aherne's headed for Oregon, and…I think I know who the next victim is. Call me."

Quickly, he stuffed the file back into the drawer, jumped out of his chair and left his office.

Dugan's door was open when Michael arrived.

"I was just going to call you," Dugan said, quickly shutting a drawer in his desk.

Michael knew that Dugan kept a flask of Irish whiskey in his desk, but, like the others in the unit, he ignored it.

"Thomas Aherne has already left the country, he's heading for the U.S. now."

"What makes you think that?"

"I just called the gallery and found that one of their artists is in Oregon. It looks like the gallery manager and owners are taking her art tour to Portland-"

"What's this got to do with the money-laundering case you're on now?"

Michael stopped for a moment, remembering that he wasn't supposed to be looking for the serial killer now.

"It's possible that...Aherne's using this tour as a front...to...uh... take paintings to his client in the States. I have a lead on who the buyer may be. I want to follow him there...to check this out. The IRS agent is in agreement," Michael lied.

"Is Neville going with you?"

Michael looked through Dugan's glass door and saw Neville's empty office. "No., he's still out on leave, after his daughter..."

Dugan grew quiet. Michael stood his ground, unwilling to let this one go. He put his hands on the edge of Dugan's desk and leaned into the man's face, just as he had done to convince his own father numerous times when he had a good lead.

"Chief, like you said, you're short of men right now. I can go alone and work with the U.S. officials."

Dugan hesitated, then said, "Let me make a few phone calls before you begin packing your bags. Remember, you're only there to ASSIST them."

"Yeah, right. What were you going to call me about," Michael asked before he turned to leave.

"Huh?"

"Just as I came in here, you said you were going to call me."

"Oh, I want you to leave William and Sarah Pearse alone. They're big contributors to our agency, and we can't have them harassed by one of our own."

Michael was silent for a moment, thinking of his last encounter with Pearse. Slowly, he understood, nodded, and left.

***

Oregon

The next morning, Jake and Shannon arrived at the ranch airstrip in the black Jeep, carrying numerous wooden crates containing Shannon's art. Jake parked next to the small, single-engine plane, where Charlie and another man stood.

As she moved her sunglasses to the top of her head, Shannon thought the new man looked familiar, but she couldn't say why.

"Good morning, Charlie," Shannon said to the older man, as she got out of the Jeep. She smiled when she saw him blush, wishing she could remember more about him. But, she knew she liked him.

"Mornin'," Charlie said as he shuffled his feet in the dirt, then turned and called to the other man. "Start loading these crates into the plane. They've got statues in them."

Shannon looked at Charlie, surprised that he even knew what was in the crates.

Charlie tipped his hat to her and said, "This here's Connor. He's helping us out until Larry is back on his feet. I found him in The Dalles, lookin' for work."

"It's nice to meet you, Connor." Shannon extended her hand to the burly man with dark hair. "That's a good Irish name. What's your family name?"

"Larkin."

The hair on the back of her neck stood up when she heard his voice and she released his hand. She saw Jake watching closely.

"Have we met before?" she asked Connor.

"No."

Connor picked up a crate and walked toward the plane. Shannon watched him load the one containing her father's bust. Her heart skipped a beat when it almost slipped out of his hands.

"Be careful with that," she yelled. "It's still very fragile."

Connor only nodded.

After the last crate was loaded, Shannon walked to the plane, noticing the dark cloud mass forming on the horizon, heading their way.

Charlie said to Jake, "Keep a sharp eye on this weather. I heard a weather alert was issued a few minutes ago."

Jake nodded, helped Shannon into the plane, and closed the door.

Shannon followed Jake to the front of the plane, noticing for the first time the soft moccasins on his feet. She sat in the seat next to him.

"How long did you say it will take us to get to Joseph?" she asked, watching his long hands as he worked the controls of the plane.

"Less than an hour."

Jake prepared the plane for takeoff. The grassy runway was

rough, but then they were airborne. Slowly, he banked the plane toward the east.

The rolling hills were ablaze as the sun rose overhead, hues of reds and yellows bursting into view when they cleared the horizon.

"How beautiful," Shannon whispered, then squinted from the bright light. She pulled her glasses down over her eyes and saw the river winding on the left, the highway threading along beside. The flat land near the river spread out below them as they followed the path of the road.

Large clusters of dark cumulus clouds seemed to be catching up around them from the west, with ribbons of blue sky still etched throughout.

She looked at Jake, who seemed lost in his own thoughts. Her breath caught as the sun glistened in his dark hair, and she wished she could reach over and touch it. She wondered if Jake heard her on the bike the night before, when she'd told him she loved him. Then, a fear grabbed her. *What if he doesn't love me?* she thought.

After awhile, she asked, "Where are we?"

"That's Pendleton," Jake said, pointing towards a sprawling city near where the river bent toward the north. "They have a huge round up every year in September."

"What're they rounding up?"

Jake laughed. "It's not really a round up anymore, it's mostly a rodeo and a reason to party - a celebration that's been going on since 1910."

"I remember the round ups on our ranch. You were gone for over a week sometimes. I always wanted to go, but Da said it was too dangerous."

"He was right."

Shannon looked at the horizon and saw mountains ahead. On one rim, there was a row of large wind generators spinning in the now gray sky.

"That's the Blue Mountains," Jake said. "See that high peak over there?" He pointed to the south. "That's called Mount Ireland."

"No kidding?" Shannon laughed. When she saw the hue of the mountain, her mood changed as she thought of her father.

"We both know about Da's cancer," she finally said.

Jake looked at her, then back at the sky in front of the plane.

"I'm really cheesed off," Shannon continued, "that he's not even interested in taking any of the treatments. He's just giving up!"

"He's already done the dance," Jake said with anger in his voice. When he looked at Shannon, his face softened.

"He did some chemo, which made him really sick. When the doc suggested surgery, Dan just seemed to give up. There're two types of surgery, but it all depends on how advanced his tumor is. He doesn't seem to want to know what he has, he's so stubborn. Once he's made up his mind, there's no changing it. He always does everything his way."

Shannon looked away for a moment, wishing she had inherited some of her father's independent attitude instead of the weakling she felt she was.

"When he wrote that last letter to you, I didn't think you'd return, but Dan always believed you would."

Shannon was silent, then said, "When I first came back to the ranch, I was jealous of you."

"Of me? Why?" Jake asked.

"Because of all the time you've had with him."

Jake looked at her, then finally nodded in understanding. "He's a good man."

"Yes, I know - now."

They flew in silence, then Jake asked, "Tell me about this Thomas you mentioned the other night, the one your mother wants you to marry."

"My mother doesn't understand that I'm not looking for a husband. She thinks that all women aren't whole unless they're married and have someone to provide for them."

"What do you think?"

"I don't need a man for that."

Shannon looked out her window, then back straight ahead. "She also thinks she has to make my decisions for me, that I'm not capable of making good choices. Thomas was her decision."

They passed over another range of mountains.

"Those are the Wallowa Mountains," Jake said. "We're crossing the Columbia Plateau, the summer home of the Nez Percé tribe. The town of Joseph is just on the other side."

Shannon sighed at the beauty. "I don't see why anyone would

ever want to leave this land. It's breathtaking!"

"It wasn't by choice…" Jake became very quiet. Then, he added, "Every year, I ride with people from the Appaloosa Horse Club on what is called the Chief Joseph Trail."

"Chief Joseph? Wasn't he the one who led the Nez Percé tribe away from the army toward Canada, because he refused to agree to live on a reservation?"

"Yes. Dan's a lot like him…" Jake smiled at Shannon, then banked the plane a little north. "I'm going to take a little side trip over the Snake…"

The canyon below was rugged, with a narrow river carving its way through the purple haze at the base. Shannon stared in awe at the landscape, seeing few flat areas for man to settle and wondered how people could live there. They continued up along the deep Snake River until it was met by another.

"That's the Grand Ronde River," Jake said pointing to the tributary. Grasslands framed each side of the river, dotted by evergreens.

After a few minutes, Jake added, "See where it joins the Snake?"

Shannon nodded.

"Near there is the beginning of the trail. To the east, around where the Snake and Salmon River meet was the first battle along that trail."

Shannon saw an elk climbing up the side of one hill. "I can see why your father started the Appaloosa herd, besides their origin," she said, nodding toward the elk.

"The Appaloosa were perfect for this rugged country around here. Their hooves are striated vertically, which gives them protection from breaking on rocky ground."

"They're a marvelous breed."

***

Oregon

Harry Blake walked into his office, carrying a cup of dark liquid he used to call coffee, just as the phone was ringing.

"Detective Blake," he answered.

"Is this Harry Blake of the Portland FBI?" the voice said.

"Yes."

"I'm in Oregon now," the voice said.

Harry recognized the voice of the IRS Special Agent he'd been as- signed to work with and frowned. He was beginning to hate this new assignment. This guy was a pain in the ass, taking himself way too seriously - like some cloak and dagger detective from the CIA.

"It's about time you called in," Harry yelled into the phone. "Where the hell have you been?"

"You know I'm working undercover. I've met the target," the voice continued.

Harry rolled his eyes and took a sip, almost choking. Target? he wondered. He opened the file on his desk and noted the date and time of this call, then drew a target next to it. "Who're you talkin' about?" he asked.

"Aherne, of course."

"So, where is he now? I just received notice that Pearse's plane is missing. They're flight plan listed Paris, then Rome, but after that, they just disappeared."

There was silence on the other end, then Harry heard, "I'll be out of touch for a day or two, but will call in as soon as I can."

The phone went dead.

Harry stared at the phone before hanging up. He'd been on the force for over thirty years now, but never ran into anyone as crazy as this guy. He snickered now as he wondered what his dad, an ex-PI, would think about this IRS agent.

CHAPTER EIGHTEEN

Jake's plane landed at the small Joseph airstrip, dwarfed by the mountains surrounding it. Jake taxied toward a hangar where a man stood with his hands on his hips.

Through the window, Shannon saw a Native American in his seven- ties, with weathered skin, eyes like a hawk, and a long, black and silver pony tail tied behind his back, standing next to a beat up red Ford pickup. He chewed on what was probably a large wad of tobacco as he looked up at the sky, which was now dark with storm clouds approaching. As the plane stopped a few feet away from him, the man shook his head and spat in the dust at his feet.

Jake and Shannon stepped from the plane and walked towards the man. In the distance, Shannon could see a small fenced cemetery, with several whitened tombstones standing in the tall dry grass that bent in the wind.

"You're late!" the man said to Jake.

Jake winked at Shannon and smiled. "We got sidetracked. How the heck are you?" Jake asked the old man, offering his hand.

"Aw, come on, son," the man ignored Jake's hand and hugged him.

Jake looked embarrassed, but hugged back.

"I've been better. Surprised to hear from you. It's been, what, six months?"

"I know," Jake said, nodding, scratching his chin. "I've been pretty busy at the ranch."

Shannon watched as the two men glanced at each other, a look of silent understanding passing between them. Then, Jake turned to her.

"This is Hank Whitebird, my uncle."

Shannon stared at Jake. Then she remembered her manners, turned to Hank and smiled, offering her hand.

"I'm glad to meet you. I'm Shannon O'Toole."

"Shannon's the sculptor I told you about," Jake said.

"I know who she is," Hank said, pumping Shannon's hand vigorously. "It's a pleasure to meet you."

Shannon smiled, amazed that anyone in this remote location had ever heard of her.

The wind grew stronger, stirring the dust around their legs. Shannon saw two dust devils swirling in a dance.

"We'd better get going," Hank said.

They rode in the pickup with the crates in the back, a trail of black smoke following them. The engine was loud and the gears ground each time Hank shifted.

Shannon saw old wooden buildings that were rotting away in amongst the pine trees. The foothills nearby looked like grass-covered fingers of a giant reaching toward the valley floor with rock surfacing like knuckles where the soil had eroded away. She was amazed that they didn't see anyone during the ride.

"Have you always lived in Joseph?" Shannon asked Hank.

"Naw, I grew up in The Dalles with my family. That's where Jake's dad met my sister. When she died, she was my last living sibling. A cousin of mine wanted to come here to work, we started this foundry together. He's gone now, too."

Hank stopped the truck in front of a large weathered barn that stood at the outskirts of town. A wide sign advertising THE WHITEBIRD FOUNDRY hung above the green double doors. Leaving Jake to begin unloading the crates, Hank led Shannon through a side door.

"It's not much, but it's mine," he said in a soft voice, almost a whisper, as if he were entering a shrine.

The interior was dark, with two small skylights lighting the rough-hewn, wooden walls. Hank flipped a switch by the door and large over- head lights illuminated the room. Worktables stood against each wall, some covered in dust from plaster. Each shelf on one table was marked with labels for different stages of readiness. The next room contained rubber molds in various stages.

"This is the last of them," Jake said as he struggled with a large crate.

Hank went to help him, while Shannon walked over to the finished shelf and looked at a six-foot horizontal sculpture of a large stagecoach with a team of horses captured in a full-speed gallop.

"This is marvelous!" she exclaimed. "Who's the artist?"

Hank looked at Jake and smiled. "Me," the older man said.

"Fantastic, I love the patina you've given it and the definition makes it looks almost alive."

"Thanks," Hank said shyly. "It's one of my favorites... Now, Shannon, what can I do for you?"

She went to the largest crate and slowly opened it, her excitement beginning to bubble. She carefully unwrapped the piece. "I won't need any enlarging for any of these. How long will it take for you to cast them?"

"Once I make the molds..." Hank began, then stopped as the light from a skylight beamed down on the clay bust of Dan.

Shannon saw Hank look at Jake, a look of surprise on each of their faces. She reached into another crate and pulled out a ceramic mold of the bust.

"I've made molds for all of these...to save time," she said. "I hope you can work with them."

"Sure...No problem," Hank stammered, then stopped. "I've never seen anything like this. It's so lifelike." He looked at Shannon and smiled. "What type of finish do you want?"

"I'd like a patina for the swan and horses, similar to the colors you used on the stagecoach. But, not the bust. I want to leave it natural."

Hank nodded in agreement. "Good choice. I can call in some more help and have this one ready for you to view in no time."

"I appreciate it," Shannon said, touching the clay of her father. "This means a lot to me."

Shannon saw a faint light toward the back of the room and walked to it. A sculpture in progress of two large rocks facing each other stood on what looked like opposite shores of a river, with a wide waterfall cascading down between them from a mountain ridge as a backdrop.

"Those rocks are in the Columbia Gorge, with Horsetail Falls between them on the Oregon side," Hank said from behind her, making her jump. "It's not to scale."

"There's an old native legend," Jake began, "about two sons who fell in love with the same woman. The woman was killed and buried by the father. Later, her hair became known as Horsetail Falls. The Indian god, Coyote, found the brothers arguing, so he turned them into rocks. One became Rooster Rock on the Oregon side of the river, the other, Beacon Rock, on the Washington side."

She recognized the rocks that she'd passed while driving to The Dalles and doubted if two men would ever argue over her.

Once outside, the menacing wind whistled through the trees and black clouds loomed overhead, threatening rain.

"I'm not flying in this soup," Jake said above the noise.

"Nobody's going anywhere tonight," Hank yelled. "These storms flare up like wildfire here, because of the mountains."

"But, where will we stay?" Shannon asked.

"You won't be able to stay at my place," Hank said, nodding towards a small house next to the foundry, a stream of smoke from a chimney blending with the wind. "It's too small."

A woman stepped out of the house. Shannon recognized her as the woman in the painting at Gina's gallery, her long, dark hair flowing around her. The woman smiled and waved to Hank.

"Go on over to the Joseph Inn. They'll put you up 'till this blows over," Hank continued, smiling.

"How long will that be?" Shannon asked, looking up at the dark sky.

Hank smiled. "That could be days," he said, winking to Jake.

Jake looked down at the ground with his hands in his pockets.

Then, Hank saw Shannon's face and straightened himself. "Well, anyway," he said, clearing his throat, "you two take the truck. I'll probably work through most of the night here. See you sometime tomorrow."

Shannon watched as Hank walked over to the woman and put his arm around her shoulders. The couple walked together into the house, slowly closing the door behind them.

CHAPTER NINETEEN

Ireland

Brid walked onto the plane at Dublin Airport, her stomach queasy. She never liked flying, but she was more worried about Shannon than the plane crashing. She placed her bag in the overhead compartment and settled into the window seat. The stewardess came over and asked if she wanted a pillow, but Brid politely declined.

Shortly after she heard the door of the plane close, a man walked up and sat in the seat next to her. She looked up and gasped.

"What're you doing here?" she asked.

Michael smiled. "I guess I'm going to the same place you are."

"Detective O'Sullivan, I—"

"Michael. My name's Michael. Are you always this jumpy?"

Brid stared at him, then slowly tried to make herself relax. "Flying makes me bloody nervous."

One of the attendants began the usual flight instruction. Brid was surprised to see that most of the people ignored it.

The plane jerked, and Brid grabbed for the armrests. It wasn't until they had started taxiing toward the runway that she realized she was holding onto Michael's arm. She let go and crossed her arms in front of her.

"It's okay if you hold on…," Michael said, leaning toward her. "I've done this many times. There's nothing to worry about."

"Easy for you to say," Brid retorted, taking deep breaths.

"The liftoff's the best part," he winked.

A few minutes later, the roar of the engines echoed in her ears. Just as the plane raced down the runway, Brid grabbed onto Michael's arm again and shut her eyes until they had lifted off. Once in the air, she let go and willed herself to breathe again.

"You see," he said smiling. "There's nothing to worry about."

Brid turned to him and glared. But, when she saw his smile, she softened. "Thank you for the support. It did help."

"You're welcome!"

After awhile, the stewardesses came down the aisle pushing the beverage cart.

"Would you like something to drink?" a tall blonde asked Michael.

"Guinness," he said, then looked at Brid. When she shook her head, he added, "and two glasses."

"But, I didn't…"

"It'll make the flight easier," Michael said, leaning toward her. He poured the dark liquid into the glasses and handed one to Brid.

Brid took a long pull of the bitter beer and leaned back in her seat with a sigh of relief. She looked at Michael.

"I've always believed in the magic of things that happen in threes."

"Threes?" Michael said, his brow furrowed.

"This is the third time we've met. Well, sort of met. The first time was in my father's pub."

"I remember." He took a sip of his beer. She noticed that when his face relaxed, he had a permanent frown over his left eyebrow.

"You have an incredible voice," he added.

"Thank you. I've been very blessed."

Brid looked out the window and saw Dublin below, now very small as the plane climbed. She turned back to Michael.

Just then, a very large woman got up from the seat across from Michael, causing him to lean in toward Brid to give the woman room to turn and walk to the restroom. Brid smiled when she saw Michael's embarrassed expression.

Sitting back up, he asked, "Why're you going to the States?"

"I'm going to visit my friend, Shannon. And, you'll be going where?"

"Same," Michael answered, shifting uncomfortably in his seat.

"What? Why're you going to see Shannon?"

Michael leaned closer to Brid and lowered his voice. "She's connected with the Pearse Gallery and I'm working on a case that involves the manager."

"Thomas? What the bloody hell has HE done now?"

"You know Thomas Aherne?"

"Know him, I despise him. He's a bleedin' arse."

Michael smiled. "Well, that pretty well sums him up. I'm in total agreement."

"Does this have anything to do with Maggie?" Brid said softly, looking around at the other people nearby.

Michael leaned in again as the large woman returned to her seat. "No."

Brid watched his face and knew that he was lying. She became frightened and grabbed his arm, this time on purpose. "Michael, if Shannon is in any danger, I need to know about it."

He was silent for a moment. A small bell sounded, indicating that the seat belt sign had been turned off. He started to get up, but Brid held on tighter. When he turned to look at her, she held her breath.

"I don't know, yet."

***

Oregon

"I want to show you something," Jake said as he drove past Black Angus cattle, horses, and donkeys grazing together in one field at the foot of the rolling hills. As they entered the town of Joseph, the landscape gave way to civilization. Shannon looked at the mix of rustic, antique buildings and newer replicas that lined the main street. Large, life-sized bronze statues of animals stood along the white sidewalk. "Are those Hank's?" she asked.

"No, recently this has become a sculptors' paradise, and they seem to flock here like birds."

"Is Hank the uncle you told me about at the ranch?"

"Yeah." Jake was silent for a moment, then he added. "He's all I've got, besides Dan."

They turned a corner and seemed to be leaving Joseph. "Where're we going?" she asked.

"Wait, we're almost there."

Shannon saw the excitement in his face as he pulled off the highway onto the gravel shoulder. The truck came to a stop in a cloud of dust next to a high embankment.

She followed Jake past a cobbled wall and through gateposts

opening to a path. He stopped as two large mule deer crossed in front of them, a ten-point buck and a younger one. Shannon held her breath, watching the magnificent animals until they were out of sight.

The path wound uphill through the trees leading to a large monument. As Shannon and Jake drew near, she noticed a colorful array of ribbons and bandanas waving in the wind. For a moment, it seemed that the breeze had quieted while she stood in front of the tombstone. She was amazed to see various trinkets, dolls, toy cars, coins, and crosses wedged in every open crevice around the stone. Some were in the branches of the Juniper tree that stood next to it.

"What are these?" she asked in a whisper.

"Offerings to Chief Joseph's father, the elder," Jake answered as he stood next to her. "He signed the treaty in 1855 for peace with the white man."

"Where's his son buried?"

"In Okanogan County, Washington." Jake looked out over the land. "My people have come to this area for generations on a spiritual quest, seeking power and guidance through visions that would reveal the Great Spirit to them. Sometimes the visions come as dreams, but places like these are sacred."

Shannon circled the tombstone, then saw the inscription: *To the Memory of Old Chief Joseph, Died 1870.* She tried to imagine going on a quest or having a vision of her own. Once, she'd thought some- thing like that happened, while she created her first statue - the spotted horse. She turned and noticed that the path continued up the small hill.

She followed it until she saw two smaller, flat stones, almost buried by the brush. Shannon reached down and touched one, the stone was cold. A few letters were visible: *A friend of Chief Joseph and his people.*

A blue dragonfly landed on the stone, lingered for a moment, then flew away. Jake came up and stood behind her, placing his hands on her shoulders to shield her from the wind. For a moment, they seemed suspended in time in this quiet place. She reached up and held his hands.

"Thank you for bringing me here," she said.

Looking up, Shannon was surprised to see a large lake below, the water reflecting the mountains in the distance and dark clouds overhead. Suddenly, the wind pushed her back, returning to its full force.

"Come on," Jake yelled over the roar. "We'd better get out of here."

They drove back into Joseph and parked in front of a two-story red- brick building with tall windows and a balcony on the front of the second level. Across the street was a statue of a woman, her skirt cast as if it was blowing in the wind.

Jake and Shannon walked into the inn. The clerk behind a large counter was a short, elderly woman, who looked very tired as she talked on the telephone.

"This used to be a stage stop," she said into the receiver. "Some say it may have been a brothel in the late 1800's, but that can't be true, since it wasn't built 'til 1909. People are always making stuff up…"

Shannon walked over to look more closely at a bronzed eagle, standing next to an enormous stone fireplace. The large bird looked down from its perch, a tree stump that stood shoulder high.

"That's one of Hank's," Jake offered to Shannon.

Shannon smiled, then, followed Jake to the counter, which stood next to a tall, wide staircase.

"Do you have two rooms for tonight?" he asked after the woman hung up.

"There's only one room left, with twin beds," the clerk said, smiling sweetly at Jake.

When Jake looked at Shannon, she nodded.

"We'll take it," he said. "Is Muldoon's open tonight?"

"Oh, yeah, they're always open," the woman said, a wishful look on her face. "Couldn't you smell their ribs cooking before you came in?"

"The wind must have been blowing the wrong way," Jake said, taking the key and led the way up the stairs.

The large room was sparsely furnished with a few antiques: a dresser with an old-style bowl and pitcher, two rocking chairs in front of the large stone fireplace. The twin beds, with plaid tan bedspreads, stood against one wall.

Shannon was surprised to see no television, telephone, or radio. One chimney-style lamp was lit in the room, giving off a soft light. It was white porcelain with brass fixtures and feet. She looked more closely and was glad to see that it was electric.

She walked to the large mantle above the fireplace, a tall window on each side of it. Outside, she could see the mountain range near the airport.

"Are these ever used?" she asked Jake, pointing to two kerosene lanterns sitting on the mantle.

He looked up. "They come in handy when the power goes out."

"Does that happen very often?"

Jake looked out the window at the trees bending in the raging wind and smiled. "Only during storms."

Shannon frowned, looking out the same window, then watched Jake remove his jacket. His blue Chambray shirt with pearl snap buttons he wore was neatly tucked into his dark jeans. She saw that this time, he was wearing an older wide leather belt with an oval silver buckle. Her gaze traveled slowly back up to his face, and she was embarrassed to see him staring at her.

She turned away and pulled her cell phone out of her purse.

"Who're you calling?" Jake asked.

"Da. I want to let him now we're not getting back tonight."

"Hank will have already done that. Besides," he added with a shrug, "cell phone reception can be pretty iffy here, especially in a storm."

She nodded, looked at her phone, then put it away.

"Which side do you like to sleep on?"

Shannon stiffened as she looked at him, confused at first. Then, she realized he meant the beds and relaxed. "My left."

"Good," Jake smiled. "I like the right. I'll take this one," he said, pointing to the bed nearest the door. "Let's go eat."

CHAPTER TWENTY

William and Sarah were checking in at the counter of the Portland Marriott Hotel. Through the front doors, Sarah could see people walking and biking along the waterfront and wondered what would drive some- one to get all sweaty like that.

"Your Executive Suite is ready," the clerk said, "but one of the other suites you reserved will not be available until later this afternoon."

"That won't be a problem," William said, holding his hand out for the keys. "Thomas Aherne will be checking in later."

"Thank you, Mr. Pearse. Enjoy your stay in Portland."

On the ride up the elevator to the sixteenth floor, Sarah looked at her husband. She placed her hand on his neck, touching just above his shirt collar. "Cut yourself shaving recently?" she asked.

The bellman kept his eyes toward the doors.

"Yes," William said curtly, pulling the collar up higher. "What do you plan to do this afternoon?"

"I thought I might go shopping, and possibly get a manicure," Sarah replied, looking down at her nails. "They have a Saks near here."

The elevator doors opened. Sarah followed her husband and the bell- man to their suite. As William tipped the bellman, she walked from room to room, comparing it to the Ritz in Paris.

"These rooms are so tiny! Don't they have anything larger?" she ex- claimed, standing in the bathroom doorway.

The two men exchanged looks, and the bellman shook his head.

"That will be all," William said, then watched as the bellman walked out, softly closing the door behind him.

Sarah walked to the desk, which sat next to the window overlooking the waterfront. She picked up the receiver on the phone.

"I'll call Shannon—"

"No, wait," William interrupted her, taking the receiver from her and placing it back in its cradle. "We don't want to warn her that we're here just yet. Then, before the show, you and Thomas will go to that ranch and get her. She won't have time to refuse."

Sarah thought for a moment. She didn't like the idea of trapping Shannon, but considered the alternative and decided William was correct. *Besides*, she thought to herself, *I'm looking forward to seeing D.J. Hamilton again.*

William grabbed her by the arms. "Are you fantasizing about that rancher again? Ever since we decided to come here, you seem different," he yelled at her.

Sarah's smile disappeared. "Darling, I was only wondering what Shannon is going to say when we arrive."

William released her and walked to the wet bar. Sarah rubbed her arms, which stung from his strong fingers. His temper had grown more explosive lately. At first, she'd been attracted to his power. Now, she felt she had to watch everything she said or did.

"What time is Thomas arriving?" she asked as a diversion.

"He's taking the crates to the gallery now. Then, he's meeting us here for dinner."

"Good, we can talk about their wedding arrangements then."

Sarah was surprised when William turned and glared at her. "Why are you so obsessed with Shannon marrying Thomas? He's not good enough for her."

Sarah looked at William in disbelief.

"You're the one who pointed out his family background. I just don't want her to think she can select anyone she chooses. God forbid, she might pick that Indian she grew up with on the ranch. She could end up there - like I did."

She saw William's face flush with anger and patted his cheek.

"Careful, my darling. Someone might think you were in love with my daughter. I'm going shopping."

Sarah picked up her purse and walked out of the room.

***

The wind howled and rain pounded sideways as Jake and Shannon left the Joseph Inn. He led her to the red door of Muldoon's. Music blared and a blast of voices greeted them when they entered. The smell of sweet barbecue sauce and smoke hung in the air.

Jake saw Shannon looking at the small area crowded with bodies dancing to the music of the trio of bearded men in jeans and red suspenders. One man played a piano, another, a guitar. A heavy-set man beat on a set of drums. The name on the base drum was 'The Miners.' He steered Shannon to an empty table, as numerous people called out to him in greeting. He waved to them, then helped Shannon to a seat.

"I'll be right back," he yelled to Shannon over the music.

"Where're you going?" she asked.

"To get us some drinks. Do you want a beer?"

"Sure, Guinness, if they have it."

Jake smiled. "This is Muldoon's! Of course, they'll have it."

He winked at her, then walked toward the bar. A young blonde passed Jake and smiled, the sequins from her fringed, turquoise cowgirl shirt glinting in the overhead lights.

Howie Muldoon, a large man with big hands, handed a waitress two mugs of foam-topped beer. His hair was salt and pepper and his eyes crinkled in a smile as Jake approached.

"Hey, Jake," Howie yelled. "You're back."

"Just till the storm blows over."

Howie looked over at Shannon, and Jake followed his gaze. She sat alone at the table, watching the dancers. Jake thought she looked exceptionally striking tonight. Her red blouse tucked into slender, dark jeans set off her fiery hair. When he turned his head to one side, he could see that one toe of her red boots tapped under the table to the music, and he chuckled to himself.

"Now, who's the Irish beauty you've brought into me pub tonight?" Howie roared.

When Shannon noticed them staring at her, Jake turned back to Howie.

"Dan's daughter. She'd like a Guinness, and I'll take a draft."

Howie looked again at Shannon. When he could see that she was becoming uncomfortable under his gaze, he waved to her and smiled.

"Well, in that case," Howie said, setting the two mugs on the bar, "these are on the house."

"Thanks, man," Jake said and started to pick up the beers. He stopped when he saw a stand of silver necklaces hanging near the cash register. He took one off the stand and yelled to Howie, "Add this to my bill, will ya?"

"Sure thing," Howie winked at Jake.

Jake wound his way around the tables back to Shannon, holding the mugs high overhead. The necklace was now in his shirt pocket.

"What were you two talking about?" Shannon asked when he returned.

"You."

"I thought so. And, what were you saying about me?"

Jake looked over at Howie and saw him smiling at them. He waved his mug in a salute to the large man.

"Howie Muldoon's from Dublin, like yourself. He was just asking who you were." Jake paused and took a long draw of beer. Then, he smiled at Shannon. "I told him you're my girlfriend."

Before Shannon could respond, a six-foot brunette waitress with big breasts came up to their table. "I see you got your own beers," the brunette said, chewing a large wad of gum. "Are you wanting dinner, too?"

"We heard you've got ribs cooking," Jake said.

"You heard right."

Jake looked at Shannon and saw her nod in agreement.

"We'll take two," he said, smiling to the waitress.

The waitress nodded, blew a large bubble, then, walked away.

"What did you mean—" Shannon began, but was stopped when a woman with long dark hair began to sing an old Irish song about a sailor. The guitarist was now playing a fiddle.

Jake lit a cigarette. He saw her stare, but decided to ignore it this time. The whole room was filled with smoke, anyway.

She leaned across the table toward him, just as he lifted his beer to his lips. "Why'd you tell Howie I'm your girl?"

Jake's hand stopped as he looked at Shannon. Then, slowly he took a sip and swallowed hard, wiping the back of his hand across his mouth.

"I didn't...I was just kidding you."

The people around them began singing the chorus to the song.

"Do you have a girl?" Shannon yelled, then, sipped the creamy foam off the top of her stout.

Jake looked out at the crowd, his jaw tightening.

"Is there anyone out there you love?" she continued.

"I thought I did…once, but that was years ago. Besides, the ranch is no place for a woman."

"What do you mean?"

"They never stay."

He was quiet for a moment. Shannon waited, then, asked, "Are you sure about that? I didn't want to leave here. Back then, I had no choice."

Jake's eyes narrowed, burning at her. Then, he remembered her young face as her mother took her away and his face slowly softened. Maybe she was right, he wasn't so sure anymore.

The band started to play an old Patsy Cline song about love at last. He stubbed out his cigarette.

"Dance with me," he said, rising from his chair.

Shannon nodded and placed her hand in his.

Jake led her to the dance floor and took her in his arms. She stiffened at first, but as they swayed to the music, she began to relax. People bumped into them, pushing them closer. When Shannon slowly lowered her head to his shoulder, he pulled her to him. This time she didn't resist.

***

The room was cold when Jake and Shannon returned to the inn, even though a small fire had been lit. The electricity was out and the two kerosene lanterns were burning, casting long eerie shadows on the walls while the wind whistled outside. Jake went to the fireplace and added another log, as Shannon wrapped a wool blanket around her shoulders and came to sit in one of the rocking chairs near the fire. Jake sat down next to her.

They sat in silence, watching the flames dance. Jake wondered what Shannon was thinking about. He'd liked the feel of her in his arms when they danced, the way Shannon relaxed into him, trusting him. He thought about what she'd said the night they'd stood on the hill outside of The Dalles and doubted whether she'd ever been able to really trust anyone in her life. Slowly, he got up and pulled the necklace from his pocket.

"I bought this at Muldoon's – for you. It has the symbol of

Tsagaglal, She-Who-Watches. She's from a legend of a tribal chief on the Washington side of the Columbia Gorge. Coyote, the Trickster, turned her into a rock to watch over her people."

Jake paused and placed the necklace around Shannon's neck. "Now, she'll watch over you."

Shannon looked down at the medallion that glistened in the firelight. Then, she stood next to Jake. "Thank you."

He put his arm around her shoulder, and she sank back into him. They stood like that for some time.

"Da said he only has a month…is that really true?" Shannon finally asked, keeping her eyes on the fire.

"It all depends."

"On what?"

"If he changes his mind."

Jake was quiet for a moment. He turned and looked into her eyes. "I'm not sure what I'm going to do without him. Dan's been there for me for so long…" He stopped when he saw a single tear slowly trace down Shannon's cheek.

"You were lucky," she said, letting the tear drop from her chin. "I just wish there was more time."

"He talked about you all the time," Jake said as he reached up and ran a thumb across her cheek.

"He did?" she exclaimed, wiping her eyes.

"Sure. He always wondered where you were, until Gina saw your website on the Internet. Then, he'd check it every day, just to see what you were doing."

"Da told me he came to Clifden to find me, shortly after we left. But, my mother wouldn't even tell her own parents where I was."

"But, why didn't you contact him?" he asked, watching her face in the soft light.

"Mother told me he didn't want me," she said in a small voice. "I didn't know until now that he even cared and that she lied to me all these years. Shortly after we arrived in Clifden, she took away the small wooden statue of a horse that my father had made for me – the only thing I had left of him."

Jake tried to imagine what it must have been like to feel abandoned and unloved, but couldn't. His life had been full of so much love around him.

"Up to now, I've always let others run my life," Shannon added, "pushing me toward what they call success. But, here, in Oregon, I can see that my father's success isn't built on money, but heart. Here, I can be myself."

Jake was silent.

"I don't care about the money or the fame," she continued, taking off the blanket and standing closer to the fire. His gut tightened as he stood and watched her.

"I just want to be in my studio and work. I control my world then. But, they're always running my career - and, me.

"My mother complains about everything I do. That's why I wear these boots. It's my only expression of independence I seem to be able to get away with."

He saw Shannon look at the dark window, where the storm was still raging outside. "Sometimes, it's easier to do as I'm told," she added.

"But, that's no way to live," Jake finally said.

Shannon looked at him. Just then, a large flash of lightning lit the room, followed by a rolling thunder that rattled the glass in the window panes. Shannon screamed and Jake went over to her, taking her in his arms. Her body trembled against his. He put his hands in her hair, looking into her eyes, a faint smell of lavender coming from her.

"When I knew you..." Jake said, caressing her hair with one hand, "before you left, you never took any guff from anyone. You even punched me in the stomach, right after I kissed you."

"I remember the kiss...but not hitting you."

Jake ran his thumb along her cheekbone and looked down at her lips. He lowered his head and softly kissed her, waiting for her punch, but this time she hit him in a different way. He felt his heart roll over in his chest. When her lips opened to him, he deepened the kiss as she wrapped her arms around his neck and pressed her body against his.

Slowly, he traced the curves of her body with one hand, still holding the back of her head as their lips tasted each other. Her tongue darted out to him and he held on.

One by one, he slowly undid the buttons of her blouse, his fingers trembling at the touch of her skin. He kissed her neck and shoulders as he pulled the material away, letting it fall to the floor.

"You're beautiful!" he said softly.

No one had ever told her that in her life. She smiled and pulled his shirt from his jeans, popping the snaps until it was open. He took a deep breath and looked skyward when her fingers ran across his chest.

Jake picked her up and carried her to one of the beds. Slowly, they came together, thunder sounding in the distance as the storm passed by and the wind began to calm. Willingly, she opened to him, touching him in a way that only she could - she touched his heart and he was lost.

The fire was down to warm embers. Jake softly slipped his arm from under Shannon's head and added some logs to re-kindle the flames.

He walked back to the bed where she was sleeping and quietly slipped in beside her. He'd been surprised to know that he'd been her first. He cradled her in his arms now, unwilling to let her go. Staring at her long lashes lying against her milky cheeks, he finally fell to sleep.

***

Jake saw himself as a young boy, walking beside his mother. She led a horse pulling a travois, which contained all of their possessions.

He walked into the mat-covered long house, a meeting place for his people. A large fire was lit in the center, the smoke rising toward the circular opening in the roof. Women in the Nez Percé formal dress danced in a circle, while seven men beat an age-old rhythm on their drums. As he passed the elders sitting to one side, he heard the old language, which he couldn't fully understand. Yet, he knew they were telling the story of 'the long walk' - where many of their people, young and old, were buried along the way north as they fled from the Calvary. The elders sang to the souls of the lost in their native tongue.

A young woman walked past him, carrying a small baby in a beaded cradle board. The woman's tan buckskin dress swayed with the beat of the drums. An elder leaned over to Jake and said, "A symbol of the younger's desire to carry the traditions of their people - to help the world see the heart of Mother Earth."

Just then, a white feather floated down slowly from the night sky. Jake knew that it signified the spirit of a fallen warrior and he thought of Dan...

Jake awoke with a start, his body covered in sweat. The lantern beside the bed was the only one still burning. He found Shannon lying naked in his arms, still asleep with her head resting on his shoulder. He gently pulled the covers up over her.

He thought about his dream and believed that what they had just shared was much deeper then anything physical, it was a return to a bond that had been created before they were born.

When they were young, he'd fallen in love with her innocence, her adventurous spirit. He'd known that he loved her, that they would always be together. But, then she left. When he saw her again, he'd been afraid that she'd turned out to be like her mother, but Shannon was much different. She was actually vulnerable, afraid, someone he wanted to take care of.

Looking out the window, he allowed himself to face the one thing that had frightened him since her return. *Would he lose her again?* With this question running through his mind, Jake reached up and turned down the wick until the last lamp went out.

Now, as the sun came up over the horizon, he pulled her closer to him. He'd heard her words that night on the bike, but had kept it to himself.

He softly whispered into her hair, "Shannon, I love you."

***

The man stood in the dark room, staring at the lights of the park below. He didn't really see the people on the walkway near the river's edge. The only sound in the room was the blades of the fan whirling slowly overhead.

On a table next to him lay a local newspaper opened to a page of the Art and Entertainment section with a photo of Shannon. The article announced her upcoming show at the Portland Gallery.

Rigid as a statue, he stood with his hands in front of him, slowly coiling a wire around them.

Maybe after this one, he thought, *I'll finally be free from your ghost.*

A door slammed across the hall.

CHAPTER TWENTY-ONE

Harry Blake stared through the window of the Portland terminal, glad that his FBI badge had gotten him past the airport security, so he could wait at the gate. He never understood why people liked to take these long International flights in one day. He hated to fly. Period. He looked down at his watch. The plane was two hours late, and he was tired. He'd already put in a twelve-hour shift. He was so close to finishing the case he'd been working on when his captain had pulled him off to baby sit this guy.

He'd talked to O'Sullivan on the phone and read about the perp he was after. He knew O'Sullivan had dual motives for following this guy. Harry wanted to be the one to bring down this creep.

What kind of detective would hound a serial killer from Dublin to the States, even if he had to use some money-laundering trail to get here? he thought to himself. Then, he saw his own reflection in the window and grinned. *I think I'm going to like this guy!*

Checking his cell phone for messages, he was hoping there was a message from the Special Agent at the IRS - the "invisible man" as Harry liked to call him. "No messages," the voice on his phone said. Harry closed his phone and slipped it into his jacket pocket. He still wasn't used to all the new techie toys, being in his late fifties, but he appreciated a few in his line of business.

The jet appeared and was directed to the gate by a short, stocky woman wearing a bright orange suit and protective earphones. Harry watched as the ramp was extended to meet the plane.

It seemed like an eternity before the plane's door opened. Harry held up a sign with Michael O'Sullivan's name on it, feeling like a limo driver. He watched as the crowd of people disembarked from the jet, passing him without notice.

One petite woman with an impish face stepped through the

doorway into the terminal. She looked as if she'd only taken a quick flight from Seattle instead of halfway around the world. She stopped to use her cell phone.

Right behind her was a big man in a tweed jacket walking down the ramp, carrying a black duffle bag. His head was above the crowd. Harry was reminded of the John Wayne movie, "The Quiet Man," he'd watched with his wife the night before. Immediately, Harry knew this guy had to be O'Sullivan. It was something in the way he walked, a learned gait that men in the military or police work acquired. The long flight had the man looking like he needed a stiff drink or a bed - maybe both.

"Detective O'Sullivan?" Harry called to the tall man who stopped and turned.

"Yes," Michael answered, looking down at Harry, then at the sign Harry held.

"I was sent to meet you," Harry said, holding out a hand, which Michael only looked at at first. "I'm Harry Blake, FBI."

When Michael heard the man's name, he smiled and shook his hand. "Sorry, I wasn't quite sure who you were. Call me Michael. Blake, that's County Galway, right?"

Harry rolled his eyes as he remembered that in the movie, an old man wouldn't buy John Wayne a beer until he knew who his family was. "Not sure. My father was born here, so was I. Do you have bags checked?"

"No, just this one."

"I do," a voice said behind Harry. When he turned, he looked at the pretty young woman he'd seen before. He'd expected she'd moved on with the other passengers, but now she was standing next to Michael.

"Are you two together?" Harry asked, looking between Michael and the woman.

"You might say that. This is Bridget McDonaugh. She's a friend of Shannon O'Toole."

"Nice to meet you, Officer Blake," Brid said, pumping Harry's hand. "Just call me Brid."

"Right," Harry said, somewhat confused.

"Did you reach Shannon?" Michael asked Brid.

"No, only her voice mail again."

As they walked through the terminal, Harry looked at Brid over his shoulder. She was following a few paces behind. In a low voice, he said to Michael, "The suspect has checked into the Marriott Hotel downtown. I understand he's at the gallery now, getting things ready for a show tomorrow. I have you booked at the same hotel. It's close to the waterfront."

"Thanks," Michael said. "I'll want to look at your reports later."

"Sure thing, I'll take you down to our office when you're ready. Pearse's plane went missing for a while, but then reappeared. They landed late yesterday. We need to talk to him about that!"

Michael only nodded.

"There's one more thing..." Harry said, lowering his voice. "We got a fax from Interpol. There's been a murder in Paris with the same M.O. as your Dublin murders. We're waiting for more details."

"Paris?" Michael said, then lowered his voice as Brid looked at him. Shannon's Paris show had been canceled, but it was too much of a coincidence for him to ignore.

Outside, Harry took Michael and Brid to his personal car - a green, unmarked Impala. He winced when Brid pointed to a long scrape down the left side of the vehicle.

"A Hummer tried to run me off the road last week."

When Harry opened the front passenger door, food and gum wrap- pers fell out onto the pavement.

"Sorry," he said to Michael and began to toss the papers and empty coffee cups into the foot well behind the driver's seat. "I was just getting off a stakeout when I got the call to pick you up."

"You fellows know how to travel in style," Michael said as he climbed in. "I've always wanted to ride in a Chevrolet."

"You're going to get your chance right now."

Harry opened the back passenger door for Brid and moved a stack of papers to the other side. A skycap arrived, pushing a cart with Brid's multiple bags.

After all was loaded and they were inside the car, Harry adjusted his rearview mirror so he could see Brid's face. "Will you be staying at the same location, Brid?"

"Yes. For tonight, anyway."

Harry saw Brid's eyes move to the back of Michael's head.

Michael looked at Harry. "Are you aware that we've had another murder in Dublin?" Harry nodded sadly. "Maggie Murphy lived in the same building as Shannon...and Brid."

Harry glanced back and saw Brid's eyes now looking down at her lap. He was beginning to see why she was traveling with Michael. He turned the mirror back toward the roadway and drove in silence, turning onto I-84 going west. He wondered whether he should call in for a second room at the Marriott, but felt Michael could work out that detail.

"You look beat, man," Harry said, looking over at the young man next to him again.

"It was a long flight."

Harry took the left bend in the highway, and the city skyline came into view. It always took his breath away, no matter how many times he drove this road. Portland was small in comparison with other cities, but he loved it. He smiled when he saw the stag on the "Made in Oregon" neon sign across the river , a classic that was first used to advertise White Stag clothing years ago. During the Christmas holiday, someone always put a red light on the stag's nose.

"After you check in," Harry said, "You two want to get a bite to eat?"

"Yes!" Michael exclaimed. "I never eat airplane food."

***

At the hotel, Michael and Brid walked toward the reception counter, while Harry dealt with the bellman handling Brid's luggage. The elevator doors opened and Michael saw Sarah walk into the coffee shop to the left of the entrance.

"That's Sarah Pearse," Brid whispered to Michael. "I'm glad she didn't see me."

"Why?"

"She doesn't like me very much."

Michael watched as Sarah sat at a small round table.

"Why don't you finish checking in to your room and go on up?" he said to Brid. "I have some business to take care of."

Harry followed Michael.

"Mrs. Pearse," Michael said, his badge open in his hand. "Do you remember me?"

Sarah looked up, a blank look on her face. When she read the name on the badge, her face grew pale.

"I thought we left you in Dublin," she said brusquely.

"I'm working with Detective Blake here on an International case. Do you mind if I ask you a few questions?"

Sarah looked at the two men, then, saw Harry's badge and shook her head. Michael knew he had to be careful with her, remembering Dugan's warning.

"You knew both of these women, right?" Michael asked Sarah, pulling photos of Nikki and Maggie out of his breast pocket.

Sarah stared at the photos, her mouth gaping. "Maggie?!"

"I'm sorry to have to tell you that Maggie Murphy is dead - strangled, like the other women in Dublin," Michael told her.

"I knew about Nikki…but Maggie, too?"

"Both Nikki Conroy and Maggie Murphy worked at your gallery, correct?" Harry cut in.

"Yes…"

"Who hired them?" Michael asked.

Sarah looked away. "Thomas."

"What can you tell me about him?" Harry asked.

"He's worked for us for two years now. He came highly recommend- ed," Sarah said, raising her head.

"Did you know that these last two women were also connected with the same art school as your daughter, Shannon?" Michael asked, watching her closely.

Sarah stared at Michael. She slowly licked her lips, then said, "No, I didn't."

"Where did your plane disappear to—" Harry began.

"You'll have to speak with my husband about that. So, if you will excuse me." She got up as if to leave.

Harry held out his card to Sarah. "If you think of anything that may help us, please call."

Sarah looked at the card.

"I'm staying here at the hotel, Mrs. Pearse," Michael added before Sarah walked away.

"She's hiding something," Michael said under his breath to Harry.

"You got that right." Harry sighed, shaking his head. Then, he turned on Michael. "Okay, I'm beginning to see the link with the murders and our money-laundering case, but how do you know so much about both?"

"Before I was assigned to this case, I was tracking the Dublin serial killer. I'm only working on a hunch here."

Harry stared at Michael for a moment. "Got it. I'm going to go see Pearse about his plane while you get checked in. Afterwards, you and I are going to talk," he said, then went around a back hallway to the elevators.

Michael followed Sarah. He stopped when he saw that she recognized Brid.

"Now, what are YOU doing here?" he overhead Sarah ask Brid.

"I…I'm on holiday," Brid answered quickly, looking at Michael over Sarah's shoulder.

"Just stay out of my way!" Sarah shouted, then turned on her heel and stomped into an empty elevator just before the doors closed. Michael watched as the light on the numbers above the elevator door stopped on the sixteenth floor.

***

Sarah was frightened. She'd seen the similarities in those two women and her daughter. It had never occurred to her before this. She'd also seen something in Maggie's photo that scared her to the bone.

She turned the corner and stopped. Detective Blake stood outside her suite.

How the blazes did he get here so fast? she wondered.

"You can't come in here without a warrant," she heard Thomas say.

"That won't be a problem," Blake replied. "In the meantime, tell me why William Pearse's plane seemed to disappear without a trace, after you left Rome."

"William said…the pilot told him he had to make an emergency landing at a small airstrip near Seattle for repairs before proceeding to Portland."

Sarah walked up to Thomas and placed her hand on his arm. "Thomas, is this man bothering you?" she asked.

"Where is your husband, Mrs. Pearse?" Blake asked Sarah before Thomas could reply.

"I don't know - he said he had an errand to run." Sarah looked at Thomas, took his arm, and said, "We need to leave."

Thomas nodded, closed the door, and the two walked to the elevator together.

In the elevator, Sarah sighed.

"What's the matter?" Thomas asked.

She released her hold on his arm and took a step away. "Maggie has been murdered in Dublin," she said as she watched Thomas carefully.

CHAPTER TWENTY-TWO

Shannon watched as Jake placed the last carton into the Jeep at the ranch airstrip. She was glad that they were able to bring the smaller pieces back with them, along with her father's bust. Hank was going to ship the other items to Gina at her gallery when they were finished.

"That's the last of them," Jake said to her as they climbed into the Jeep together.

"I can't wait to see Da's face when he sees his bust."

When Jake smiled at her, she could see he was relaxed; his eyes were soft, with small laugh lines at the corners. She looked at his square jaw and soft mouth as she fingered the silver medallion he'd given her.

Jake leaned over, placed his hand on the back of her neck, and pulled her mouth to his. She wrapped her arms around him and held on.

As the Jeep arrived at the ranch house, Shannon saw Thomas getting out of a long, black limo.

"Oh, no," Shannon sighed, dread grabbing her stomach.

A driver got out and opened the other door. Sarah stepped out, wearing a pink, tailored suit, her jewelry glinting in the sun.

"What?" Jake asked.

"My mother. And...Thomas."

The look of jealousy on Jake's face made Shannon smile for a moment. It was probably the same look that she'd had at David's, when that young woman walked into the bar.

Just then, her father came out of the ranch house and smiled at her mother. When Jake parked the Jeep, Shannon stepped out and stood between her parents. There was an eerie silence in the air, except for the humming of the limo's engine, the driver waiting behind the blackened windows.

Jolly came running toward Shannon, but when the dog neared Thomas, she stopped and growled, the hair on the back of her neck rising.

Thomas cowered and tried to step behind Sarah.

"Jolly, come here, girl," Shannon called.

"Control that beast, will you?" Thomas demanded.

Shannon saw Jake smile as he got out and leaned against the Jeep, folding his arms.

"She's not a beast," Shannon said to Thomas. "What on earth are the two of you doing here?"

Thomas began to speak, but Sarah stepped forward. "Shannon, we've come to take you home."

Shannon looked over at Jake and smiled to him. Then, she walked up to her father and placed her arm around him.

"I am home, Mother."

Sarah glanced between Dan and Shannon, her face twisted in anger. "Nonsense!" she yelled, placing her hands on her hips.

"Hello, Sarah," Dan said in a soft voice. "You're still as beautiful as when I first met you."

Shannon watched as her mother looked at Dan for the first time in over twenty years, a different man then when they were married. Shannon was surprised to see her mother's face soften.

Thomas stepped in front of Sarah, laying his hand on Sarah's arm. "Remember what we came here for," he said softly. Then, he walked to Shannon and pulled her away from Dan.

"Actually, Darlin'," Thomas said to Shannon, rubbing a hand up her arm with a sideways glance at Jake. "We've come to take you to your show in Portland."

"Portland?" Shannon said, stepping back out of Thomas' reach. "What are you talking about?"

"I've arranged for some of your work to be shipped here, to be shown at the Morrison Gallery in Portland. It opens tonight."

"Tonight?!"

Thomas looked back at Sarah slyly. "Didn't you write her about the show, Sarah?"

Sarah looked at Dan again, then turned away, the anger returning to her face. "Yes. But, I recall that the mail doesn't always arrive here in a timely manner."

Shannon stared at her mother.

"Come with us now," Sarah said to Shannon as she stood next to Thomas. "Soon, you'll be back in Dublin, where you belong."

Dan placed his hand on Shannon's shoulder protectively.

"Shannon belongs here," he said in a strong voice that surprised Shannon.

"In this god-forsaken place?" Sarah said, looking around her. "I'm glad I took her away from this dust bowl—"

"But, Mother," Shannon interrupted, "you told me it was Da who wanted us to leave."

Everyone was quiet for a moment, as Sarah looked between Shannon and Dan, slowly licking her lips.

"It was for your own good - for both of us…" Sarah began, but stopped. Shannon knew her mother was finally caught in her own lie.

"I never wanted to leave," Shannon said, glancing at Jake.

Sarah looked at Dan with rage in her eyes. "You've done this to her," she yelled at him. "She was never rebellious until you wrote that damned letter—"

"I've done nothing to Shannon, but love her since the day she was born."

Tears began to well in Shannon's eyes.

Thomas placed his hand firmly on Shannon's arm, pulling her away from Dan again.

Jake dropped his arms and started to walk toward them, but a look from Shannon stopped him. He stood near Dan, his eyes never leaving Shannon's face.

"Remember your career, Darlin'," Thomas said. "It was necessary to add Portland, since you were already in America. We go back to Dublin for a short stop, then on to London from there."

Thomas waited for a moment and looked between Jake and Shannon. Then, he smiled.

"We couldn't get married in Paris," he added, "so your mother has started the wedding plans for when we return to Dublin."

Shannon stared at Thomas in disbelief. Then, she saw the confusion in Jake's face.

"Go get your things, Shannon," Sarah said. "We must leave now.

Portland is waiting for you."

"But, I…I already have a show scheduled at the gallery in The Dalles," Shannon said, still stunned by the hatred she saw in her mother's eyes.

"In The Dalles?" Sarah said. "That small wayside? It's no bigger than Clifden."

"I promised Gina—" Shannon began.

"I'll take care of that," Thomas said. "You're expected in Portland by five." Thomas looked at his watch. "It's almost three now. If you hurry, we'll just make it. William is waiting there."

Shannon saw the pain in her father's face and made her decision.

"All right, I'll go," Shannon said finally.

Jake walked over to Shannon.

"Shannon," he said softly to her. "You don't have to do this, if you don't want to."

Thomas looked at Jake. "Who the hell are you?"

"He's that half-breed that Shannon's father took in," Sarah said with a wave of her hand as if she were swatting a pesky fly from her face. "Never mind him."

Dan stepped toward Sarah and looked down at her with rage in his eyes. "Sarah, I can't believe you said that."

Sarah began to say something, but Dan cut her off. "I always believed the good in you would overcome your greed. I never stopped loving you."

"I let your smooth talk over-power me once before," Sarah yelled. "But, I'm not letting that happen this time. You always thought more of your precious ranch than anything else in your life."

"You're no longer the woman I married. I thought I'd never say this, but I want you to leave this ranch - now!"

Shannon saw the hurt in her father's eyes. "It's alright, Da. I'll go pack my things," she said and turned.

Dan took Shannon's hand in his. "Jake's right, you don't have to do this."

Shannon smiled up at her father and gently touched his face. Softly, so only Dan could hear, she said, "Yes, I do. But, I'll be back as soon as the show is over, I promise."

She kissed her father on the cheek, then walked toward the house. Sarah and Dan's voices could be heard arguing in the background.

In her room, Shannon threw clothes into her suitcase, tears streaming down her face.

Jake walked in and took Shannon by the arms to stop her.

"I can't believe you're going."

Shannon wiped her face, then turned away from him, holding herself.

"I told you, sometimes it's easier that way."

"That's a cop-out—"

"I know, but I don't want to see…" She stopped and continued packing.

"I didn't believe that guy was your fiancé."

"I told you. It's what my mother wants."

"You don't have to do what she says."

Shannon didn't respond and closed her suitcase.

"You're not going to marry him, right?" Jake demanded.

Shannon stood shaking. She turned to the window and looked down at the three people outside. After a moment, her father walked slowly toward the barn. She could see his frustration from his demeanor.

"Didn't last night mean anything to you?" Jake asked softly.

"Yes…, but you don't understand." She went to the bed and picked up the suitcase.

"I understand one thing, I—"

"Would you do me a favor?" she asked quickly, knowing what he was going to say.

"What?" Jake looked confused.

"Please take the statues that are in the Jeep to Gina? I don't want those to go to the Portland gallery."

Shannon grabbed her purse and suitcase and ran toward the door. "I have to go see Da."

There was so much she wanted to say to him, but the old, familiar feeling of futility was enveloping her and she couldn't respond. Suddenly, everything that she'd hoped for was crashing around her. She was afraid she'd say something that would stop her from leaving, but she knew she had to go - to protect her father. At the bottom of the stairs, she turned and saw Jake standing in the hallway.

Once outside, she started toward the barn, but Thomas intercepted her. He took her bag and threw it into the front seat of the limo. Her mother was already in the back of the long car, waiting.

"What're you doing?" Shannon yelled at Thomas.

"What I should have done a long time ago." Thomas quickly grabbed her arm and forced her into the back seat of the limo, next to Sarah. He got in beside her and ordered the driver to leave.

Shannon turned and saw Jake watching from the porch as the limo drove away. Then, he started walking toward the barn. It was a familiar scene, only the last time, Shannon had been eight years old.

***

Dan was grooming Skye when Jake walked into the barn. He hated to see the older man's shoulders bent in defeat, but he knew he needed to respect Shannon's decision.

The two men stood in silence, just as they had once before. Then, Skye whinnied.

"Shannon asked me to take some of her work to Gina's gallery," Jake said, kicking at the dust on the barn floor with his boot.

"Then, you'd better do what she said."

"You going to be all right?" Jake asked, seeing Dan's hand shaking as he ran the brush along Skye's coat. He knew what it'd cost Dan to see Sarah again. And, to see how much she'd changed.

"Shannon'll be back this time. I know it," Dan said. He turned to Jake. "I've made a couple of decisions."

Jake waited, holding his breath.

"I'm going to schedule the surgery Doc Newman wants me to have... just as soon as Shannon gets home." Dan looked down at the brush in his hand, then back up into Jake's eyes. "I don't want to die - not yet, anyway."

Jake nodded, fighting to tamp down the threatening tears. "What's the other decision?"

"I'll tell you about it when you get back."

Then, Dan turned to the horse and continued brushing the mare's coat.

Jake walked out, heaving a long, quiet sigh.

***

Just as Jake arrived at Gina's gallery in The Dalles, Thomas got back into the limo and the driver pulled away. Jake stared at the long vehicle until it was no longer in view. Then, he entered the gallery.

He walked over to Gina, who was standing at the counter with a bewildered look on her face. "What did that guy want?" he asked, nodding back at the door.

"He was canceling Shannon's show...said she had a bigger one scheduled in Portland."

"She's not canceling. She's...just not going to be able to be here... until later." Jake really wanted to believe it. "I have her statues in my Jeep."

"I don't get it," Gina began. "What happened?"

"Shannon's mother came to fetch her."

"Sarah was at the ranch? And, Shannon just went with her?"

Jake only nodded.

"How's Dan taking it?"

"Pretty shook up."

"Who was that guy, anyway?" Gina asked, nodding back toward the door where Thomas had left.

"Shannon's fiancé."

Jake frowned, then tried to smile. Just as Gina was about to ask another question, his cell phone rang.

"Jake, Dan's down!" Charlie's voice said. "I called the doc—"

"I'm on my way."

CHAPTER TWENTY-THREE

Shannon walked out of the bathroom in her slip. CNN World News was on the television. She looked around her and shook her head. The large Marriott suite was such a waste, since she was only going to be there until after the show that night. But, then, her mother didn't know that.

She remembered the look on Jake's face as she'd left the ranch earlier and shivered. She knew she hadn't asked him to come with her because of her father. He needed Jake there. But, that didn't help the ache in her heart. She also knew that she needed Jake. In just a few short hours, he'd become very important to her.

She sighed in frustration as she saw the yellow dress lying on the bed that Thomas had brought to her earlier. She recognized the expensive Versace design. Slowly, she slipped the dress over her head, the billowy chiffon softly caressing her body, resting just above her knees. She looked down at her long, tanned legs and was thankful for the few days in the sun she'd had since she'd arrived in Oregon.

As she stepped into the satin heels, she wished she'd remembered to bring her red boots. At least she still was wearing the necklace Jake had given her, which seemed to give her strength.

Just then, a woman on the newscast caught Shannon's attention. "To date, a total of ten women are dead from strangulation in Dublin, Ireland, possibly linked to the Dublin Serial Killer. The most recent woman was found in an apartment building in the Temple Bar area. The authorities believe that the killer is now in the United States."

Shannon stared at the image of a body being carried out of her own apartment building in Dublin. Photos of the victims appeared on the screen. Many of them she didn't know. She gasped when she saw Nikki Conroy's photo, but the photo of the last face made her slowly sink to the bed. *Maggie Murphy*! She watched, unable to turn away, as tears spilled from her eyes. When the newscaster moved on to sports, Shannon turned off the set with a shaking hand.

Suddenly, she froze. *Oh, my God! They all look like me*! The room seemed to spin around with her own thoughts. *Why is the killer here?* Then, she remembered the strange man at the Pearse Gallery.

"Shannon, it's time," William called from the other room.

"How did you get in here?" she asked, coming out of the bedroom. She saw that the door wasn't fully closed.

"I have a key." He walked up to her.

"William, I just saw—" she began.

"You look lovely in that dress, just as I knew you would," he said as he took her by the arms.

"But...the news," she said, trying to pull away. "I...I have to talk to Thomas—"

"That bloody *eejit*."

William pulled Shannon to him. She could feel his breath on her face. "You can't marry him," William said softly. "You are my—"

Just then, Thomas and Sarah walked in.

"See, I told you she was..." Thomas started, then trailed off when he saw Shannon in William's arms. He looked at Sarah nervously.

Sarah walked over to Shannon and jerked her away from William. "You little slut," Sarah yelled.

"It's not what—" Shannon began.

"This is the last time I ever want to see you two together like that again!" Sarah demanded.

Shannon had finally had enough. "You are right about that!" Shannon yelled back, standing taller and stepping away from the three people who'd managed to run her life, until now. "After this show, I'm contacting my father's attorney to dissolve my contract with your gallery, William. I'm not going back to Ireland."

"That is absurd!" Sarah said, shoving Shannon at Thomas. "Take her to the gallery, now! I'll deal with her later."

Thomas grabbed Shannon's arm tightly and they left.

When the door closed, Sarah turned. "What're we going to do? We can't just let her walk out on us like that."

"She won't," William said as he stared at the door. "I won't let her."

"Why is it that my daughter can't seem to resist you?" she asked.

"We were just talking. I think you're actually jealous of her."

"Jealous? Rubbish!"

"Yes, she's young and sensuous, like you once were." William turned back to Sarah and smiled.

"Don't try to charm your way out of this one. I saw that look on your face. You had more on your mind than just talk." Sarah said as she began pacing the room. "This would never have happened with Dan."

"You're right. D.J. Hamilton loved you...and his daughter. He wrote about—"

"You're the one who intercepted his letters. All these years, I believed he didn't give a damn about either one of us."

Sarah stared at her husband as he looked down at the ring on his right hand, the 'family crest' he called it.

William started for the door. "It's time we go to the gallery and make our appearances."

"I'm not going."

William stopped and turned. "What? You're becoming as obstinate as your daughter."

"Maybe I am. But I don't like how much time you're spending with her. Maybe you're right. I am jealous."

Sarah's chin came up as she looked at her husband. "I know about the other women."

William slowly walked up to Sarah. "Maybe, if you were more like your daughter, the others wouldn't have been necessary."

"This has got to stop!"

William backhanded Sarah across her face, and she fell onto the couch.

"You've bored me for years now," William hissed. "But, you're still useful...I'll wait for you in the lobby while you do something with your face."

After the door closed behind him, Sarah got up and looked into the mirror. She raised a hand to straighten her hair, but stopped. She looked more closely at her face and saw the mark William's ring had made.

"That son-of-a-bitch! He'll never touch me again," she swore.

She applied some concealer from her purse. As she replaced the makeup, her hand stopped. Looking behind her to make sure she was alone, she unzipped a small compartment in the cloth of her purse. Inside was an old black and white photo taken on her and Dan's wedding day. Turning the photo over, she saw that the ink was faded, but the phone number for the ranch was still visible.

She dialed the number and waited until the fourth ring. When a woman answered, Sarah quickly hung up. She slipped the photograph into her jacket pocket and began pacing.

Images of her life since her divorce from Dan circled through her mind. She'd made many mistakes, knowing that her obsession with money was at the root, but she didn't know how to change. It's who she was.

She stopped pacing when she recalled the recent newscast and the faces of the murdered women in Dublin. Suddenly, William's words flooded back to her. '...*the others wouldn't have been necessary...*' she thought. She stared at the door.

"Shannon..." she whispered, suddenly frightened as she remembered the similarities between her daughter and the dead women.

Sarah ran to the phone.

"Michael O'Sullivan's room, please."

***

"Damn it!" Michael yelled, turning off the television. "Who the hell leaked that information?"

He raked a hand through his hair, then picked up his cell phone. Looking at his watch, he dialed Neville's home phone.

"Hello," Neville's sleepy voice answered.

"Neville, this is Michael. Someone over there talked to the press about why I'm here."

There was silence on the line for a moment. Then, Neville said, "Whelan opened his bleetin' mouth. He didn't like it that you were the one selected to go to the States."

"That idiot!"

"Any new developments?" Neville asked.

"Nothing yet."

There was a knock on his door.

"Someone's here. I'll call you again tomorrow." Michael hung up.

"Hi," Brid said when he opened the door. "I brought some sandwiches from the coffee shop downstairs." She went to the desk and set down a bag and two cups of steaming coffee. "I hope you like pastrami on rye, it's all they had."

"Fine," Michael said abruptly. He paced the room as he dug into a sandwich, chasing it down with the strong coffee.

"What's eating you?" Brid asked.

"Nothing."

"You look like hell," she said.

He placed his hand on his chin and felt the stubble from yesterday's growth. He'd been so busy, he'd forgotten to shave. Then, he noticed that Brid was only picking at her sandwich. *Had she also seen the news?*

Brid looked up and saw him watching her. "Downstairs, I saw Shannon leave the hotel. I tried to catch her, but I was too late. She didn't look too happy."

Michael started to get up, but Brid held up her hand to stop him. "Before I came up here, Harry told me he'd put a tail on them."

"Well, at least we know where she is."

"How can you be so cool, doing this type of work every day?" Brid asked. "Don't you let any of this ugly stuff get inside of you?"

Michael was silent for a moment, then said, "If I do, I can't do my job. And, victims...like Shannon...don't have a chance."

As soon as he'd said it, he was sorry. Brid didn't know that he suspected that Shannon was the next victim.

Just then, his phone rang.

"O'Sullivan."

Michael avoided Brid's eyes.

"This is Sarah Pearse," Michael heard. "I need to talk to you. I...I think I know...Please come to my daughter's room right away."

Michael noted the room number on the pad next to his phone. "I'm on my way, Mrs. Pearse."

Before he hung up, he heard something - like the sound of a door opening. He looked at his closed door and frowned.

"What does SHE want now?" Brid asked.

"She's ready to talk. Stay here, I'll be right back."

Just as Michael opened his door, Harry ran in.

"We just received this," Harry said, handing Michael a fax. "The results of the tests from your M.E. in Dublin."

Michael glanced at the report, then looked up at Brid and Harry.

"Picture wire's the weapon?!"

Harry beamed. "Yep. I'm going down to that gallery and arrest the psychopath."

"I knew I didn't trust that *bastard*!" Brid exclaimed. She looked at Michael. "If Shannon's in any danger…"

"I'm on my way!" Harry said, as he ran for the door.

"Wait!" Michael put his hand on Harry's arm. "I'm not sure…" Michael stopped. Maybe he was just being overly-cautious, for the first time in his life, but something just didn't feel right about this case. "Never mind," he said, shaking his head. "I'm going to talk to Sarah Pearse."

Harry nodded and left.

Michael turned and looked at Brid. "Want to come with me?"

"Gladly," she said, relieved not to be left alone.

CHAPTER TWENTY-FOUR

Shannon stepped out of the taxi and walked into the entrance of the Morrison Gallery. She was amazed at the volume of the large crowd of people already at her show. Nervously, she looked around the room of glass and steel, but saw no sign of Thomas. A short, bleached-blond man came up to her.

"Miss O'Toole," he said, bowing to her with a theatrical flair. "We are honored to have you here tonight."

"And, you are?" Shannon asked.

"Oh, I'm Jeremy Renta, the gallery director. William didn't tell you about me?"

Shannon could see he was disappointed, his lower lip pushed out into a pout, one hand on a hip.

"Of course he did," she said in her business tone she'd learned from Thomas. "Thank you for sponsoring my work."

"We've invited the best of Portland to come meet you."

"We?"

"William and myself, of course. He's such a gracious man."

"Yes." Shannon continued to scan the room. "Have you seen Thomas Aherne?"

"No, he's always…"

Just then, William walked through the entrance of the gallery. Shannon looked for her mother, but didn't see her.

"Ah, here's William now," Jeremy said, waiving a hand.

Shannon saw Thomas enter from the back room and go up to a couple standing alone; a woman in a red, sequined gown and a large, tailored man. She recognized the Greenburgs.

William came up to Shannon and put his hand in the small of her back. "Hello, my dear," he said and leaned in to kiss her cheek. Shannon pulled away.

"William," Jeremy said with glee. "Oh, it's always a pleasure to see you."

"Thank you, Jeremy. May I have a word in private with my step-daughter?"

"Of course," Jeremy bowed again and went to a cluster of people standing in front of one of Shannon's sculptures.

"Where's Mother?" she snapped at William.

He frowned at her sharp tone. "When I left, she said something about final travel arrangements to make."

Before Shannon could reply, Thomas walked up to her with the well-dressed, older couple.

"Shannon, you remember John and Laura Greenburg," William said, pouring on his most charming smile. "You met them at your show in Dublin."

William turned back to Shannon, and she shook hands with the couple.

"I was wondering why you chose such basic subjects for your work," Laura said. "They are, as we say, primitive. It seems a waste of your talents, my dear."

Shannon's chin came up, but she continued to smile. "I only use what nature gives to me."

"It's a pity," John said. "We would like to sponsor a show in Seattle of your work, provided you use more…shall we say…sophisticated subjects, like ballet dancers…or nudes. That's the sort of work I'd like to see you do more of—"

"I work from my heart, Mr. Greenburg, and I don't see any dancers or nude statues in my future."

John Greenburg harrumphed, then took his wife's elbow and led her away. Thomas ran over to them, looking back at Shannon over his shoulder.

William took her arm firmly and hissed in Shannon's ear, "Those people are very wealthy and influential in the art world. You will do well to take their advice, young lady."

Shannon winced as his fingers dug into her skin, but she remained silent.

"I have some business to attend to in Seattle later tonight," he continued. Whispering softly to her, he added "I will find you when I return."

"Don't bother." She straightened her shoulders and took a deep breath. "I'm through being your puppet."

"We'll see about that!" William said and walked towards the Greenburgs.

Just then, Shannon saw a face that sent chills up her spine. Seeing Connor at the gallery, instead of the ranch, jarred her memory. He'd been the man back in Dublin who'd approached her and scared the hell out of her! As she walked towards the front door, Shannon shivered when she saw the look in Connor's eyes as he followed her. She looked around to find someone to help her.

***

Michael knocked on Shannon's door, surprised that Sarah was here instead of her own room.

"I wonder what Sarah wants to see you about?" Brid asked.

"Beats me."

There was no answer.

As Michael knocked again, the door opened slightly. Michael entered, but stopped and turned to Brid.

"Go back outside—"

"Oh, my god!" Brid screamed as she looked over his shoulder at Sarah, lying on the floor.

Michael ran to Sarah and checked for a pulse.

Brid started to reach for the phone, but Michael stopped her.

"Don't touch anything."

Brid stopped, her body shaking. Michael went to her and wrapped his arms around her, shielding her view of Sarah's body with his own.

"It's too late," he whispered. "She's dead."

***

As Shannon neared the entrance to the gallery, Thomas stepped in next to her and grabbed her arm.

"Where do you think you're going?" Thomas asked, smiling.

"I'm going to the police. That man over there—"

"Police?" His grip tightened. "Once we're married, you'll never be able to—"

Shannon looked behind her and was relieved to see Connor stop, watching her from a distance. "Thomas, I'm never going to marry you!"

"But, you're mine…we belong together—"

"That's what you think. Oh, I heard that Maggie knew where my stolen statue was," Shannon said in a shaky voice.

Thomas dropped his hand and stared at Shannon.

"What?"

"She's dead, you know…and…I intend to tell the police."

"What're you talking about?"

Shannon looked at William standing behind Thomas. "I think you know."

Just then, Jake rushed into the gallery. The look on his face filled Shannon's heart with dread and she ran to him. "What's wrong? Is it Da?"

"Yes…I flew here to get you."

"Holy Mother of God!"

Shannon and Jake ran out of the gallery, just as Harry Blake arrived with a team of detectives.

She looked back and was surprised to see Thomas being hand-cuffed.

CHAPTER TWENTY-FIVE

Jake and Shannon entered Dan's master bedroom, the four-poster bed sat in the shadows along one wall with only one light next to the bed. A tall oxygen tank stood on the opposite side of the bed, a clear tube connected to Dan.

Gina sat next to Dan, holding his hand, while a tall, lanky man in his late forties, was leaning over Dan, giving him an injection.

Shannon gasped when she saw her father's pale face. She ran to his side, relieved that he was still alive.

"Oh, Da. We got here as fast as we could."

Dan tried to respond, but he was too weak, his breathing, labored. He fell back against the pillow and closed his eyes.

Jake watched from the foot of the bed, his hands in his pockets.

"I'm Dr. Newman," the man said to Shannon. He took her by the shoulders and walked her toward the door. Jake and Gina followed. "Dan rejected any further cancer treatments I've offered. Now, he refuses to go to the hospital. I've given him enough morphine to make him as comfortable as possible, but that's all I can do for him."

"But, he told me today he wanted to do the surgery," Jake asked, looking over at Shannon.

"His heart is giving out," the doctor said with defeat in his voice. "I doubt that he'll make it through the night."

Shannon's eyes welled with tears. She turned and looked at her father, then she wrapped her arms around herself. "I did this to him, when I left today."

Jake put his arm around Shannon.

"Don't blame yourself—" Dr. Newman began.

"Isn't there anything we can do?" Gina asked.

"Just be here with him," Dr. Newman said. "That's what he

wants."

Shannon looked at Jake. Then, she saw the pain in Gina's face and went over to her.

"You know where to reach me if you need me," Dr. Newman said to Jake, then gathered his bag.

Jake nodded and followed the doctor out of the room.

"I'll walk down with you," Gina said and left Shannon alone with her father.

Shannon sat beside Dan, gently taking his hand.

"Can I do anything for you?" she asked in a soft voice.

Dan shook his head slowly. "When you know you're going to die," he said between short gasps of breath, "you think about the things you wish you'd done differently."

"Da, it's—"

"I shouldn't have given up searching for you—"

"We could've had more time together," she said, tears welling as she looked down at their hands intertwined.

Dan tried to smile. "We'll always...have each other, baby," he said. "Never forget that family is everything."

Shannon's tears fell as she leaned over and kissed her father's forehead. His breathing seemed easier now, and she knew the medication was kicking in.

He turned his head slightly and cleared his throat. "I have to ask... do you love Jake?"

Shannon looked at her father, surprised by the question. She wiped her tears away and smiled.

"Yes...I think I always have."

"Thank God." Dan smiled, and Shannon gently hugged her father.

She looked up as Jake and Gina returned. Jake swallowed hard and went to the other side of the bed. Gina stood near Dan's feet, laying one hand on his leg.

Dan slowly raised his other hand to Jake, which he held with both of his hands.

"Now, my family is together. I just wish..." Dan stopped and coughed. He looked between Jake and Shannon, then smiled at Gina. Slowly, he inhaled and said, "Remember...you have nothing...unless you have love..."

Shannon saw Dan's body relax and knew he was letting go. After a moment, as he exhaled for the last time, his hand slowly slipped from Jake's.

Jake stared at Dan's face, then looked over at Shannon. Their eyes meet.

Without a word, Jake left the room.

***

The den was dark and empty. To Shannon, it seemed lifeless without her father. She turned on a floor lamp, then sat down in Dan's overstuffed leather chair and thought of the few precious moments she'd had with him in her lifetime. Even when she was small, he was always teaching her lessons that are part of her being. Now, free of her mother, Shannon realized that she was who she is more because of her father.

Charlie walked in. "I'm sorry, Shannon. Dan was such a good man."

"Thank you. I know you meant a lot to him."

She saw the bundle of blue paper in his hand. "What's that?"

"It's Dan's will. He told me to…You need to read it." The older man stopped and handed the bundle to her. "I don't know if Dan really meant it, but here it is. I'll be in the kitchen with Maria if you need me." Charlie left the room.

Shannon opened the black ribbon tied around the bundle. Her eyes skimmed over the words, which were a standard format of Dan's wishes. She stopped when she read the legal description of the ranch property with Jake listed as the heir.

"What?! Why would he do such a thing? I'm his daughter…" Shannon saw the case of trophies across the room and she remembered what others had said of Jake. "*D.J. thinks of Jake McLeod as his son.*"

The bundle dropped from her hands to the floor.

Now what do I do? Where do I go? She slumped back into the leather chair and wept. She wept tears of pain, of sorrow. She'd let her father down and was ashamed that she hadn't come sooner, in spite of her fears. She hadn't been there when he needed her.

***

Harry walked into the Marriott hotel room and sighed when he saw the local forensic team scouring for evidence, dusting for prints.

He spotted Michael and Brid over by the windows.

"What're you doing here, Blake?" Detective Simpson asked.

Harry liked Matt Simpson, a young blond detective with the Portland Homicide Department. Matt was the same age as Harry's nephew, John, who wanted to be a cop someday.

"I was called here by my assistant, O'Sullivan." Harry nodded towards Michael. "We've been working together on a case involving this woman, Sarah Pearse."

"Well, she's my case now," Simpson said, smiling.

Harry went over to Michael. "Glad you caught me – Aherne isn't talking yet."

Brid looked pale, staring out the window with her arms wrapped around her.

"Detective Simpson," a black woman on the forensic team said as she handed him an evidence bag. "I found this in the victim's jacket pocket."

Harry and Michael walked over to the detective.

"I thought you said her name was Pearse," Simpson said to Harry.

"It is."

"Why does this say her name is Hamilton? And, who's the guy in this photo?" Simpson asked, as if he didn't really expect an answer yet.

"That's Daniel Hamilton," Brid said from behind the men.

They all turned and looked at her.

"He's Sarah Pearse's first husband, who lives in Dufur," Harry added smugly. "I told you we've been working on this case. Pearse is also a citizen of Ireland, which makes her a high-profile case."

Simpson turned the clear bag over, and both he and Harry noted the phone number written on the back of the photo.

***

Shannon felt someone gently shaking her. She realized that she had fallen asleep.

"Are you okay?" Gina asked.

Shannon sat up and nodded. She saw the will lying on the table next to her and her heart ached.

"Has Jake come back yet?" Shannon asked. She looked at her watch and was surprised to see it was almost midnight.

"No," Gina said, sitting across from her. "I doubt if he'll be back for a day or two. He did the same thing when his father died."

"He ran away like that?"

"Yes. It took Dan two days to find him up at the cabin in the hills. He was so worried…" Tears began to well in Gina's eyes.

"You loved my father, didn't you?"

"Yes." Gina looked up at Sarah's portrait and frowned. "But, he always loved Sarah."

Shannon stood up and looked at her mother's face, then turned back to Gina. "No, I think he loved her memory. Once he saw what she has become, the memory was shattered. I could see his love for you when you two were together."

Tears slowly fell from Gina's eyes. She rose up and hugged Shannon. "You meant so much to him. A day didn't go by when he wasn't talking about you."

"That's not what his will said," Shannon said. "D.J. left the ranch to Jake."

Shannon shrugged, trying to remain calm, even though she was shaking inside with fear. "This is just another place…" she began, but stopped, looking around the room that she had grown to love all over again. She sighed, then continued. "I guess life has a plan for me, but I'm not sure what that is. I thought I knew."

Gina stood in silence.

"It's so ironic," Shannon continued. "Here I am, a successful sculp- tor, yet I can't have the two things I've wanted all my life - my father and my home."

***

After Gina left, Shannon ran to the barn. One bare light bulb was lit.

"JAKE!" Shannon yelled into the near darkness, hoping that Gina was wrong. "Jake, where the hell are you?"

The only answer was Skye's whinny. Shannon walked down the aisle between the stalls and found Skye with her nose over the stall door. Shannon rubbed the horse's nose and stroked her long neck. She hated to leave the horse, but didn't even know where she was going herself.

There was one more place she had to go. Her new studio held her tools, her work, the models she brought from Ireland.

Shannon walked through the darkness, her steps growing longer as anger began to build inside of her. She flipped on the light switch and began shoving her tools into the canvas bag she'd brought them in.

She saw her father's bust and sank down on a stool next to it, her emotions riding on a roller coaster. She stared at the likeness of her father and realized she did love him and didn't blame him, but her life at the ranch was over. There was only one other place left that she had ever felt welcome.

"OK," she said to the bust. "I came here alone, and I'll leave the same way."

She picked up her tool bag. Just as she turned to leave, she saw the clay model of her nude bronze. She realized now that the image she had used when creating it was the woman she thought she was. But, in reality, it was the woman she wanted to be. She placed the model in the canvas back and stepped outside.

In the distance, Shannon saw the lights of a car on the road from Dufur, but as it neared the ranch driveway, the headlights went out. Shannon shrugged and walked to the house.

In the kitchen, Maria and Charlie sat at the table.

Shannon asked, "Have you heard from Jake?"

"Nope," said Charlie.

"Then, I'm leaving for Portland to catch the first flight back to Dublin."

"Tonight?" Maria asked. "But, aren't you going to stay for the funeral, Lupita?"

"No…" Shannon hadn't thought of that, but knew she couldn't stay any longer. "Charlie, will you pack the rest of my stuff in the studio and ship it to my grandparents' in Clifden? I know D.J. had the address around here somewhere."

CHAPTER TWENTY-SIX

Michael and Harry stood in the small area behind the two-way mirror of the Portland Police interrogation room and waited.

"I'm still not convinced..." Michael began, then watched as Detective Simpson brought Thomas into the stark room. Simpson sat Thomas down in a straight-legged chair. Then he went to the other side of the table, lay the file down, and sat with his back to the mirror.

"Thomas Aherne, I'm Detective Simpson of Portland Homicide. You know why you're here, right?"

Thomas was silent, staring at the opened file.

"You murdered Sarah Pearse in her daughter's room at the Marriott tonight," Simpson continued.

Michael watched Thomas' face closely, but there was no change in his expression. Turning to Harry, Michael said, "He was like that when I talked with him back at the Pearse Gallery in Dublin. The guy shows little emotion."

"What's it going to take to get him to confess?" Harry wondered.

"We'll just wait him out. He'll break soon enough."

The two looked back into the room when Simpson asked, "We won't extradite you right away. You'll go to trial, be convicted, and sent to prison here before Ireland and France get their way with you."

"Extradite? What the bloody hell are you talking about?" Thomas yelled at Simpson.

"You're the main suspect in the Dublin Serial Killer cases."

At last, Michael saw what he was waiting for. Thomas looked away from Simpson, directly into the mirror and there was fear in his eyes.

***

"Just what I need," Shannon said out loud, staring at her reflection in the bathroom mirror at the ranch house. "My period!"

Surprised that it was lighter than usual, she went down the hall into her old bedroom and check that her bags were ready. She looked at the closet, her red boots were the only items left.

She went to the bed, picked up her cell phone, and saw that Brid had called. Clearing the screen, Shannon dialed directory assistance.

"United Airlines, please," she said.

When connected to the airlines, Shannon asked, "Are there any flights to Dublin tonight?"

She booked a first class seat and hung up. With one last glance around the room that she'd only known for a short part of her life, she walked to the dresser. While watching herself in the mirror, she slowly removed Jake's necklace and placed it in her blazer pocket.

Turning off the light, she walked out carrying her bags and D.J.'s will.

Shannon went to the den. She looked one last time at her mother's portrait. "You were right, after all," she said softly to the painting. "The ranch was more important."

She leaned the copy of the will against the stone of the fireplace and draped the necklace over the blue paper, then walked out of the house.

As she put the last of her bags into her car, Shannon heard Maria call to her. She turned and waited as the small woman ran over to her and hugged her.

"I wish you would stay," Maria said, wiping her eyes. "This is all so wrong."

"No, I can't."

"We'll miss you," Maria sobbed as Charlie joined her, putting his arm around his wife.

"Tell Jake…" Shannon began, then stopped.

"Tell him what?" Charlie asked.

"Oh, never mind. Goodbye."

Shannon got into her car and drove down the lane. After she turned onto the road to Dufur, she pulled out her cell phone and dialed Brid's number. She didn't see the car that followed her.

"Shannon!" Brid's voice said as she answered.

"Where are you?" Shannon asked.

"Here, in Portland. I—"

"Portland! But, when did you—"

"Shannon," Brid interrupted. "I've got to see you...your mother... she's dead."

CHAPTER TWENTY-SEVEN

The taxi whisked by the brightly lit buildings of downtown Portland. It was four in the morning, and Shannon was amazed to see the number of people still walking along the damp sidewalks. The rain that had begun just after she'd left the ranch had mirrored her feelings of despair and disappointment.

"Are you sure you want to do this?" Brid asked.

Shannon only nodded. Detective Simpson and Agent Blake had met her at the hotel where Brid said they should meet. They'd explained the circumstances of her mother's death.

"I was glad we were able to book me a seat on your flight," Brid said.

Shannon didn't answer.

"Are you alright?" Brid asked next to her.

"No...It's like I'm in a freaking nightmare. I wish I could just wake up and find it's not real."

"I know. Same for me, too."

"I can't believe you've been in Oregon all this time, and I didn't know."

"We've both been busy," Brid said, then looked away. "I called, but you must've had your cell phone off."

"I'm sorry...I just don't know what's going to happen next."

"I understand," Brid said, touching Shannon's hand. "You've been through so much."

They rode in silence for a few moments.

"Did you know that Thomas was arrested - just after you left the gallery..." Brid began.

"Thomas? Why?"

"They think he, huh, is the murderer."

Shannon put her hand to her stomach. "What? I can't believe it.

Why would Thomas want to kill…"

The taxi came to an abrupt stop in front of a tall, red-brick building. A silver plaque announced that they were at THE CITY MORGUE. The two women got out.

Shannon suddenly felt a thick fog of denial wrap around her, making her numb to the bone. First her father died. Now, her mother was murdered. *What the bloody hell is going on?* she screamed inside.

"Wait here for us," Brid told the driver, then led the way into the building.

At the front desk, Shannon and Brid saw a young woman bent over a book titled *Forensics for Dummies*. The woman looked up, pushing her horned-rimmed glasses up her nose.

"Are you here to see the new body?" she asked.

"Yes," Shannon answered, not sure what she was supposed to say.

"Sign here, then go down the hall through the double doors at the end."

Following Brid, Shannon felt a cold chill. She pulled her light jacket more closely around her, but it didn't help. She began to shake, dreading the doors ahead.

"In here," Brid said, a sadness in her voice. "I wish there was…" she began, but stopped.

Shannon nodded, understanding her friend's concern. "I'll be fine," she said softly, attempting to smile at Brid. "It wasn't as if we had a lot of love between us…"

The room was stark and cold. Walls of vaults and the sterile, stainless steel atmosphere made Shannon shiver. She wrapped her arms around herself, hating what she saw ahead of her. Her mother lay covered in a white sheet, still and pale. Slowly, Shannon walked up to her, not seeing the two men in the room. She gasped when she saw the long, ugly welt around her mother's fair neck.

"Miss O'Toole?" Shannon heard from a distance, as if she was standing in water up over her head. She turned and saw a tall young man in jeans and a tan jacket.

"I'm Michael O'Sullivan, of the Garda," the young man said. "I'm sorry—"

"Garda? You're a long way from home." She turned and looked

at her mother again, then back to Michael. "Unless you did this to her, you have nothing to feel sorry about."

Anger was stirring deep within her now, and she wore it as an armor to protect her heart. She saw the older man dressed in white standing next to Michael. "And, who are you?"

"Jim Mitchell, the Medical Examiner here. Everyone calls me 'Mitch.' Your mother has been identified by Detective O'Sullivan…"

Just then, Harry Blake walked through the doors.

"Then, why was I called down here?" Shannon asked, ignoring Blake. "She's dead, I can't bring her back. You've arrested her killer…" Shannon could hardly breathe.

"Shannon," Brid said, wrapping an arm around Shannon's shoulders. "It was necessary for you—"

"Stop it!" Shannon yelled, stepping away from Brid. "You know what it was like with her, Brid. I couldn't wait to get away…" Shannon stopped as she looked at her mother. Icy tears streamed down her own cheeks and she felt confused, betrayed. Angrily, she wiped them away.

"Aherne lawyered up," Shannon heard Harry tell Michael.

Shannon saw the red patch on her mother's cheek. "What the hell is that?" she asked, pointing to the red mark, shaped like a crescent moon.

"I've noted that, as well," Mitch said. "Based on the color, she was hit shortly before her murder. O'Sullivan here seems to think it's an important clue to the serial killer cases in Dublin."

"Serial killer—" Shannon whispered, looking at Michael. "Are you saying that Thomas was…" She stopped, putting the back of her hand to her mouth. When Michael nodded, Shannon's knees weakened.

Michael reached out and caught Shannon, helping her to a nearby chair.

"Can I get you anything?" he asked.

Shannon shook her head slowly. She looked at her mother as tears once again welled up in her eyes.

"We have been unable to find your step-father, William Pearse," Harry said, his voice echoing in the large room. "Do you know his whereabouts?"

Shannon looked at the shorter man. "At the gallery…" she

began, her voice shaking. She turned her focus to each full breath in an attempt to slow her racing heart beat. "At the gallery, he said he was going to Seattle tonight…on business."

"Do you know if he has any business contacts in Seattle?" Harry continued.

"John Greenburg's the only one I know. He was at the Dublin Gallery and then again at the one in Portland last night."

"Have you talked to William since then?" Michael asked.

"No."

Harry walked softly to Shannon and showed her the evidence bag with the small black and white photo. "This was found on your mother… when she was brought in."

Shannon looked down at the photo of her father and mother on their wedding day. She began to sob.

Brid went to Shannon and knelt down next to her. "Honey, you've been through so much. Are you sure you want to fly to Dublin to- night?"

Shannon nodded. Then, after a moment, she slowly got up and walked back to her mother's body. Out of the corner of her eye, she saw Brid motion to the men to step away.

"I've got a phone call to make," Harry said, then left the room.

Shannon looked down at her mother. "You did love Da, after all," she whispered, hoping that her mother's spirit could hear her. "I thought you despised him." At that moment, she felt that her life had been a lie.

"When can her body be released?" Shannon asked.

"I beg your—" Mitch began.

Harry returned.

"We're flying to Ireland tonight," Brid said, looking quickly at Michael. "When can Shannon's mother's body be sent there?"

The three men looked at each other.

"I'm leaving with Shannon," Brid added softly. "She shouldn't be traveling alone."

Michael cleared his throat and looked at Harry. "We'll take care of the arrangements."

***

"Shannon!" Jake yelled as he ran into the ranch house and raced up the stairs. He turned into her bedroom and stopped. The room looked as if she'd never been there at all.

A small overhead light bulb beamed from the closet. Jake slowly walked to it and saw Shannon's red boots lying on the floor. "Damn!" he swore and left the room.

As he passed the doorway to the den, he heard Charlie call his name. Jake stopped and went to the older man.

"Where's Shannon?"

"She's going back to Ireland," Charlie said sadly.

"Ireland? What the hell are you talking about?"

"I gave her a copy of Dan's will, just like he'd asked me to do... months ago, before—"

"What? You old fool!" Jake yelled. "Dan was going to—"

The phone rang in the den and Jake answered it. "Diamond H Ranch."

"This is Detective Blake of the FBI," the voice on the other end of the line said.

"FBI?"

"Yes, who is this?"

"Jake McLeod, the ranch manager. What's this all about?"

"Your phone number was written on the back of a photo that was found on a dead woman's body. Do you know Sarah Pearse?"

Jake was silent for a moment. He looked at Charlie, then up at the portrait of Sarah.

"Yes...she's the mother of Shannon O'Toole."

"Sarah Pearse was murdered last night at the Portland Marriott."

"Jesus," Jake whispered.

"Is Daniel Hamilton there?"

"No, he passed away yesterday."

"How did he die?" Harry asked.

"Heart failure," was all Jake could say.

"What's going on?" Charlie asked, but Jake held up his hand to stop his questions.

"Where is Shannon?" Jake asked the detective.

"She's leaving on a plane to Dublin. I was just following up on some loose ends on this case."

Jake looked at his watch and knew he wouldn't get there in time. "Why is the FBI involved?"

"I'd rather not discuss that over the phone. Can you come down to my office later today?"

"Give me the address and I'll be there. I have some things to take care of here first."

Jake noted the Portland address, then hung up and looked at Charlie.

"Shannon's mother was murdered."

"What?!"

"And, Shannon's on her way to Dublin right now. I have to go to Portland later, but there's still so much to do here…for Dan."

"Tell me what you need and it's done."

Jake began pacing the room. He walked to the fireplace and leaned his elbows on the mantle. Then, he saw the necklace dangling over the copy of Dan's will. Slowly, Jake turned back to Charlie.

"I know what I have to do," he said softly, then left the room.

CHAPTER TWENTY-EIGHT

Ireland

Shannon sat in the kitchen of her grandparents' cottage and looked out the window at the Twelve Pins as she was used to calling them, a mountain range of a dozen peaks on the western coast of Ireland. She thought of the numerous times she'd sat in the very same spot when she was young.

Moyna was making soda bread, and Liam rifled through his morning newspaper, just as they had every day of her small life. But, today was different. It had only been two weeks to the day since her parents had died and she'd left Oregon.

"I liked it better when I used to cook this bread in me open fire," Moyna said as she turned the bread over. Shannon watched her grandmother wipe the tears from her eyes. "The edges don't get as nicely brown on this griddle as when the heat was comin' up 'round it."

Shannon knew she was needed here. Her mother was buried shortly after her body arrived from the States. At first, she was sad when she thought of missing her father's funeral, but then she remembered why she left.

The phone rang.

"It's probably that young man of yours again," Liam said to Shannon.

"I'm not talking to him!" she yelled. "Don't answer it."

"I don't see what harm it would do to just talk to him," her grandmother said. "It's not his fault what your father did."

"He's the last man on earth I want to talk to right now."

"Liam here," her grandfather said into the mouthpiece. "No, she still won't have a thing to do with ya'."

He hung up the receiver and picked up his paper again.

"Father Eugene did a nice service for our little girl," Liam said from behind the newspaper. Shannon knew he was using the paper as a shield so the women wouldn't see his tears.

"It was interestin'," Liam continued as he turned to the sports page, "that 'Sir' William couldn't even be here for his own wife's funeral. I never understood what my daughter saw in 'im."

"Aye, you did," Moyna said as she lifted the last pieces of bread from the griddle, the heavenly smell wafting through the small room. She wiped her hands on her apron, then dabbed at her eyes, "'Tis his money she was after!"

Shannon sighed sadly. "I think she was happiest with William." The smell of bacon filled the air as her grandmother opened the oven door. Normally, she couldn't wait to dig into the traditional breakfast she'd known when living here, but today, it turned her stomach.

"I'd bet the farm that he's somewhere lookin' for new investors, like he always did," Liam spat, his face grimaced with hatred now.

"You're looking awfully pale, dear," Moyna said to Shannon. "Maybe you should go lie down."

"I'm alright…probably just the stress…"

Shannon put her hand to her mouth and ran out of the room. In a few moments, she was vomiting in the bathroom. She flushed the toilet and returned to the kitchen, wiping her face with a damp cloth.

"I'm calling Dr. McKenna," Moyna announced.

Shannon saw her grandfather nod in agreement.

"Granma!" Shannon moaned.

***

Patrick McKenna had been Shannon's physician as a child when she lived at the cottage. His hair was grayer now, but he still had the softest touch as he completed his exam.

Shannon was lying on the bed, with her grandmother at her side as McKenna put away his stethoscope. The shadows on the walls were getting longer as the sun traveled across the sky.

"What type of virus do I have?" Shannon asked.

"I'm afraid it's bigger than a virus," Dr. McKenna said with a look of mischief in his eyes.

"Oh, dear. I told you—" Moyna began.

"I won't know for sure until I run some tests," the doctor began, then smiled, "but, I think you're pregnant."

"WHAT?!" Shannon exclaimed. "But, it's only been—"

"Based on what you told me and about your light spotting, I'd say you're around three weeks along. I'll call you as soon as the test results return."

Shannon was embarrassed as her grandmother and the doctor left her room - the shame she'd felt when she had to confess to making love with Jake, when she was still a virgin. Looking out the window as tears streamed down her cheeks, she now only felt lost and confused.

Moyna returned with Liam.

"Oh, my dove," Moyna cooed, wiping Shannon's eyes with her linen handkerchief, "don't you be cryin'. We'll be takin' care of you and the wee one - just like before."

Shannon looked at the two people who had taken her in when she was young. She turned her face into her pillow and sobbed.

"I need to tell Jake…"

"Don't you be talkin' like that," Moyna said sternly. "I don't want you repeatin' the mistakes of your mother, may she rest in peace."

Shannon stared at her grandparents. Liam looked embarrassed and Moyna was twisting her handkerchief in her hands.

"What're you talking about?" Shannon asked.

Her grandparents glanced at each other. Then, Liam blurted out, "Didn' ya know? Yer mother was pregnant with you when she married yer father—"

"And, look how THAT turned out," Moyna interrupted, frowning at Liam. She turned to Shannon. "Oh, my lord, child. You had no idea."

Shannon shook her head sadly.

"Sarah didn't find out 'til after yur father had left for his ranch," Moyna continued. "She wrote letters, but we had no reply. Four months later, praise the Lord, he came back for her. They were married and left for America shortly after that. You don't want yur child to go through the life you had, now do you?"

"Ah, Moyna," Liam said. "Maybe yur meddlin' in somethin' ya shouldn't be." His face softened as he looked at Shannon. "Let the girl make up her own mind about what's good for her."

***

Brid sat in her Dublin living room, listening to a CD of Irish ballads, the male voice singing loudly. She was so glad to be home.

She wondered how her friend was doing. On the plane ride back, Shannon hadn't faired very well - being sick most of the time. Brid thought it was probably due to the upheaval she'd just experienced in her life. She still couldn't believe what Shannon's father had done to her by giving the ranch to Jake.

After their arrival in Dublin, she drove Shannon to her grandparents and stayed with Shannon until after Sarah's burial. It felt good to know that her friend was now safe.

Brid heard a knock at her front door. She got up, turned the music down, and called out, "Who is it?"

"Michael."

She opened the door and let Michael enter. His clothes were disheveled and wrinkled, as if he'd been sleeping in them for days.

"I thought you were still in the States," Brid said, noticing the dark circles under Michael's eyes. "Didn't you say—"

Michael grabbed her shoulders. "Brid, Where's Shannon? She's not in her apartment."

She saw the panic in his eyes and became frightened.

"Why're you looking for Shannon?"

Michael looked away for a moment. "It's important." He tightened his grip on her. "Do you know where she is?"

"Yes, she's at her grandparents' cottage in Clifden."

Michael looked around the room and picked up Brid's coat hanging next to her door. He held the coat out to her.

"The Air Support Unit has a helicopter waiting at the airport. Come with me and show me where the O'Toole's live. It'll save time."

"Yes, but I still don't understand—"

"She may be in danger. Thomas Aherne is not the serial killer!"

CHAPTER TWENTY-NINE

The light in Shannon's old bedroom in Clifden was growing dim as the sun began to set low in the sky. She could see the ocean from her window, the wind blowing the tops of the waves.

Shannon paced like a trapped animal, her cell phone in one hand. She'd just hung up from Dr. McKenna's call.

"Okay, Shannon," she said to herself. "You've fucked up. It's confirmed. You're pregnant, just like your mother. Now will you call the man and tell him or just take this next step in your life without him?"

She stopped when she saw a sideways beam of sunlight illuminate the clay statue she'd brought with her from Oregon. She stared at it for some time, letting her thoughts disappear.

Then, as if the sunbeam encased her in the light, she knew what she would do.

"It's time to end this."

She pulled her Aran sweater over her head and gently smoothed it over her stomach, holding her hand there for a moment. Her grandmother had made the sweater for her on her twentieth birthday. That seemed so long ago now.

She picked up the statue and walked out of the room. Stopping in the kitchen, she said to Moyna, "Is it okay if I take the car and go for a drive, Granma?"

Moyna dried her hands on a towel hanging near the window above the sink. "Aye. You know the keys're always hangin' near the door. Where you be off to now?"

"Just around the loop. I need some fresh air - to think."

Moyna gave Shannon a kiss on her cheek.

"Take my cape with you. It looks like rain. And, be back before dark."

"Promise."

Shannon hugged and kissed her grandmother and walked out. A strong wind began to blow around her, making it hard for her to put on the cape. Finally, she managed to clasp the one button at the neck and wrap the scarf around her. She was grateful for the warm wool material.

She shoved the statue into a deep pocket, got into the old Austin, and started the engine. It sounded like a motorized sewing machine.

She pulled out of the gravel driveway and started along the coastline, not seeing the dark car that followed her at a distance.

***

On the Galway Road in Ireland, a blue and white Mini Cooper wound along towards Clifden, the gears grinding as the driver downshifted for a curve.

"Damn left-handed shift," Jake swore, finally getting into second. "Give me a horse any day."

He saw a sign that said Clochan and wondered if he'd taken a wrong turn when suddenly a large truck came around the corner at him. He swerved back to the left side of the road, having forgotten for a moment where he was.

His thoughts hadn't been on the road. He'd been thinking of what he was going to say when he saw Shannon.

It'd been weeks since he'd seen her, and he missed her. Wishing he could have made this trip sooner, he knew there was no possible way. He'd had to stay and take care of the arrangements for Dan. Jake understood why Shannon wasn't there for her father's funeral.

Looking at the box on the passenger seat, he smiled. *She's going to be surprised*, he thought.

He came into the center of the village and knew that he was in the right place when he saw a tall spire, which he'd seen pictures of when Dan had returned from Clifden.

Seeing a man sitting outside a small shop, Jake pulled over to the side of the road and stopped. Slowly pulling his long torso out of the small car, he stretched a moment before walking over to the man.

"Can I help ya?" the man said with a lilt, his eyes crinkling with his broad smile. He held a large drum that he was cleaning with a soft cloth.

"Yes, I'm looking for Liam O'Toole's house."

"Aye, Liam and Moyna. Great folks. Been here longer than me."

"Where do they live?" Jake asked.

"Down the road apiece," the man said, pointing along Main Street. "Ya can' miss it - white cottage with green shutters."

Jake looked down the street and could see numerous cottages with the same coloring. "But, how will I know which one is his?"

"'Tis the one with the big barn at the end of the street. He's got the finest Connemara ponies around here."

"Thanks," Jake said and turned to leave.

"Are ya friends of the O'Toole's?" the man asked as he picked up a small hammer and lightly tapped one of the tacks on the side of the drum.

"I hope to be," Jake said and left.

***

Shannon took a left to the lower Sky Road. The clouds tried to hide the sun, but once in awhile, it would peek through, painting the landscape with a rose hue. A herd of sheep were grazing near a thatch-roofed cottage. The water in Arbear Harbour, an inlet of Clifden Bay, was roiling from the strong winds. The Atlantic Ocean was visible to the west.

As she passed an ancient castle, she saw an old woman approaching on the road in a two-wheeled cart driven by a white horse, a 'Jerusalem Jeep' she remembered they were called. The woman smiled and waved to her, and Shannon waved back.

It was dusk when she arrived at the cemetery by the cliffs. She stopped the car and got out, pulling the scarf up into a hood. The ruins of the old church lay in the soft, boggy soil with seas of waving grass all around. Her mother had once told her that this was her favorite place when she was young because she could see the ocean from here.

Shannon stepped through a stone arch that still stood as the entrance to the graveyard. Slowly, she made her way to her mother's grave. She wasn't sure if the tears stinging her eyes were from the crisp, briny air or the loss of her mother. She knelt down close to the stone cross over the new grave, trying to find shelter from the wind.

Bowing her head, she cried.

"Oh, Mother, look at me now. I've gone and got myself in the same place you were once - pregnant and alone."

Shannon wiped her tears with the backs of her hands.

"I now know why you married my father...and why you always felt trapped. But, that's not going to happen to me."

Slowly, Shannon stood up. She thought of a song she'd heard long ago about learning the greatest thing in life.

"I never said this much...but, I love you, Mother. I just wish...I wish we could have been...different, closer. I'm not sure what made you so unhappy, but I hope now that you've found peace."

Walking closer to the edge of the cliff, she stood looking out over the ocean to the west just after the sun had set. The wind pushed at her, but she stood her ground.

"Goodbye, Mother."

CHAPTER THIRTY

Liam was lighting the fire in the fireplace when he heard a car stop outside of his home. From the sound of the engine, he knew it wasn't his own Austin.

"Someone's here," he yelled up the stairs to his wife.

He wiped his hands on his pants and opened the door, surprised to see a young man about to knock, carrying a large box under one arm.

"Hi," the man said. "I'm Jake McLeod, a friend of Shannon's." Jake extended his hand.

Liam was stunned for a moment by the handsome-faced stranger. Then, he yelled into the cottage, "Moyna, you'd better come down. Shannon's young man is here."

With that, he shook Jake's hand and stepped aside.

"Come in with ya', lad."

As Jake entered, Liam looked outside at the weather. Then, he looked up and down the roadway in front of his house, hoping to catch sight of Shannon returning. Sadly, he closed the door.

Moyna entered the living room and came to stand by her husband.

Jake laid the box down on a table in front of the couch.

"Hello, Ma'am. I'm Jake—"

Moyna's face lit up and she grabbed Jake's hand. "Thank the Lord! You've come in good time."

"Time for what?" Jake asked, looking around the room.

Liam leaned into his wife. "We'll be lettin' Shannon do the explainin'."

"Explain what?"

"About the baby!" Moyna exclaimed, then saw the look on Liam's face. "I couldn't help it, it's all so exciting."

"Baby? What're you talking about? Where's Shannon?"

Just then, the phone rang.

"O'Toole's," Liam said into the phone, his eyes on his wife.

"Mr. O'Toole!" Brid's voice yelled from the earpiece. "May I speak to Shannon?"

Liam held the phone away from his ear, sure that Jake and Moyna could hear Brid, as well.

"Hello, Brid. What's that noise—"

"I'm in a helicopter…I need to talk to Shannon!" Brid's voice insisted.

"Helicopter? Now, settle yerself down, girl," Liam said calmly. "She's not here at the moment, but—"

"There's no time to explain. Find Shannon and keep her safe!"

"Safe? Safe from what?" Liam insisted.

"The Killer! They arrested the wrong man in America. The Garda thinks Shannon is…just find her. We're about sixteen kilometers from Clifden. We'll be there in a few minutes."

"Tell her she may be on the Sky Road," Moyna said. "That's where her mother's buried."

The phone went dead. Liam looked at Jake and Moyna with fear in his heart.

"Jake, you can ride a horse, can't ya?"

"Sure. But, why?"

"Our Shannon usually takes the smaller loop to Beach Road. I'll use your car and search from here. But, you'll get to her faster if on horseback down on the beach."

***

The sharp wind whipped around Shannon as she slowly pulled the statue from the pocket o! her grandmother's cape. She looked at the figure for a few moments. Just as she was about to throw it into the ocean, a hand grabbed her wrist. Startled, she turned.

"William! What the devil are you doing here?"

"It took me some time to find you. I…came here today to pay respects to my wife—"

"Respects? THAT's a joke!" Shannon said, laughing. "You didn't even bother coming to her funeral—"

"I couldn't…I…had business—"

"Business? It's always business with you, isn't it? You never let up."

Just then, a dark car raced toward them and came to a stop. The door flew open and Shannon recognized the man. "Connor!"

She turned to William. "He's the killer, William. I saw him in Dublin and again in Portland."

Just then, Connor ran toward her, but William stepped between them.

"Shannon, I want you—" Connor began, just as William slugged him, knocking him cold.

William grabbed Shannon by the shoulders, his fingers cutting into her skin.

"How many women do I have to go through to get to you?" William yelled.

"What the bloody hell are you talking about?"

"I've waited a long time for this…Nikki and Maggie…they could never satisfy me. Not like I know you will. Unfortunately, you're getting too smart, young lady. The statue - you know where it is… "

"Let me go! Have you gone mad?" Shannon struggled against his hold as rain began to pour down on them.

She turned her head away as William tried to kiss her. She saw a rider on the beach dismount and start to climb the rocks below. In a flash of light, she recognized him.

"JAKE?!" she screamed into the wind.

A loud roar was heard overhead and the wind circled around them in forceful gusts, pelting them with rain. Shannon freed one arm, the one still holding the clay statue. She hit William on the head with it, but the statue shattered. It stunned him for a moment, allowing Shannon to pull away and run. The hood of her cape fell back and her hair whipped around her face.

Slowly, the helicopter began to descend as she ran towards Jake, not daring to look behind her. Just as she reached the cliff's edge, a hand grabbed her from behind.

"You'll die before that man touches you," William's voice yelled over the cacophony.

In that fleeting moment, when she thought she would plunge to the ocean below, she saw everything in slow motion: the helicopter landed; Brid ran towards her, followed by Michael; William's angry face came close to hers as he tried to kiss her again; as she turned her face away and looked down, Jake's hand reached up and grabbed William's ankle, pulling him off balance; Michael grabbed her, just at the moment when William fell over the edge.

"NO!" Shannon yelled into the wind, her soaked hair plastered to her face. When she looked down, William lay on the rocks below, her grandfather's horse standing near his twisted body. She looked for Jake, but didn't see him. Something more than fear grabbed her.

"JAKE! JAKE, where are you?" Shannon began sobbing, falling to her knees near the cliff's edge.

"I'm right here," Jake said behind her.

Shannon stood and turned, throwing herself into his arms.

CHAPTER THIRTY-ONE

In her grandparents' living room, Shannon sat on the couch, wrapped in a blanket and Jake's arms. Rain beat against the windows, and the howl of the wind sounded like a lonely wolf, searching for his mate.

Liam and Moyna talked softly with Brid near the kitchen entry.

"I knew he was a good for nothin'," Shannon heard Liam say. "But, to come to this...I just wish I could've had me own bare hands on 'im."

"William...," Shannon said, leaning her head onto Jake's shoulder, "I can't believe it. My own mother, all the others..."

Michael walked in, his overcoat whipping around his long legs. When he turned to close the door, Brid went up to him.

Shannon shivered, and Jake pulled her closer.

"Are you all right?" Michael asked Shannon.

She nodded and reached up to push her hair back from her face.

"Shannon, you remember Michael..." Brid began. "He was at the morgue—"

Just then, the door opened again. A dark-haired man entered.

"YOU!" Shannon yelled. "I thought you were the killer."

"Connor Larkin? A killer?" Jake asked, a look of confusion on his face.

"Sorry to disappoint you," Connor said. "I know I wasn't up front with you at the ranch, Jake, but I work for the Intelligence Division of the American Internal Revenue Service. We've been investigating your step-father, Miss O'Toole, on a money-laundering scheme."

"Money-laundering?"

Connor looked at Michael, who came to stand beside him.

"We've been working together on this," Michael began. "You see,

William was laundering money for Greenburg…but, we found that he was also selling reproductions, keeping the originals to sell in a European underground."

"But, what made you suspect William as the serial killer?" Shannon asked Michael.

Michael took off his coat and began pacing the room. "When I saw your mother's body, she had a mark on her neck that I'd seen before, but couldn't place it. Then, I remembered seeing a similar mark on Maggie Murphy's body."

He stopped and looked at Brid. "On a hunch, I went back to the Pearse Gallery. I'd seen a large portrait of William there. We think his crest ring could have made those marks."

"But, why was Thomas arrested?" Shannon asked.

"At the time, he was the main connection to Nikki and Maggie. He'd hired them to work at the gallery. And, picture wire was used in all the killings, except your mother's."

Shannon saw Michael look over at her grandparents. Her heart ached to see the sadness in their faces as they hugged each other.

"When did you know Thomas wasn't the killer?" Jake asked Michael.

"We found a motel suite outside of Dublin that William had leased, near the racetrack where he kept his horses. He'd made the mistake of keeping…something of each of his victims there. Your stolen statue was in that suite."

The room was silent for a moment as Michael's words echoed.

"It is fitting that he died near my mother," Shannon said softly.

Then, the wind began to calm as Brid walked over to Michael. She took his hand in hers. "If you're finished, I think we should leave. Shan- non looks like she needs some rest."

Michael nodded. "Connor, it's time we go back to Dublin." He turned to Brid, kissing her lightly on the cheek. "I'll meet you outside," he said to her, then guided Connor out the door.

Brid went to Shannon and hugged her. "I'll call you tomorrow, so we can talk. I'm so glad you're finally safe."

She turned to Jake. "It was nice meeting you." Brid looked over at Shannon, winked, and said, "Take good care of her."

After the door closed, Shannon looked at Jake. "I wish I could have been there for Da's funeral."

"The whole county seemed to turn out for it," Jake said, then his face grew sad. "Dan stepped in to fill the void after my father died. It must've been hard for you, but I know he loved you with all his heart."

"Yeah, right up to the moment when he gave you the ranch."

Jake ignored her comment and leaned over to Shannon, his dimples deepening in his face. "I know about the baby," he said softly.

"WHAT? How do you..." Shannon looked at her grandparents.

"I think I'll make us some tea," Moyna said, slipping into the kitchen. Liam smiled at Shannon and followed his wife.

"You weren't going to keep it from me, were you?" Jake asked Shannon.

"I hadn't decided. I'm not my mother, you know. I won't use it as an excuse to get a husband."

"Well, maybe this will change your mind." Jake got up and went to the box he'd brought. He carried it to her and gently placed it on her lap.

Shannon slowly lifted the lid and stared at the contents.

"My boots!"

She picked one up from the box and an envelope fell out. Slowly opening it, she saw that it contained a deed to the ranch - with HER name on it. She looked at Jake in disbelief.

"But, I thought Da left the ranch to you?"

"He did. That's where I was after he died, his attorney's office, getting that changed. After you came back, Dan told me he was going to do this himself. He just ran out of time."

Shannon thought for a moment.

"Well?" Jake asked nervously.

Shannon re-read the paper in her hand, then looked up at Jake.

"Well...do you think you might marry a pregnant ranch owner from Oregon?"

Jake's face lit up with a smile. "If that's a proposal...I accept." With am impish grin, he took a ring from his pinky finger. "I picked this up in Dublin before I came here - just in case."

Shannon watched as he gently slipped the ring onto her finger, the raised Claddagh on the wide silver band shimmered in the firelight.

"They told me at the store that for an engagement, you wear the heart pointing toward your heart." Jake swallowed hard, then continued. "After we're married, we'll need to turn it around."

Shannon threw herself into Jake's arms and kissed him. "Then, I think it's time for the three of us to go home."

THE END